THE COVEN'S Son

THE COVEN'S Son

PRESTON ALLEN

Columbus, Ohio

This book is a work of fiction. The names, characters and events in this book are the products of the author's imagination or are used fictitiously. Any similarity to real persons living or dead is coincidental and not intended by the author.

The Coven's Son

Published by Gatekeeper Press
2167 Stringtown Rd, Suite 109
Columbus, OH 43123-2989
www.GatekeeperPress.com

Copyright © 2020 by Preston Allen
All rights reserved. Neither this book, nor any parts within it may be sold or reproduced in any form or by any electronic or mechanical means, including information storage and retrieval systems without permission in writing from the author. The only exception is by a reviewer, who may quote short excerpts in a review.

The cover design, interior formatting, typesetting, and editorial work for this book are entirely the product of the author. Gatekeeper Press did not participate in and is not responsible for any aspect of these elements.

ISBN (paperback): 9781642379631
eISBN: 9781642379648

Library of Congress Control Number: 2020940616

To my mom, my #1 fan and biggest cheerleader.

Prologue

The room was alive. Tables shook, lights swayed, instruments fell. The delivery nurse with long, painted nails and sweat dripping from the tip of her nose steadied the wailing woman from falling off the gurney. She lifted the arm rails and clicked them into place, providing the laboring woman with something to hold onto, giving her bruised hand some relief from the woman's vise-like grip. The other two nurses awaited further instruction from the doctor who steadied himself at the feet of the patient, looking more like he was ready to catch a football than a baby.

"Hold the gurney steady!" he instructed one of them.

The floor trembled as the earthquake gained strength. The door to the room swung open. It was the father. Without a word he ran to the woman and wrapped his arm around her and wiped the dampness from her forehead. Plaster from the ceiling flaked onto the floor all around them.

"Nurse!" the doctor yelled, as he reached for a platform of tools on wheels that had rolled just out of reach during the commotion. The nurse hurried to move the table back into place.

The panting woman screamed from her hospital bed despite being comforted by the father of her baby. She wanted a natural birth, free from any forms of treatment that would ease her pain. She wanted her baby untouched by pharmaceuticals that could be transferred into the child's body from her own. She thought it selfish to want to numb the joys of childbirth, but at this moment, between heavy breathing, shaking walls, moving ceilings, and excruciating pain that could only be described as being ripped in two, she began to regret this decision.

"One more push," the nurse with long and seemingly out-of-code acrylic nails said, urging the soon-to-be mother.

With one final bloodcurdling scream, the woman pushed her baby completely out just as a blinding flash of lightning cracked across the sky from the window on the far end of the room. There was a deafening pop as the cabinet just behind the doctor tore halfway from the wall and crashed onto the foot of the nurse holding the bed still. She screamed in pain.

"It's a boy," the doctor said, clearly relieved that the ordeal was over. "The first baby I've ever delivered during an earthquake." He smiled, obviously exhausted and shaken. The father beamed with pride on seeing his new baby boy for the first time. The doctor handed the woman her baby as the nurse tinkered with the fallen cabinet, mustering the strength to move it from her colleague's foot.

"What is this made of?" she questioned as she struggled to heave the cabinet off.

The doctor glanced back. "Oak," he said as he turned back to the parents. The father smiled and shook the doctor's strong, clammy hand. The mother's long strawberry-blonde hair was plastered to her forehead from sweat, but a weight was lifted from her shoulders. She held her baby in her arms knowing full well that the earthquake they had experienced was not natural. It was her son.

Chapter 1

The teenager pulls his head through the neck of his black T-shirt printed with snakes in the style of old tattoos running along the side as he runs from his bedroom at the end of the long hallway. "Oak! I'm getting in the car, let's go!" a female voice yelled.

"I'm coming!" he yells as he slides around the corner and slips on his shoes. He opens the door to the outside and looks at his mother standing in the driveway. Her long golden hair blows in the gentle breeze as she looks directly at him with her baby blue eyes.

She puts her hands on her hips and asks, "Did you take your garlic?"

Oak shivers and reluctantly goes back inside to grab a clove of garlic off the kitchen counter. He always makes it a point to run late for everything in the hopes that his mom will be too distracted to remember the raw garlic clove he is required to take every day for his safety. He unwraps the clove from its papery shell and pops it into his mouth. The overwhelmingly strong scent hits his nose the second he bites it open and begins to chew. Hot and overbearing spiciness fills his whole mouth as his eyes water. He chews as fast as he can while heading back out the front door to his mom waiting outside.

She hands him a bottle of water as he gets in the car. "Your grandmother just finished performing raindrop therapy on a client of hers and is on her way to pick up dinner. I told her we would pick up some rosewood oil on our way to see her tonight."

Oak chugs the water as they drive down the street on their way to his grandmother's house. He wipes off his mouth with the back of his hand. "Can we get some mistletoe while we are there?" His eyes are large as he desperately hopes his mother will agree, although the way she is side-eyeing him doesn't lead him to believe she will go for it.

"You know the garlic works better. It's stronger and less risky."

"But raw garlic is so disgusting. I just want a break!"

"I'll think about it," she tells him as they turn into the parking lot of a small building with a tall pointy black roof, wind chimes, and streamers decorated all along the front entrance.

Oak looks down at his feet. *I'll think about it* usually means no. He knows that mistletoe is a parasitic plant that if pinned to his clothing will absorb the abundance of energy flowing through his body at all times, but the risk of it falling off during the day puts him more at risk than ingesting garlic, which contains his power from the inside. "But, I'm getting older and it's much more under control now than it was!"

"Enough," his mother interrupts. "I said I'll think about it." Her stern gaze turns soft as she remembers how much she hated eating garlic as a child. She can't even step foot into an Italian restaurant without her stomach churning. Oak steps out of the car and kicks the front tire of the car before walking around to enter the store. "Are we still throwing tantrums at fourteen?"

He ignores her and heads to the front door of the pointy-roofed building. He pulls the door open and allows his mother to enter first while he reads the name of the shop imprinted in bold letters on the glass of the door. "Divinity." They have been here many times. Oak likes to peruse the walls looking at all the colorful crystals and inhaling the heavy incense perfuming the place. He always winds up with smudges on his nose from getting too close to the powdery sticks.

As soon as he enters behind his mother he catches the smell of warm lavender and freshly burned sage. Immediately his shoulders fall and both he and his mother relax instinctively.

"Merry meet!" exclaims the robust gray-haired woman behind the counter, a small lilac streak of hair falling just below her eyebrow. She holds her arms out in welcome as what seem to be hundreds of bangles and bracelets jingle around her arms. She has on at least twenty necklaces, with endless earrings pierced all the way up and down her lobes and cartilage, some dangling, some studs.

Oak's mother walks over and gives the woman a hug, stretching over the counter, barely able to reach the woman. "Merry meet to you, Hyacinth."

"Dev, it's been too long. You can't possibly have been working this whole time without a visit," Hyacinth says.

"Business is a bit slow at the moment because of that new book of affirmations. Everyone is a do-it-yourself witch now," Dev tells her. "But I was just here last month." Dev works as a freelance spirit catcher, observing spirits through the use of a special camera. She is the firstborn child of Pepe and Marion Melt.

"That book has every woman on earth thinking they can conjure the craft with sticky notes," Hyacinth says as she rolls her eyes and lets out a sigh. "I've lost so much business because people think they can take things into their own hands," she tells Dev as she begins to rifle through a box underneath the counter.

Dev responds, "Luckily it's just sticky notes. My mother, Marion, needs some rosewood oil for her raindrop therapy sessions and there's no one trying to replicate that." Marion runs a healing touch clinic where she employs a government-certified Reiki healer while she herself performs raindrop therapy.

Hyacinth pulls a bag out of the box she was fiddling around in and holds it up to Dev. "Just got this in. Palo Santo. I know you like it more than sage so I saved it."

Dev's eyes light up as she snatches the bag from the clerk. "Yes, yes yes yes," she says excitedly. Ever since the mysterious book of affirmations hit the market and caused the mainstream media to bring light to the occult, Palo Santo has been a rare commodity. "That stupid book says to burn Palo Santo while posting your affirmations to your mirror. It's sold out everywhere, and bought by people who have no idea what they are doing, let alone have the ability to use it. Second and third children, even!"

Hyacinth scoffs at the idea that a second- or third-born child could have any abilities beyond being able to tell if milk has soured without smelling it. "Yes, that book makes no mention of the fact that the first-born is the only child able to perform any rituals due to siphoning the majority of the energy a mother produces during pregnancy, leaving the second child and onward with nothing but a slight hint of knowing when their food is burning on the stove," Hyacinth says, turning her stern sentence into a joke as they both chuckle.

"Where is Oak?" Dev asks, looking around the mystical shop.

Oak rounds the corner holding many things in his arms. "Here I am." He plops the items onto the counter.

"Looks like he's done the hard part for you," Hyacinth says, ringing up the Palo Santo first and then beginning on the other items. Two chicken feet, rosewood oil, cascarilla.

"Oh!" Dev realizes. "We need mugwort!" She jogs from the counter to the other end of the store. Hyacinth gives Oak a narrowed look as she scans the last item and bags it just as Dev comes back with the final purchase. She places the bag of mugwort into the clerk's hand and removes her wallet from her deep burgundy leather purse with a sigil burned into the side. A swirl and a loop create a magical pattern that distracts a thief's attention away from her bag.

Dev pays Hyacinth and turns and walks away from the counter toward the exit of the store. As Oak begins to follow, Hyacinth gives him a mischievous grin and he tries to pretend he doesn't see it. In the car, Dev hands Oak the bag of goods. But, not before noticing a dripping from the bottom of the bag.

"What's wet?" his mother asks, swaying the bag away from them so as not to drip water on their clothes. Oak cringes as he reaches into the bag and pulls out a small snippet of a green plant with two tiny white berries attached to the end of a vial of water. Dev looks at him sternly. "Fresh mistletoe?" Oak's eyes plead, on the verge of tears, to let him keep the only break he can get from eating raw garlic.

"Three days. That's it. I don't trust it to be strong enough to go on any longer than that," Dev says, half angry and half saddened. She hates how miserable the garlic makes Oak. If he loses control of himself though, he is going to hate much more than just garlic.

Oak's eyes shine with tears of happiness as he places the plant gently back into the bag as they head off to his grandmother's house. Halfway there, Oak hears a rumbling from his stomach as he feels the bubbling of bile and acid gurgling around in his lower belly.

"Are you okay? Is it the garlic?" his mom asks him.

Oak hesitates to answer but realizes that's not what it is. "No, I don't think so, just hungry," he says and he looks over at his mother and gives her a reassuring smile. This was a perfect opportunity to continue to paint the garlic in a bitter light but he decides it isn't worth it to complain too much.

"Well, we're almost to Grandma's and she'll have dinner ready for us. Don't pin your mistletoe on until the morning. Since you already had your garlic today, we don't want your ability fully suppressed. I want you to work on some enchantments tonight with your grandmother while I go out with your father after he gets home from work," Dev says as she brings the car to a slow stop at a red traffic light.

"What kind of enchantments?" Oak asks, curious because it seems she has something specific in mind.

"I want you to enchant your own safety pin for the mistletoe." Impatiently, Dev taps her hands on the steering wheel of the car, waiting for the light to turn green.

"Oh." Oak shakes his head in agreement.

Oak is the first son born as a first child to the family in over two hundred and fifty years, and Dev tends to be overprotective at times, so Oak is cautious not to express too much excitement when she gives him a little wiggle room. Males born of the occult tend to carry much more power than their female counterparts and siphon far more magic from their mothers during pregnancy. Which is why Dev is so overly cautious about suppressing Oak's power. No one really knows how to handle the strength of a firstborn male.

They round the corner and head toward the end of the cul-de-sac while passing by beautifully aged oak trees that are sensually dropping gold, red, and brown leaves onto the ground that flutter up into the sky and twirl before dropping back down onto the slowly yellowing lawns below.

"We're here," Dev says as she puts the car in park and opens the door.

Oak puts his hand on his mother's shoulder as she is about to exit the car. She turns back to look at him. "Thank you," he says quietly, and opens his side of the car and gets out. Dev is glad she allowed him the mistletoe after seeing such pure appreciation from her usually moody son.

They walk together to the front door of Pepe and Marion's beautiful two-story Victorian-style home. Every detail of the home is painted a different color of mesmerizing hues. The scalloping details above the windows are a salmon pink while the trim that outlines the entire house is a deep fuchsia. The base of the house is painted a purple so deep it is nearly black, but the intricate little nooks of wooden ornamentals are a flashy gold. They walk up to the bright plum door and use the large brass lion's head knocker to indicate they have arrived.

"Did you know a bright plum door means witches live here?" Dev asks her son as she smiles at him.

"Witches?!" Oak screeches as he playfully pretends to run away from the house, nearly tripping on the concrete edging details lined around his grandmother's walkway. The plum door swings open, light shining on every angle of the door, showing a subtle glittery sheen as they come face-to-face with Marion. The crone of the family is wearing a long black cloak, open in the front, allowing you to see her lilac flower-print dress that stops just at the knee. Her hair, somewhat outdated, gray with blonde highlights, is layered all the way from the top of her eyebrows to the bottom of her shoulders. She smiles when she sees her kin.

"Grandma!" Oak yells as he gives her a giant hug, being careful not to be too rough on the old woman's back.

"Hi, Mom," Dev greets her, walking in.

Oak hands Marion the bag of goodies they purchased at Divinity. "Oh, what's this? This is far more than rosewood oil." Marion fumbles through the bag and pulls out the mistletoe. "I suppose this is for you?" she questions, handing it over to Oak. Oak shyly takes it from her.

"Yes, we thought we could give it a try. But only for three days!" Dev interrupts, looking for approval from her mother.

"Oh, lighten up, Dev," the old crone says, smiling at Oak and giving him a nod. "We would've given you this choice if fresh mistletoe were readily available during your younger years," she says as if Dev were still a child, making her feel small.

"But he is a male," Dev protests, only to be interrupted by her mother

"And you are a female!" she says, throwing up her hands in mockery and wiggling her fingers in the air around the house, stomping around like an angry spirit.

Oak laughs and is relieved that his grandma is supportive of the idea of suppressing his energy in a way that doesn't make him smell like the son of Van Helsing.

Marion leads them into her apothecary to restock the newly bought rosewood oil. The room smells of a powerful incense that makes everyone who enters feel motivated. "What is that smell, Mother?" Dev asks.

"I'm burning a combination of purple statice and vervain together. It's a little cocktail I mixed up to make you feel creative and ready for crafting!" Marion answers excitedly.

The room is covered from floor to ceiling with shelves filled with books and row upon row of jars, intertwined with vines and greenery. Marion takes the rosewood oil tincture and places it among a selection of many other oils in the room.

"Grandma?" Oak asks, curiously looking around the room. "What is it that you do? What is raindrop therapy?"

Marion looks at him for a moment before realizing that in his entire life of being involved in the craft, she has never taught him anything on the subject of her work. "Oh my dear. Raindrop therapy utilizes aromatherapy oils and reflexology massage to cleanse and renew the body. I use a combination of oils based on the person's ailments to create a cure."

Oak thinks for a moment, remembering the smell and how it changed his mood when entering the magical shop, and how his grandmother's apothecary affects him in the same way but gives him a different feeling. He figures that this is how his grandma's massage works, using different types of oils to change the mood of the person she's working on. "Oh okay."

Dev, unsure of how Oak never realized what exactly his grandmother does, reaches her hands up to pull her light strawberry-blonde hair away from her face. As she does, she catches a glimpse of her watch. "Let's have dinner. I've got to get going soon, and this one needs to learn how to enchant a safety pin," she says as she exits the room, twirling around the corner as if she is gliding on air. She has a date with her husband—she hasn't had one in a very long time—and her excitement is starting to show.

Marion places a hand on Oak's shoulder and begins walking him out of the apothecary, closing the door behind them. "Once your mother leaves, we will get to work on that enchantment. I have some ideas to try!"

Oak smiles. He can barely stand the excitement of enchanting the pin so that he can go three whole days without that stupid garlic. They head to the kitchen where Dev is laying out the food Marion bought for dinner. A rotisserie chicken, steamed vegetables, coleslaw, and potato wedges all come out of the bag. Marion takes over and motions Dev to have a seat.

Dinner is mostly silent aside from the periodic tapping of Dev's fingernails on the table. She is clearly very anxious and excited for her date with her husband. Oak smirks as he eats the rest of his dinner, knowing that it has been a long time since his parents have been able to get some alone time, what with how much his father works.

Alan is a hardworking provider for his family whom Oak almost never sees because of his work schedule.

Dev stands up, taking her plate and moving it to the sink. She sighs. "Guess I ought to get going," she says, with a twinkle in her eye.

There's a sudden loud grinding sound as Marion jumps up out of her seat, causing her chair to slide against the rich, dark hardwood floor. "No, I don't think so."

Dev and Oak look at each other in confusion.

"You're not going anywhere looking like that!"

Oak shows a sign of relief when he realizes nothing is wrong, but Dev looks even more panicked.

"We are a family of the occult! We mustn't ever attend company with a man without ensuring he is completely bewitched!" Marion cackles heartily. She grabs Dev by the hand and pulls her out of the kitchen. "Come, child, we shall show you our women's secrets to enchanting our men," she says to Oak while they disappear up the stairs to the second floor of the house. He really doesn't care to know these secrets, but this is the perfect time for him to watch some magic.

Oak hurries after them. He finds them in Marion's bedroom, Dev sitting at a brightly lit vanity in the corner of the room, just outside the master bathroom. "We redden the lips for seduction," Marion says as she dips her lip brush into a deep red lipstick then sprinkles cinnamon dust over the tip and begins to apply it on Dev's mouth.

Oak notices many candles strewn throughout his grandmother's bedroom. Without taking his eyes or ears off the primping women, he goes around the room snapping his fingers between the wicks of each candle, bringing them to life instantly, their red-hot flames dancing atop the warming wax, setting the perfect mood.

Marion plucks some dried petals from a wilted rose in a dried-up vase on the right of the vanity and tosses them into a dark wooden mortar and pestle. She begins to crush the petals and stirs in what appears to be makeup powder. "We blush the cheeks to imply we are shy, but the petals woo him to think of love." Marion brushes the makeup and rose-dust mixture onto Dev's high cheeks.

Oak notices Dev has been mixing something together in her lap the entire time. Marion sets everything down and reaches for the concoction. She finds an eyeshadow brush from a cup of brushes up against the mirror of the vanity. "We deepen the eyelids to maintain control." She swipes the dark, sultry powder onto Dev's eyelids.

"What is that mixed with?" Oak asks curiously.

"Ah, good. You are paying attention. Licorice root," Marion answers. She leans back to check Dev's eyes for symmetry. "That should about do it. Oh yes, one more thing, Oak. Run downstairs to the apothecary and get me the helichrysum oil."

Oak nods and heads downstairs. Once in the apothecary he is struck by the eagerness to practice the craft. To do spells, to mix herbs, to make magic. He is fully aware that this feeling is caused by the incense his grandmother has burning in the room but nonetheless, he excitedly finds the tincture and runs back up the stairs with a whole new motivation. He heads back into the master bedroom where Dev is adjusting her hair and Marion is wiping away makeup and herb residue from the counter.

"Here it is," Oak says, handing the oil to his grandmother.

"Perfect." She unscrews the top of the helichrysum oil and shakes a few drops into a spray bottle. "Now, Oak.

With your knowledge of plants and herbs, what is this helichrysum oil going to do?" his grandmother asks as she puts the nozzle on the spray bottle and gives it a shake. Oak hesitates. "Come on, now. I know you know this."

The motivation he had a second ago is sucked away by the unexpected question. He doesn't like to be tongue-tied or caught off guard by things he knows he should know. He's done so much research to try to eliminate garlic from his daily routine that he should know exactly what a particular herb does. Marion uses the bottle to spray Dev all around and over her body as if she is trying to liven up a wilted flower.

"Helichrysum oil is used to open your heart..." He hesitates. "And restore love!" he says enthusiastically, proud of himself for remembering.

"Precisely!" Marion says, pointing at Oak in approval. His mother looks ravishing. A sight to behold. "Now, let's head downstairs for some tea while we let your mother get dressed," Marion instructs as she shuffles Oak out of the room. Dev gives him a loving smile, squinting her eyes so that they wrinkle just slightly in the corners, indicating the authenticity of her warmth toward her son.

Back in the kitchen, Marion puts on a kettle for tea and Oak sits at the table swinging his feet beneath his chair. "I've been doing some research, Oak," Marion says abruptly.

"Yeah?"

"On firstborn children. Males specifically," she says, her tone slightly lowering into what seems to be a sudden sadness.

"O-okay?" Oak says now, nervous.

"It seems that your power may be a little too concentrated to ever be able to fully stop suppressing it."

Oak starts fidgeting. "You mean. The garlic? Forever?" he says, his voice quivering.

"Unfortunately, yes, and I know right now it seems like a miserable thing to have to do. But, you are young and will see soon in the future that eating a raw clove of garlic every day is truly not as horrific and life-ruining as it may seem to you now," she says, trying to reassure him.

"It burns when I eat it," he says in frustration. "My chest hurts for hours afterwards. I burp it up all day long. My sweat smells like it, and there's a faint scent of it seeping out of my pores ALL THE TIME!"

Marion motions with her hand for him to calm down. "That's why I have some ideas for this pin we'll enchant tonight for you to wear by Monday. If all goes well, we will be able to give you some relief," she says calmly, trying not to rile him up any more. Oak is just about to respond when there is a high-pitched squeal from the stove.

"Tea's done," Marion says as she stands up to quiet the kettle. She pulls two cups and saucers from a cabinet as she prepares a tray with various options for the tea. Fresh cream, almond milk, sugar, honey, agave nectar, and two large herbal bulbs, tightly tied up. She brings the tray to the table and sets it in front of Oak. She sets a saucer on the table and places one of the herbal bulbs into a teacup and sets that on the saucer. Then she pours the boiling water from the kettle into the cup, over the bundled herbs, and takes a seat for herself.

Oak watches as the bulb swirls in the hot water, spinning and twirling. It branches out and plumps, slowly opening, revealing bright, beautiful, brilliant colors in the center. Oak reaches for the agave nectar as steam begins to sprout from the luscious, blossoming tea flower. The steam is lightly tinted baby blue and has a pearl-like sheen flowing through it.

Marion prepares her tea the same way, but adds a little cream as well. Her herbal bulb begins to twirl just as they are interrupted by Dev appearing in the entrance of the kitchen. Both Oak and Marion turn to her and see that she has floated down the stairs in a slinky black dress that hugs every dip and curve of her body. The bottom of the dress hits just below the top of her ankle but a long slit on the side reaches just to the top of her left knee. The dress ends at her chest with a plunging neckline that reveals just about three inches of cleavage, leaving her shoulders bare. Over her shoulders she wears a black mesh lace shawl that blurs the appearance of skin but tantalizes nonetheless.

She looks to her family with her best 'come hither' stare, trying not to laugh, but the corners of her mouth turn upwards. Marion and Oak begin to clap and cheer, wolf-whistling and howling at Dev's makeover. Dev can't help but smile as she spins and poses, using her shawl as an accessory to add flair.

"NOW you may leave," Marion says as she lifts the hot cup of tea to her lips, burning them immediately but not giving a reaction so she does not take the attention off her daughter.

Oak gets up and hugs his mother goodbye. "Have fun tonight, Mom, and mesmerize Dad using your powers of Satan," he says into her hair as they are hugging.

She pulls back from the hug and playfully slaps him on the shoulder. "Good night, everyone," she says as she heads for the door, gliding effortlessly across the floor. "I'll be back Sunday night to take you home for school Monday, Oak."

Oak locks the door behind her and turns to look at his grandmother from the kitchen. "Did you bring a pin?" she says to him from across the house, mischievously smiling at him.

Chapter 2

Marion and Oak sit with their backs to each other in the apothecary as they flip through pages of books and charts, trying to find the perfect combination of things to adorn the mistletoe with. Oak sits at a writing desk pressed up against the wall, checking pages of a book about infusions, and Marion sits on the floor at a glass coffee table adorned with wrought iron legs that look like snakes, unrolling a scroll that charts precious symbols. The room is dimly lit with small lamps and candles that cause light to dance upon the oddities in the room. A twinkle bounces off the eyeball of a taxidermied bat hanging upside down from a string dangling from the ceiling.

Oak reaches up to a bookshelf, past a wall of framed pinned butterflies and jeweled beetles, and grabs a leather-bound book just next to a glass display of a fully articulated cat skeleton. The room is silent aside from the shuffling of papers. Oak is leaned so far forward into his book that he barely notices Marion getting up and walking quietly out of the room. His stamina to solve this dilemma is amplified tenfold because of the incense combination Marion continues to have burning throughout the night. He traces his finger along the lines of text in the book.

Enchanting objects over long periods of time may require the use of an outside power source.

Oak looks up from the page and stares at the wall, contemplating what this means. Books on the craft are never really straightforward enough to come right out and tell you how to do what you are trying to do because there are so many things you could be trying to accomplish. A lot has to be figured out by interpretation, and trial and error.

"The use of an outside power source," he mumbles to himself. "Like a battery?" He leans back in his chair, slightly frustrated. He has never had to do anything this advanced with magic before. He knows herbal usage very well and can do basic tricks like light candles without fire, and make his reflection move differently than his actual self in a mirror, but he hasn't had any need to really learn a lot of the craft. His grandmother has an extensive knowledge of everything occult and his mother has less. As the years have gone on, the need for magic in society has dwindled significantly and there just hasn't been such a fuss over learning anything other than things that help your day-to-day activities go a little bit smoother than the average person's.

"Precisely like a battery," his grandmother says as she enters the room holding up a large safety pin, the light from the candles causing it to glisten. Oak is so caught off guard by Marion entering the room that he fumbles the book from the desk onto the floor. He leans over to pick it up as Marion praises him for the discovery.

"You found exactly what I was considering." She sits on the floor by the coffee table. Oak holds his hand out for the pin she brought into the room. She reaches over, her bones cracking in her back at the stretch, and drops the pin into his palm.

"What were you considering?" Oak turns the safety pin over and over in his hand, looking at the shape and size. "This is a big safety pin," he says. "I was considering exactly what you said, a battery. Not in the literal sense but as the book states, an outside power source."

She takes her cold cup of tea off the table and takes a sip, slightly cringing as the old bloomed flower tickles her top lip with its stiffening petals. Oak stares at the safety pin, carefully considering how you would add a power source.

Marion smiles and sets down her stale tea. "Crystals, my dear. Crystals are the energy source we need to power any enchantments done to this pin. That shall be our first step. We must figure out which crystals we need to keep energy running through our makeshift boutonnière." She reaches behind herself to a pile of books sitting on the floor where she's been researching. She finds the one she needs and opens it while setting it atop the coffee table. "Come, let's figure this out."

Oak slides out of his chair and onto the floor next to her. A few of the dangling plants from the wall of herb jars sway and fuss, almost as if they are alive. In the magical house of a witch, you never know what can happen although it's probably just the result of a gust of air from Oak switching positions to the floor. He sidles up next to his grandmother, pushing his shoulder against hers. Peering down at the book, he sees it has many photos and diagrams, along with illustrations of every crystal you could think of.

"There are so many kinds. How will we ever choose?" Oak says, sounding defeated.

"Oh, honey, this is how the craft works. You must have patience. Creating this pin is going to take the entire weekend."

Oak dramatically puts his head down onto the coffee table with a groan and a thud. Marion slides the book over to him. "You work on this. I'm going to see if I can use that book of infusions to find the perfect material to attach the crystal." She stands up and goes over to the desk Oak was at.

Oak reads page after page about the four types of crystals. He reads about covalent crystals and ionic crystals. He yawns as he flips through the book, glancing at the time. It is two a.m. He's just getting to the part about metallic crystals. Marion calmly thumbs through the book about infusions, clearly showing she has done this many times and understands the involvement in this creation. She shows no signs of fatigue. Oak has been mumbling softly to himself as he reads and so, Marion knows exactly where he is in his search.

"Don't forget to brush up on molecular crystals!" she says loudly, scaring Oak to attention just as his head starts to sag forward. He doesn't make any noise but the shock has given him a second wind and he goes back to work with a little more enthusiasm. Marion giggles quietly and continues on in her own research.

Oak eventually comes across an illustration of a crystal that is swirled with a deep rich purple and soft cloudy white. It contains twists of teal and small traces of blue hues.

Supplies energy along with productivity and amplifies mental abilities and focus.

Oak's eyes widen. "Grandma, I think I found something."

Marion lifts her head from the book and twists her back around to look at Oak. "What is it, dear?" she says calmly, a hint of grogginess creeping in.

"Fluorite."

Marion puts her finger to her lip in thought. "Yes. Yes, I think if I recall correctly, that may work. What does it say? It increases focus, right?"

"Yeah, it says it supplies energy which will power the enchantment. It helps with productivity, which will help with the workings of the enchantment. Also, it amplifies mental abilities and focus, which will allow me to self-suppress my powers in case of an emergency," he says, slightly adding a questioning tone to each sentence, asking Marion for confirmation.

"I think that is absolutely the one. We can add quartz to it as well, which increases the power of any crystal it is used in unison with."

THE COVEN'S SON

Oak takes in that information. He knew quartz would increase the power of other crystals but hadn't thought of using it for this. He is amazed at how well the craft works with all of its available elements to create something new, each ingredient feeding off each other in perfect collaboration.

***

Oak lifts his head from the hard glass tabletop. There is a blanket around his shoulders and he is a bit confused. He wipes the sleep from his eyes and realizes he passed out shortly after discovering which power source they are going to use for his pin. His grandmother must have covered him before going up to bed.

He slowly gets to his feet, his knees creaking from the bent position they were set in all night. He stumbles around a bit, stretching his legs and stomping out the rigidness of his joints. With the blanket wrapped around himself, he heads out into the hallway. Everything is quiet. He doesn't smell any coffee or breakfast. He checks the time. Ten a.m.

He walks along the bottom floor of the house, searching for Marion. "Grandma?" he calls. No answer. He starts up the stairs and about halfway up yells, "Grandma?" No answer. Just as he begins to make his way up the rest of the flight of stairs, he hears the front door unlocking. He turns to the door to see Marion coming inside.

She holds up a small plastic bag. "Fluorite!" she says excitedly as Oak walks back down the stairs to greet her.

He glances down at her other hand. "What's that?"

Marion eyes him strangely. "Something you will both love and hate." She hands him a small brown paper bag. He peers inside and scrunches his face up. "It's black garlic," she says. "It's much more potent and stronger than regular garlic, so it will last you two days instead of one. It's more expensive and a lot harder to find, but since we are working on extending the life of your mistletoe, you don't want to start using it today and weaken it without the proper enchantments. You need to suppress today so I thought it would be nice to splurge just this once." She looks at him with understanding eyes. "Also, it tastes a little sweeter and more vinegary than normal garlic so, it might be a bit of a nice change?"

Oak realizes if he puts the mistletoe on today, it will begin utilizing its parasitic abilities and immediately start to wear down and he doesn't want to enchant mistletoe in a weakened state. He forces a smile, trying to appear grateful even though he can already feel his stomach churning at the idea of eating the garlic.

Marion moves to the kitchen with Oak behind her. "No time for breakfast today. We've got work to do," she says as she pours water into the back of the coffee machine.

Oak tosses the brown bag onto the table and slumps into the chair next to it. Marion is rinsing out the blooming teacups from late last night and setting up mugs for the java slowly dripping into the glass pot.

A kitchen cabinet door slowly creaks open from the opposite end of the kitchen. Marion hears the sound and turns to face it. She narrows her eyes and walks over to gently close it. As she reaches for the gaping door, one by one each cabinet door around the room slowly opens like a domino effect. Oak lifts his head as now the drawers all around the kitchen begin to slide open, ever so slowly.

Puzzled, Marion begins to ponder. It doesn't take long before she realizes what's going on. "Oak Leigh Black," she says sternly, just as the windows in the room slide up and open on their own. "You are hours past your normal time to suppress," she notes as she realizes that his abilities are beginning to take control as the garlic from yesterday begins to slowly fade from Oak's system. She walks over to one of the windows and tries to pull it shut. "You need to eat the garlic. Now."

Oak doesn't normally get the chance to see his power come out because his mother always ensures he has garlic first thing in the morning. Seeing the room move, the cabinets open and the windows lift, Oak begins to scare himself. He opens the brown bag and feels around inside until he grabs hold of the crunchy outside of a bulb of garlic. He pulls it out and snaps off a clove. He hesitantly holds the black garlic up to his nose. The aroma is slightly sweeter than normal but there is no mistaking it for anything other than garlic. He nearly gags as he slips it into his mouth, a smoky caramelized flavor hitting his tongue.

Marion manages to get the one window shut as the cabinet she just closed behind her creaks open again. She turns and looks at it and then darts her gaze over to Oak, impatiently tapping her foot for him to finish. He swallows the clove, just barely holding it down as each cabinet door ceases to move and the kitchen windows glide shut on their own. Marion mumbles something under her breath, low and deep. Unable to make out anything she is saying, Oak turns his gaze to all the cabinets as they slam firmly shut.

"Whoops!" Marion giggles. "That was a bit more aggressive than I had intended. Feel better?" she asks him. He doesn't answer her but gives the slightest of nods, not sure if he is going to vomit, hands trembling from both a combination of forcing down the food he hates and scaring himself after seeing his power to do things he was entirely not in control of.

Marion brings a hot mug of coffee to the table and sets it down in front of Oak. "We have quite a bit of spell work to do still, so drink up," she tells him as she makes her way out of the kitchen and back into the apothecary.

Oak finally decides he is feeling okay to move again and won't get sick, so he takes his mug from the table and follows Marion. The door to the apothecary is slightly open and as Oak gets closer he hears a banging coming from inside. He slowly pushes through the door and finds Marion hammering at an object. "What are you doing?"

She takes another small swing at the small hard object. "I'm breaking pieces off the fluorite and next

I'll do the quartz," she says, narrowly missing her finger as the small hammer hits more of the writing desk than the crystal. "The pieces need to be small enough to tuck under the latch of the safety pin." She tosses a book to Oak between swings. "Go to page 367."

He just barely catches the book with his free hand, the mug in his other splashing coffee. He takes the book to the coffee table and sits on the floor. Oak sets down the mug and opens the book to the page Marion requested. A section of the page is highlighted and he reads it out loud.

"The sap from an oak tree provides the best adhesive properties for infusing magical items as it contains the ability to allow energy to flow through it unlike man-made glues and tapes." He looks at his grandmother.

"So, we need oak tree sap to use as a glue to stick these crystal pieces to each other and the pin," she says, dealing one final blow to the crystal in her hand. She slides her palm around the surface of the desk to gather the fragments of rocks into a small pile. "Take this and go outside to the front yard. This entire neighborhood is lined in oak trees. Make a small puncture in an oak tree and allow the sap to spill out. Gather it onto this piece of parchment and bring it back here. We only need a small amount." She hands him a small, sharp metal tool and a tiny square of parchment paper.

Oak takes the items from her hand and slowly walks outside, realizing he has hardly any drive to perform this task. He only now realizes just how powerful Grandma's incense combination has been on him to energize him to create. It's a new day and she hasn't lit anything new yet so he feels like his normal, hard-to-entertain self again. Once outside, he notices what an amazingly cool and breezy day it is. Crunchy leaves swirl on the ground as he walks to the oak tree on the side of the front yard. He is not quite sure if this tree is still considered to be on his grandmother's property line but figures no one will care if he steals a few drops of sap. He uses the tool Marion gave him to drive a tiny hole into the side of the tree, indenting his palm as he uses it as leverage to push the tool through the bark and then pulls it back once more.

Oak looks at the puncture, waiting patiently for it to begin to drip. He watches the tree as a tiny bubble of sap begins to form on the hole he created. Filling up until the sap reaches about the size of half a pea, it begins to drip. Just before it's about to start running down the side of the bark, Oak uses the metal rod to scrape off the drip of sap and slides it onto the small sheet of parchment. He places his thumb over the puncture wound of the tree and when he removes it, the hole is gone, leaving a trace of stickiness on his thumb. He smirks because his limited use of magic is still impressive to him and not scary when he uses it for small tasks.

He heads back inside and finds his grandmother putting a piece of quartz into a small black velvet drawstring bag. She motions to the pile of tiny crystal pieces on the desk. Oak peers down and sees that she has mixed the fluorite and quartz together. "This entire project will work better if you create this piece yourself," Marion says, motioning for Oak to sit at the desk. "Your own creation will be more compatible to you than someone else using their form of magic to enchant it."

He pulls the large safety pin from his pocket and unlatches the sharp end as Marion waves her arms around the room causing a gust of wind that instantly lights every candle around them. Oak admires the show of magic as that is a little too advanced for him to be able to accomplish just yet.

Marion lights her famous combination of incense and places it in the room. Oak now feels ready to work. He loves this incense enchantment; it feels so good. "Now, take this." She hands him a pin with a tiny black ball at the top. "This needs to be precise. Use it to dip into some of the oak sap and gather a few crystal pieces."

He holds the pushpin steady as he dips from the parchment paper to the pile of fluorite and quartz on the desk, carefully spinning the pin as the stones collect in the sap.

"Now, reapply more sap. We want to use it like a glue and tuck it deep into the clasp of the safety pin, nice and tightly packed so that it doesn't interfere with the clasping of the sharp end."

Oak coats the fragments in more sap and begins to put the mixture into the hollow head of the safety-pin clasp. His hands tremble a little and he wishes he hadn't had coffee before doing something so precise. Though he is not sure he would even be able to be awake if he hadn't. He tucks the infusion of crystals and tree sap into the deep corners of the safety pin. He spins the pushpin by its black ball around and around until he's sure the mix has stuck to the inside of the clasp. He pulls the now-clean pushpin out slowly.

"Success!" His grandmother cheers and takes the safety pin from him. Then she props it up by driving it down into a block of foam in the room that she normally uses for pinning insects. "Now we must allow it to fully cure. In the meantime, we must get back to work to figure out the rest of this boutonnière." She heads to a bookshelf and begins to browse. Oak feels the urge to take a break welling up inside him but is immediately released as he takes a breath and smells the enchanted scents of purple statice and vervain.

Marion pulls out a large poster-like chart from the back of one of the bookshelves. "This is a chart of sigils that will help us achieve what we need," she says, bringing the large chart over to him. They peer at it together, gazing at the many symbols and patterns, reading below each one to find out what it does.

Oak's eyes wander toward the bottom. He notices the word 'life' in the description of one of the symbols. It looks like a square with none of the corners closing, and at the end of each clean straight line is another two sets of short straight lines going the opposite way.

"Grandma, look," he says as he points down toward the bottom of the scroll. *Success and life.*

"I was intending on finding a life sigil but this one also ensures success. I'm certain we won't find a sigil more perfect than this one."

Oak is pretty familiar with sigils. Dev has one on her purse to ward off thieves. Basically, it is a pattern that conjures the universe to alter whatever the intended symbols pull from the world. Once activated, through fire, a sigil protects the intention for an allotted amount of time. This sigil, however, will be powered by the crystal infusion and should last indefinitely. "So how do we do it?" Oak asks his grandmother.

"Well. You'll have to carve it into the head of the safety pin." Oak glances at the pin that's been pressed into the foam block across the room. Marion hands him a magnifying glass. "You'll probably need this," she says, trying not to laugh. She would absolutely hate to have to carve such a tiny sigil. Especially considering the particular one they need to use has such straight lines. "I'm going to make some lunch." She strides out of the room.

"Lunch?" Oak says to himself as he glances at the time. It's almost two p.m. He has no idea how it's gotten so late and realizes that she was not joking when she told him this would take all weekend. He grabs the pin from the foam and sits down at the desk. He uses the magnifying glass to inspect the outside of the clasp. He is going to have to use the pushpin's sharp tip to slowly carve the sigil into the head of the safety pin. Grinding metal against metal to create a carving is surely going to take a few hours.

Oak takes a deep breath, filling his lungs with the smell of incense, and gets to work, constantly glancing to the sigil chart to make sure he is positioning everything correctly. Marion periodically enters the room from time to time, setting down a plate of food for him, and casually refilling his drink while he works. Sometimes, she hunches over and examines his work to make sure he is doing things right.

After a few hours, Marion glances into the room. Oak is sprawled out on the floor like a starfish, asleep. She looks toward the writing desk and sees the safety pin tucked underneath the magnifying glass with metal dust all around. She gives the dust a gentle blow after she removes the magnifying glass and sets it aside. She picks up the pin and inspects it. It's perfect. She has no doubts that this will provide the mistletoe with everlasting life. Marion smiles as she sets the pin down and snuffs out the incense she's kept burning all day for her grandson. He does not need motivation right now; he needs rest. She leaves him be in the apothecary and finishes the rest of her day quietly and alone while Oak sleeps until morning.

***

Oak finds himself curled into a ball nearly halfway under the coffee table in the apothecary. The smell of coffee floats through the air and fills the house with its warm scent. He checks the time. Eight a.m. Getting up, he heads towards the kitchen as the wafting aroma fills him entirely.

"Good morning." Marion says, breakfast ready and the table set. Oak sits, rubbing the sleep from his eyes as he takes in all the smells. "Hopefully we'll finish today.

I want your mother only to know about this when it's complete." She sets a plate of hot food in front of him.

"She usually picks me up about seven. How do we convince her this will be safe?" he asks, using a fork to prod around the eggs on his plate.

"We don't." She sits down in a chair across from him with her cup of coffee. "We don't know that it is safe, so we cannot convince her of anything we do not know ourselves." She rests her elbows on the table, leaning slightly forward. "But, she has been overprotective of you all her life. We tell her what we've created, and if she pushes back, we tell her it's time for her to loosen your reins."

Oak puts a forkful of food into his mouth with a smirk and a lifted eyebrow that says 'good luck with that.'

Marion rises and starts toward the apothecary. "Take your time and enjoy your meal, I'll begin working on our final step."

Oak fiddles around with his food, smearing it across plate, kicking his feet back and forth underneath the chair. He had completely forgotten that his mother might not even go for this idea. His appetite gone, he stands up, leaves his plate on the table, and heads to the apothecary.

Marion is scooping the ashes from the incense they've been burning all weekend into her mortar and pestle. "In the closet there, get me the bottle of Florida water, please," she says as Oak enters the room.

He heads to the closet and pulls open the door. There are six-foot-tall shelves lining the inside, filled with so many various things. Jars and bottles of every shape and size, more books, statues, a cup filled with pens made from bones, doll parts, spell candles, scrying mirrors, and more.

Oak browses the shelves, trying to find the Florida water bottle. He notices a tall, thin, clear bottle with a colorful label and gold top. *Agua de Florida*, it says on the label. Reaching into the closet, he takes the bottle off the shelf. He closes the door and turns to his grandmother who is now right behind him. "Pour a little in here," she tells him, holding up the mortar while stirring the ashes with an orangewood stick.

He unscrews the top of the bottle and dribbles a bit of water in. Oak can smell various forms of citrus with notes of spiciness that he can't place. Marion continues to stir as the water mixes with the ash, creating a dark gray paste. "What is this going to do?" he asks while she walks over to the desk where they've been working all weekend.

"This mix is going to activate the sigil you so brilliantly carved and I had you add this Florida water that was sent to me directly from Peru to help your mother accept this whole thing and forget about her three-day rule. It should open her mind to let us try and see if it works."

"We're putting a spell on Mom?" Oak asks.

"Let's call it a compelling," Marion replies, smiling as she scoops up the paste with the flat end of the orangewood stick. "Bring the pin here." Oak brings the pin over. "Sigil up, so I can spread it into the carving," she tells him. He holds the symbol for life towards her and she spreads the paste across the sigil. "Make sure it fills the crevices entirely. One missing spot or bubble will ruin the entire spell."

Oak uses his thumb to spread the mixture into the tiny head of the safety pin. He spreads it around until his thumb wipes away all of the excess, revealing only the strenuously carved mark for life and success.

"Now for the fun part," Marion says, setting down the bowl on the desk and handing Oak a single match. "Light the sigil on fire."

He takes the match and hands her the pin. He holds the head of the match between his middle finger and thumb and snaps. The match roars as a large spark arises, quickly diminishing into a controlled flame, thin streams of smoke billowing off. Oak presses the head of the match to the latch of the safety pin in his grandmother's hand. It sparks brightly as it catches and sizzles and beams like an Independence Day sparkler. Marion holds it slightly more away from her as Oak takes a step back, smiling widely. The alcohol in the mixture evaporates and the flame snuffs out, leaving behind only a freshly activated sigil of life.

"The hard part is done. Your mother should be compelled to ignore the three-day trial and let you wear this forever. The only thing we need to do now is get a tiny bit more sap from the tree out front to secure the mistletoe to this and we are finished," Marion says.

Eyes wide, Oak swipes up the metal piercing rod and parchment from the desk and runs outside. He goes to the tree and plunges the rod firmly in, then out and waits for some sap to begin to drip.

While waiting, he notices a little girl peering from behind the tree. "Um, hello?"

Her fluffy, pale sea-foam-green dress with a white waistband blows in the gentle breeze of the day. Her hair is dark and long with perfectly straight-across bangs. "Hello," she says in a high squeaky voice, almost as if she's inhaled a helium balloon. She stares at him, hands folded behind her back, twisting to and fro, as if she's waiting for something.

"Uh, do you need something?" Oak asks uncertainly, still waiting for the sap to drip.

"You're ugly," she says.

Surprised, he looks back towards her and finds her suddenly gone. Feeling uncomfortable at the whole interaction, he looks around and sees no one except the community lawn service doing the weekly maintenance. His foot is tingling like it's falling asleep while he waits for the sap. He sees no sign of the little girl anywhere.

Finally, Oak notices some sap pooling out of the puncture. Much more this time than before. He hits his leg just above the knee with his fist a couple times, his foot feeling very tight, tingling more now. He uses the parchment to collect the sap and turns back toward the house. His legs tangle and he falls flat on his face with a thud. Lifting his head, he looks at his legs to see his left foot is still firmly planted where it was when he was facing the tree, feeling like a thousand tiny needles are pricking him up to the knee.

THE COVEN'S SON

Oak rolls over to untangle his legs and has to physically yank his foot from the patch of dead grass underneath. He notices small mushrooms circling the area where his foot was. *Must've been suctioned in some mud,* he thinks. That would explain the mushrooms and dead grass, a wet spot in the yard.

Standing up, he brushes his clothes off with his free hand, the rod and parchment with sap sample in the other. He brings the items inside to Marion and they use the sap to coat the sharp side of the safety pin. Then they slide it through the stem of the mistletoe as it pokes out the other end. They pin it shut and Marion explains that it will need to dry in order to be secure. "You take this home with you tonight and put it on the roof of the house," she explains. "The crystals inside need to be charged by the moon for the whole thing to work."

Oak nods in understanding and places the boutonnière into a small box from the apothecary closet. The doorbell chimes. "Well, we couldn't have timed that more perfectly if we tried," Marion says, patting her grandson on the shoulder. She is so proud of what they've accomplished this weekend. She answers the door and greets Dev. "I hope you had a wonderful time!"

Dev gives a weak smile and enters the house, her hair undone, wearing no makeup and a T-shirt and sweats. Marion does not pry as to what that means but assumes her daughter's plans could probably have gone better.

"Ready to go home?" Dev asks Oak, seeing him in the doorway of the apothecary.

"Yes."

"We have something to show you!" Marion exclaims. She motions to Oak to open the box in his hands. He is hesitant to make the reveal right now but does it anyway. Slowly, the lid of the box slides off and reveals a beautiful brooch made with live mistletoe.

Dev peers inside at it. She knows exactly what she is looking at and knows how much time and effort has gone into it. She opens her mouth to protest, but hesitates. After a minute of searching for the right words, she says, "What an incredible idea! Please be careful. Let's go home. I'm tired." Then she turns and walks out the front door.

Oak stands still and moves his eyes to Marion in amazement. "Did she really appreciate something magical I did?"

"Either that or we put a spell on your mother with the Florida water. Either way, who cares? She's allowing it."

Oak smirks and closes the box. He gives his grandmother a hug goodbye and heads out the door.

The ride home is mostly quiet and smooth. They arrive at their house and head inside. Alan is not home, though he normally isn't. Not while Oak is awake.

Dev asks Oak if he is hungry. He tells her no and explains that he has to put the pin on the roof to charge under the moon tonight. He winces in anticipation of her reply but she just says okay and heads off to the living room. He is really not sure if this is the Florida water talking or if she has finally realized she has to let go a little.

Oak heads to a little nook outside the house that he can climb to access the roof. He gently sets the box on top of the house and removes the lid. By morning he will have a fully functioning suppression charm. Back in the house, he preps his backpack for school in the morning. He brushes his teeth, changes his clothes, and goes to bed.

Chapter 3

The sun shines brightly into the bedroom and onto Oak's face. He closes his eyes tightly and rolls over, pulling the blanket over his head as he groans. Then the memory hits. "The pin!"

He hops out of bed and runs out his bedroom door, dashes through the hallway past his mother, and out the front door. He rounds the side of the house to the nook and retrieves the small box from the roof. It doesn't look any different, but he figures it's not supposed to.

He heads back into the house and bumps into his mother who was coming out to see why he ran outside in such a hurry. "Everything okay?"

"Yeah, like I told you, I had to charge the crystals we infused into the pin under the moon," he says, tilting the box toward her so that she can see inside. "Do you think it's ready?"

She reaches a finger in and holds it to the pin. "Yes, it is."

"You can feel if it's charged?"

"Yes, you can feel a tiny vibration. You should be able to tell; it's quite easy."

He isn't sure why she is being so calm about the whole thing when just a few days ago she was shoving garlic down his throat like a raging madwoman. Oak touches his finger to the pin and then touches the box. "I'm not sure I can tell a difference."

"You will, just keep trying. But right now go get ready for school," she tells him.

He heads to his bedroom to put the box down and goes into the bathroom to brush his teeth and do his hair. The entire time he is prepping to leave he can't stop thinking about wearing his new magical amulet. He makes his way back into his bedroom and picks an outfit from the closet, grabs a pair of shoes out from underneath his bed, and slips them on.

Oak picks up the entire boutonnière and stands at the full-length mirror hanging behind his bedroom door. He takes a deep breath. With trembling hands he holds the plant pin on different areas of his body, deciding on what looks most subtle. He decides it looks best along the bottom left side of his T-shirt. He unlatches the sharp-pointed end of the safety pin from the crystal-infused clasp and pushes it through the bottom edge of his shirt. After securing the latch he takes a step back to see himself. A wave of coolness washes over his entire body, the kind of feeling that you get when someone gives you unexpected terrible news. The feeling settles and Oak feels perfect. He knows it is working.

"WE'RE GOING TO BE LATE!" Dev yells from the front of the house. Oak snaps out of his trance and grabs his backpack from his bed and meets her in the car.

When they get to the school, Dev pulls up to the curb to let Oak out of the car. He opens the car door, turns to her, and says "Thank you" as sincerely as possible.

Dev knows the 'thank you' is not for dropping him off at school. She puts her hand on his shoulder and gives him a loving rub. "Have a great day," she says as he stands up and heads to the school entrance, his head held high.

He marches through the hallways of lockers feeling great that he finally isn't going to smell much like garlic anymore. He knows he still does; it will take a few weeks for it to leave his system, but his confidence is still boosted at the idea. As he heads down the hall to his locker, the other students still turn away from him. A few kids even run directly into other students trying to avoid being near him. This isn't anything out of the ordinary for Oak; it's part of why he was so desperate to figure out a different way to suppress the excess energy. He feels a bit discouraged that nothing has changed even though he knows it's all different for him now.

The first half of the day goes on as usual. Nothing different from before this past weekend. He reminds himself he has to be patient and allow the scent of garlic and the reputation that precedes it to go away. At lunch he realizes he spent all of his morning messing around with the mistletoe and completely forgot to pack himself food. He checks his wallet and has enough money to buy some. He waits in the long line, sliding a tray along as the line slowly inches forward.

The gap the students leave between them and him is painfully clear. He finally gets his food and pays.

Just beyond the exit to the food line, Oak stands slightly to the side, scanning the cafeteria for somewhere to sit. He spots his friend Kyle-Ray by recognizing his unusual hair. His only friend. They ended up being friends because they both had strange names. Oak's name literally means wood and they laughed about the story his mom told him about how he was actually named after a cabinet. Kyle-Ray is his actual first name or, first names, hyphen and all. Nobody calls him Kyle, and he assumes it's to mock the strangeness of it.

Oak goes to the far corner of the room to sit next to Kyle-Ray. He sets his tray down next to him. "Oak tree! Hey!" Oak pushes him halfway off his chair for calling him that. "Where were you all weekend? I came over twice and no one answered the door," Kyle-Ray tells him, moving his long, shoulder-length black hair with sun-faded light brown ends out of his face to talk.

"I was at my grandma's all weekend. Mom was out of town."

"Oh awesome. What did you do?" Kyle-Ray asks.

"We, um, mostly did crafts," Oak says to him. No one knows very much about witches' lives. Not because it's a secret really, but because if you say anything about having magic, being a witch, potions, spells, or oils you are automatically dismissed as being crazy. It hasn't been a very big deal since the 1800s. So unless someone finds out, it's just easier to leave things untold.

"Wow, crafting. Did you knit me a scarf?" Kyle-Ray asks him, bumping his shoulder with his.

"Yes," Oak laughs. "A long floral knit scarf. Also, I made you some fudge."

Kyle-Ray stares at him. "I'm so ready," he tells Oak, striking a pose as if he is wearing a long scarf and biting some fudge.

Oak laughs, trying not to choke on his food. Kyle-Ray has never once mentioned Oak's smell and Oak has no idea if he even has a sense of smell to begin with since he doesn't believe that anyone would want to be his friend otherwise. Kyle-Ray is also much taller than Oak, so he wonders if maybe the scent doesn't travel up. But, they sit next to each other all the time. Oak has to control his overthinking.

The lunch bell rings, indicating the start of everyone's next period. Oak tells Kyle-Ray goodbye and goes to take his tray to the dishwashing window. He slides his tray to the woman who is setting them into a large machine. He turns to try to catch up with Kyle-Ray who has already left the cafeteria. Not paying attention to his surroundings, Oak slams directly into another male student, causing the boy to drop his tray and send everything on it sprawling across the floor. The boy looks at Oak and reels his hand back, slapping Oak hard across the face.

In total shock, Oak's instincts kick in and he pulls his hand into a fist and punches the boy square in the nose. The boy falls to the ground and there are audible gasps and reactions from the rest of the students around them. The boy on the ground skitters back and holds his nose. He looks flabbergasted.

Oak turns to leave the confrontation but is met with a faculty member standing over him. "Principal's office. Now."

***

Sitting in the waiting area of the principal's office, Oak keeps craning his neck to peek at the doorway of the hall. He has been waiting for over thirty minutes and seen multiple students come and go into the office but none of them were the boy he punched. He knows he is in trouble, but the boy started it. He slapped him first. Why isn't he here waiting to see the principal too?

More time passes as a few faculty members go in and out of the office, followed by a couple more students. Finally, a deep voice calls from the office. "Oak Leigh Black."

Oak stands. The principal motions for him to come inside. He has seen Principal Santora around the school but has never had a conversation or even said hello to him. He goes inside the office and Mr. Santora shuts the door behind them.

"Please, have a seat, Mr. Black," Mr. Santora says as he heads around to the opposite side of his dark mahogany desk and sits in his large, deep red overstuffed leather office chair. "So," he starts. "It seems you got into a physical altercation with another student." His cleanly shaped black facial hair moves against his lips as he speaks.

Oak can't help but stare at the single patch of gray just above his lip. "Y-yes, sir," Oak responds nervously.

"You know that is a very serious offense, Mr. Black, one that can get you suspended and possibly expelled." The principal leans forward, the light from the sun now reflecting off his bald head.

"Yes, sir, I understand. I was only defending myself though." Oak tries to sound confident through the shakiness of his voice.

Mr. Santora looks at him, confused. "Defend yourself from what?"

"F-from the boy I ran into. I didn't mean to run into him. I wasn't paying attention, but he slapped me. I had to defend myself."

The principal leans back, his hand on his chin, crossing his legs. "He slapped you? Well, you and I both know that isn't true, Mr. Black."

Oak sits up straighter now. "Yes, sir, he did. He hit me first."

"Oak, I have eight witness statements here with me; five from students and three from faculty, and not one of them mentions you being slapped."

Oak's mouth drops open slightly from shock. "What? That's impossible; that's the only reason I hit him. He hit me first!"

Mr. Santora reaches over to a small stack of papers on his side of the desk and fans them out before Oak. "Every statement here says you bumped into the student and then punched him in the face, for no apparent reason."

Oak scans all the documents. Every single one of them has left out him being slapped. "No, this isn't right. He slapped me. Why would I just punch someone? That doesn't make sense!"

"No, it doesn't make sense, does it? That's why this is such a serious matter. You cannot go around hitting students, Mr. Black. You were even the one at fault for bumping into him. The statements mention the boy was merely standing behind you quietly, waiting to turn in his lunch tray."

"It's not true! It didn't happen like that! I promise! Maybe no one noticed us until after I punched him. Maybe no one saw him slap me first!" Oak insists, his eyes welling up with tears.

The principal pauses for a moment to evaluate Oak's emotions. He has a lot of experience reading students and believes Oak is being sincere. "Well," he says, crossing his arms. "We do have security cameras in the cafeteria. It will take a day or two but if you really are telling the truth, we can go over the footage to clear your name. We may be able to lessen your punishment if we can prove he hit you first."

"I am telling the truth. Please get the footage," Oak pleads.

Mr. Santora nods and writes something down. "You are free to go while we investigate this further. Please, stay out of trouble until then."

Oak stands to leave and takes a deep breath of relief. When they pull the security footage, his name will be cleared, at least from starting the fight. Just before he heads out the door to get back to class, the principal stops him. "Your mother has been notified of this altercation."

Oak nods apologetically and heads back to class. He waited so long in the reception area that school is practically over. He makes a quick pit stop to swap out some books at his locker for the last period of the day.

When his locker opens, a small white envelope falls at his feet. He looks down and picks it up, grabbing the books he needs. After he swings the locker shut and puts his backpack on, he opens the envelope. Inside, he finds a sample of cologne, like the kind you pull out of the folds of a fashion magazine. There's nothing else.

He falls back against the locker and pushes his head back, throwing the sample and envelope onto the floor. "I'm not gonna cry. I'm not gonna cry," he says to himself over and over, holding his gaze upwards to help prevent tears from being able to fall from his eyes. "It's all over. I just need time. Just time and it'll be gone. I'm so close," he says, motivating himself to hold it together.

After a few moments of deep breathing he is able to pull himself together long enough to go back to class. He enters the classroom, disrupting the lesson, and all eyes are on him. The teacher holds her arm out for him to take his seat and continues. As Oak walks to his seat, each student he passes holds their nose or turns their face away from him.

Oak takes his seat toward the back of the class and grips his desk so hard his knuckles turn white. His head is swirling with emotion. Being blamed for the fight, the envelope in his locker, and now everyone's over-the-top reaction to him walking to a desk. He is having a hard time holding everything in.

As the teacher is talking about the ancient Egyptians, the lights in the room begin to flicker. A few bulbs burst and shatter into the clear plastic covering just below. Students scream and gasp. One student dives under her desk and another bolts for the door. "Calm down, everyone! It's just a power outage," the teacher says to the class.

Oak's heart begins to race. The charmed mistletoe isn't working. Everyone in class is talking at the same time; the teacher has lost their attention. Oak's eyes dart around. He has no idea what to do. Should he run out of the room? Should he stay where he is? There is nothing to suppress his power if his creation isn't working. His mother was right to be wary. He looks down at the pin on the edge of his shirt and stares in surprise. There is nothing there. The pin is gone.

Oak begins to panic. The clear plastic coverings on the ceiling protecting the light bulbs swing open, the ones with shattered bulbs sprinkling shards of glass down into the room, some into students' hair, the rest on the floor and desks all around. The room is still lit by the sun from the windows that line the left side of the room.

Oak stares in disbelief at all the glass on the ground. No one appears to be hurt, but he is causing chaos and can't control it. Then he sees it. His pin is lying on the floor next to some shattered glass.

"Is everyone okay?" the teacher is shouting, but she is drowned out by all the talking, screaming, and gasps. Oak stares at the pin, in full panic mode as the glass and mistletoe begin to vibrate; all the debris where he is looking is bouncing and vibrating like sand on a loud bass speaker. "Carefully, everyone out of the classroom!" the teacher says to the class, ushering students out as they stand from their desks.

The mistletoe and glass-shard mixture shakes violently across the floor, slowly moving toward Oak. Students walk by, inhibiting his view of the pin, but it continues to slide and move toward him. The board at the head of the classroom falls to the floor with a deafening crack, the metal frame making a much louder noise than one would expect. Everyone screams.

The chaos enters the hallway as the students leave. The precious charmed amulet finally reaches Oak's grasp and he immediately grabs it. He snaps into a sense of calm that instant. His heart immediately stops racing; the lights that haven't blown turn back on, and a few more students exit the room. Everything is now still. Oak takes a huge breath and reattaches the pin to his shirt. The charm *does* work; it had just fallen off.

There are only a few students left in the room, including Kyle-Ray, who shares a history class with Oak on Mondays. Oak stands and follows the rest of the students as they leave the room. The teacher takes a head count along with other staff members who have come to help after hearing the commotion. No one knows what happened, except Oak.

Kyle-Ray leans into Oak and whispers, "Did you get your plant thing back?"

THE COVEN'S SON

Oak's heart races again. "What?" he asks him, playing dumb.

"That plant thing you've been wearing on your shirt all day. When you were walking to your desk, Kate Sumpter unhooked it and it fell on the ground. I couldn't say anything, but I was going to grab it when class let out. Then, the power went all crazy and I couldn't get it."

"Kyle-Ray Stem?" the teacher calls out, doing roll call.

"Here," he says, raising his hand.

"Oh yeah, I got it. I saw it on my way out," Oak lies. He realizes when he gets home he'll have to study how to prevent anyone from unlatching the pin except him.

"Oak Leigh Black?"

He responds to his name and raises his arm.

The final bell rings and the teacher nods that everyone is free to go, jotting down that all students are accounted for and wiping her forehead.

Oak and Kyle-Ray head outside with the rest of the school to the pick-up line and search for their parents. Kyle-Ray sees his dad and pats Oak on the shoulder then runs off. Oak scans the crowd half-heartedly because the faster he finds his mother, the sooner he will be in trouble for the call from the principal. Soon, he spots his mom's car and slowly walks over to it with his head down. He opens the door and gets inside, buckling his seat belt.

"You punched somebody? What the hell, Oak?" Dev asks him, pulling around the car in front of her waiting to pick up their child.

"Sort of," he responds quietly, staring at the glove compartment.

"Sort of? How do you sort of punch someone? What happened?"

"He was standing behind me. I wasn't looking and I ran into him. He slapped me across the face, so I punched him."

"He slapped you?"

"Yes, but I guess no one saw it happen. All the witness reports said I punched him out of nowhere."

"Why would you punch someone for no reason? They didn't question that?" she asks him, pulling out of the school and onto the main road.

"No. Well, yes, the principal did. He believed me. He said there's security footage that he is going to get. It'll take a day or two though," he explains.

"If he hit you first, you know I always told you that gives you every right to strike back. So, you're not in trouble if that's the case."

"It is."

"If it's not, we have a problem."

"We won't," Oak promises.

They pull up to a red light just before the turn into their neighborhood. "You know what I just noticed?" his mom says, starting a smile.

"What?"

"I didn't need roll down the windows. It's kind of nice not having you smell like garlic," she says, giggling.

"What do you mean?" he asks, confused.

"What? You stopped taking the garlic, so you don't smell any more. Did you forget?"

Oak looks down at his pin and gently touches it, ignoring Dev's question. They make their way around the corner and pull into the driveway. Oak gets out of the car and runs into the house before Dev can even unbuckle her seat belt. He runs to his room and slams and locks the door behind him. The lock doesn't work very well and Dev has a pretty heavy hand, so she usually comes bursting in, popping the poorly designed lock, but Oak locks it anyway because the pop of the lock is much louder than just opening the door.

He paces back and forth in his room, stepping over laundry and random garbage or things lying about. He needs to clean his room but his head is so full of thoughts right now. He paces around thinking about the day and everything that happened. "Mom said I don't smell anymore." He walks to one end of the room. "She was closed in with me, right next to me, and she didn't smell anything." He walks to the other end of the room. "Then why? Why is everyone still acting like I smell?"

He stops in the middle of the rom to pick up an empty soda can and toss it into the trash. Then he realizes. It doesn't matter if he doesn't smell anymore. That's his reputation. That's how he is known. No one is going to notice that the smell is gone because everyone avoids him. This won't stop. He will never not be the kid who reeks of garlic.

He balls his hands into fists. Today was supposed to be the best day of his life and it turned out to be one of the worst. Since he missed most of his day sitting in the office, he doesn't have much homework tonight so he thinks it best to get what little he has done and put the rest of tonight to good use. He finishes two math pages and a short essay for science.

Now comes time for the real homework. How to enchant his pin so that no one can open it but him. He has a few books that his grandmother has given him lining a shelf on the wall. He has always found books on herbology the most interesting; however, Oak has only flipped through a few pages of the other books, learning a few tricks, but nothing more than that. He scans the shelf and stops at one that seems promising. *Transmutations.*

He pulls the book down and jumps into his bed, flipping the book open.

Transmutation alchemy is the process of linking various elemental symbols together to create an implosion of magic that fuses all said symbols and creates an otherwise unobtainable feature.

"This is going to be more complicated than I think I'm ready for," he says, rubbing the bridge of his nose.

He scans the contents and begins reading random sections, trying to find what he needs. There is a section on creating a customized transmutation circle. The text refers him to the back sections of the book. Oak flips to the back. There's a diagram of various symbols and meanings, used to create the magic circles. Each symbol has to directly connect with the other symbols, and the link between all symbols needs to make one cohesive circle that does exactly what you need it to do. There seem to be thousands of connecting possibilities.

Oak believes he can create the perfect effect using this form of magic, but to get the right combination of symbols is going to take a long time. He grabs a pencil and paper from his desk and gets back in bed. He begins to sketch out symbols from the back of the book. He begins by choosing a protection symbol, a warding symbol, and a locking symbol. In his head he imagines how each symbol would work and tries to figure out in what order to connect them and where the others should link up.

A few hours go by and Oak's bed is littered with sketches of circles and symbols. Connecting these symbols properly to create a fully functioning result is more advanced magic than Oak has ever attempted. A few of the papers are burnt, some of them splattered in a wet black inky mess, some of them completely exploded. The results of linking the symbols together incorrectly produces failed attempt after failed attempt.

Transmutation alchemy results often create an undesirable outcome when organic and inorganic symbolism does not create a free-flowing path to the natural order of creationism, allowing energies to conjure from manifestation to manifestation.

"Okay, I have no idea what that means." His eyes cross trying to comprehend the passage.

Oak sketches away furiously, unknowing of the time. He draws circle after circle and symbols inside circles, then he looks at what he has drawn and concentrates on the next move, another circle, this time a complicated symbol in that one.

Always remember to leave the outermost ring of your custom transmutation circle open until ready to activate. Sealing the outer ring of your circle will activate its magic.

"THAT I understand," he says, relieved that he is beginning to comprehend some of it.

He leaves the outside edge of everything he draws open about a half an inch until he is ready to try it. It takes about five seconds after he seals a transmutation circle before it activates. He draws until there are over fifty intentional markings inside the outer circle, each and every part of it linking together to create something new.

He picks up the paper and holds it in front of himself to look at it. This will be attempt number seventy-eight. He lays the paper down on the floor, reaches out with his pencil and closes the gap, sealing the circle. He backs up and covers his face with his arms; he almost lost an eye on the last attempt since the paper exploded violently. The entire circle begins to glow orange, as if embers are catching it alight. The orange embers slowly spread off the symbol, encasing the entire piece of paper, turning it a dark gray. It wrinkles and settles onto the ground, looking extremely delicate and fragile, and the glow subsides. Oak puts his head in his hands. Another failed attempt.

With a heavy sigh, he bends down to pick up the fragile paper off the floor. When he does, the paper disintegrates in his hands and falls apart, leaving soot on his fingers. He dusts his hands off and trudges into the hallway closet to find a broom and dustpan to clean up his mess. He flicks on the hallway light and reaches for the closet door. The light from the hall reflects a metallic sheen on the gray smudges on his fingers.

Oak stops. He lifts his fingers to his face, turning his hand against the light. There is, in fact, a metallic sparkle. He runs back into his room and flicks on the light to look at the paper on the floor. He gets down on his hands and knees and peers closely at it. "It's metal," he whispers to himself. "It's ... iron? IT'S IRON LEAF!" The paper turned to metal. Exactly the type of metal to create a barrier around his boutonnière that will protect it from being unclasped by anyone but him.

He rolls on the ground excitedly, covering himself in the delicate iron leaf. Now, standing up, looking like a coal miner, with metallic smudges on his face and in his hair, he jumps onto his bed and redraws the transmutation circle once more, being extremely careful to replicate it exactly. He gently places the new drawing on the floor, leaving it unsealed.

He runs to the kitchen in the dark, trying to be as quiet as possible since it's about three a.m., and grabs a piece of garlic out of the pantry. Taking a knife, he cuts a tiny piece off a clove. He tosses it into his mouth like a piece of candy. He doesn't chew or swallow; he just lets it sit. He needs to suppress his powers from firing out of control when infusing the pin and holding some garlic in his mouth should help with that. He runs back into his bedroom and detaches his pin and lays it in the circle. His excess power should remain suppressed long enough to do the spell.

He takes his pencil and seals the opening. He steps back as the orange embers outline the circle and this time, the metal safety pin of his magical brooch glows. There is a small flash of light and the paper disappears, leaving the glowing orange pin on the floor. The glow dies down and a small stream of smoke floats up into the air. Oak picks it up. The pin is now made of a magical form of iron. It will now prevent anyone besides him from unclasping it. He attaches it to his shirt and spits out the garlic he is holding in his mouth, sending it flying across the room.

Pleased and exhausted, he slumps into bed, on top of the pile of failed attempts, and falls fast asleep.

Chapter 4

"What the hell is all this?"

Oak is shocked awake by his mother yelling. Dev is standing at the doorway to his room, looking at the absolute disaster of a mess he created late into the night. He rubs his eyes and sits up. Groggily, he says, "I was practicing—"

Dev interrupts him. "Transmutation? I see that. This magic is far too advanced for you. You don't even know how to conjure!" She gazes around the room, studying all the different changes the papers have made. "You could have blown up this entire house," she says to him, hands on her hips.

"But, I did it." Oak points to his mistletoe pin and she can clearly see the pin is now made of a different metal.

"You did it? You figured out transmutation circles?" She squints at the mistletoe. "You actually did it." She stands up straight, looking impressed. "That was extremely dangerous, especially to do indoors with no experience. You're very lucky you didn't hurt yourself. Get ready for school," she tells him and leaves him to get dressed.

Oak hops out of bed, unpins the brooch from his shirt, and pins it in his hair so that he can take his shirt off. He changes into his school clothes and heads to the bathroom. Dev is in the kitchen cooking up a breakfast wrap to take on the go. Even though Oak doesn't have to run late to try to avoid eating garlic, the habit is hard to break and Dev knows they will be leaving the house at the last possible second. When he emerges and enters the kitchen with his backpack, Dev hands him a burrito and they head to the car.

On the ride to school, Dev says, "When you get home today, there is something we need to discuss."

"Is it the transmutations? I won't do it again. I just needed to secure the brooch," he responds.

"It's not that," she tells him.

"Then, what is it?"

"Not now. When you get home, okay?"

"All right, I guess." It annoys him when people start conversations and then don't finish them. The thought of what it could be will be running through his mind all day, ruining his concentration.

She pulls up to the curb of the school and lets Oak out of the car. "Have a good day," she says as he shuts the door. As Dev is driving off, Kyle-Ray is dropped off. Oak waves and Kyle-Ray jogs over to him so they can head into the school together.

"Ready for another day of knocking people out?" Kyle-Ray jokes to him.

"That's not funny," Oak says to him.

Kyle-Ray flinches and covers his face as if he is about to be hit. "Hey, watch the rage," he says, smirking and giggling.

"Go to class," Oak says to him, pushing him off in the opposite direction.

Oak winds down the hallways, getting the usual stares and reactions. "You gonna punch me too?" one kid says as he passes.

"You're enrolling in anger management, right?" another girl comments, shutting her locker loudly.

He does his best to ignore everyone. The day proceeds pretty normally until the end of third period. A student enters the room in the middle of a lesson and hands the teacher a note. The teacher reads the note out loud as the student leaves. "Oak Black, please go see Mr. Santora in his office."

Oak gathers his things as the other kids taunt him and go "ooh." When he gets into the reception area of the principal's office, the receptionist tells him he can go right in. He opens the office door and both his mom and dad turn to look at him. Oak's stomach drops. There is no way this can be good if his dad is here.

"Mr. Black, please, come in," the principal says and Oak shuts the door behind him. "Have a seat." Oak pulls a chair from the side of the room and places it in between Dev and Alan. "So, Oak. I was able to obtain the video footage of the incident yesterday a bit earlier than I expected."

Oak sits nervously, sweat forming on his forehead. He hasn't done anything wrong so he doesn't know why both his parents are here.

"We are going to let you review it now, with your parents present. They have not seen it yet," Mr. Santora says, turning his computer screen around so that all three of the Blacks can see. He hits a button on his keyboard and the black-and-white security footage shot from the ceiling begins to play. They see Oak returning his lunch tray at the window and can also see the boy standing a fair distance behind him. Oak turns around and is looking in another direction when he bumps into the boy. Then, out of nowhere, Oak punches the student in the face, knocking him to the ground.

Oak gasps. "WHAT?" His father pinches the bridge of his nose and his mother looks beyond disappointed. "No, no, no, that's not right, there's no way."

"Son, it's right here, in black and white, on video," Mr. Santora says sternly. "I'll play it again," he says, clicking the keyboard key over and over, replaying the footage in a loop. "Here you are returning the tray, you bump into the boy, and for no reason it seems, you punch him."

"HE SLAPPED ME!" Oak yells, standing up.

"Sit down, Mr. Black," the principal says. "I was very inclined to believe you were telling me the truth. That's why I hurried to get this footage. I must say I am indeed disappointed."

Oak sits and stares in disbelief.

"This will certainly be taken care of at home," his dad says, reassuring Mr. Santora.

"I'm afraid it is going to be a bit more complicated than that," the principal responds, turning the computer screen back to himself. "Oak, I'm going to need you to head to your locker and gather all your things. An escort will accompany you. Your parents are going to stay with me so that we can discuss your possible expulsion."

"EXPULSION? I'm being expelled!?" Oak exclaims.

"It's possible. We have a zero-tolerance policy on physical violence. This matter is out of my hands. The good news is, the boy's parents are not pressing charges."

Dev's eyes begin to tear up and Alan just shakes his head. Oak stands up and leaves the room. He walks slowly to his locker, escorted by a school security guard following behind, replaying the footage in his head over and over. He doesn't understand how the camera doesn't show him getting slapped across the face. He knows it happened.

Just before he reaches his locker, the bell ending third period goes off. Soon the halls fill with students chatting and opening lockers. Oak gets to his locker and loads his backpack with his things. There's a tap on his shoulder. He turns and sees Kyle-Ray smiling. "Wanna have lunch?"

"I think I've ... been expelled," Oak says, voice shaking, looking up at the ceiling.

"What!" Kyle-Ray exclaims. The loudness of students in the hall drowns him out.

"I gotta go," Oak says, visibly upset, eyeing different areas above him. "Here." Oak hands him a plastic bag that was in his locker.

"What's this for?" Kyle-Ray asks.

Oak clears his throat, lifting a fist to his mouth. The fire sprinklers being to spin, spraying a downpour of water all over the students in the hallway. Everyone begins to scream and run. Kyle-Ray puts the plastic bag over his head and runs off. Every drop of water misses Oak. Completely dry and unaffected he walks back to the principal's office, satisfied now that he will no longer have to experience the torment of this school any longer.

The car ride home is mostly quiet, aside from a cough or sigh here and there. There is so much tension in the air, you could cut it with a knife. Oak stares out the side window from the back seat, curious as to how his parents are going to handle his mess. They stop at the red light just before the entrance to their neighborhood and Oak notices a large semitruck barreling toward the intersection. Its lights are on and the horn is blaring. The semi is swerving left and right on the road and has clearly lost control. Their red light turns green and Alan, who is driving, hits the gas and they begin to go.

Oak's heart is beating out of his chest as the giant truck blares its horn once more, the headlights shining in Oak's eyes, blinding him temporarily. He screams at the top of his lungs, "LOOK OUT!", and shields his face with his arms, leaning completely to the left in hopes of avoiding the inevitable collision.

Dev screams at Oak's warning as Alan slams on the brakes in the middle of the street. Silence. Alan looks around outside frantically. Nothing happened.

The car behind them at the intersection honks. Oak moves his arms away from his face and sits up.

"Look out at what?!" Dev says angrily.

Oak looks around out the windows. There is nothing there. "There was a semi. It was going to hit us," he says as the car begins to move again.

"What are you talking about!?" Alan asks, very visibly shaken and annoyed.

"I don't know if you think this is a game or what, but you go straight to your room when we get home, do you understand me?" Dev says furiously. "Do. You. Under. Stand. Me?"

"Yes." Oak responds, still looking for the semi.

When they arrive home, Oak goes straight into his bedroom, shuts the door and swipes all the failed alchemy papers onto the floor, and slumps into bed. He pulls the blanket up over his head and curls into a ball. His parents are in another room, fighting. He can hear pretty much everything. They are asking what's wrong with him and how he ended up getting so out of control. They are yelling about him lying and making things up. Oak can hear Dev say she believes it's because of the craft. That his magic is out of control. Alan argues that her entire family has been raised with this for generations and that she needs to fix it. Dev responds, telling him that no one has dealt with a magical son in over two hundred and fifty years. This is all new territory for everyone.

Doors slam repeatedly and then there is a knock on Oak's. The door opens slightly and Alan peeks his head in. "Hey, bud. Let's chat." Oak pulls the blanket off himself and sits up.

Alan sits on the edge of his bed. "Listen," he says, putting his hand on Oak's foot, covered by the blanket. "I'm leaving tonight."

"To go to work?" Oak asks.

"No, I'm checking into a hotel."

"When will you be back?"

"I won't."

A rush of nervousness rushes over Oak. "What do you mean you won't be back?"

"Your mother and I." Alan looks down at the floor, drawing in breath, preparing for his next sentence. "We're getting a divorce."

Oak sits up straighter now. "What? Why? You just had an entire weekend together."

"That weekend was for us to see where our relationship was. It confirmed that we're better off apart."

"Is this because of me?" Oak asks warily.

"Of course not, no. This is strictly between me and your mother."

Oak slightly nods, holding back tears.

Not knowing what else to say, Alan pats Oak's foot and leaves his room. He can be heard shuffling things around by the front door and leaving.

Oak falls back onto his pillow and stares at the ceiling, tears streaming down his face, wondering how things can get any worse. He is not surprised at the news, considering how little his parents were ever together, but hearing it confirmed out loud brings his emotions forward. He loves his parents, but he hardly ever sees his dad because he works so much. Things at home won't really change much. Even so, the idea of his family splitting apart is enough to make his stomach churn.

***

After a couple hours, Oak opens his eyes and realizes he fell asleep. He hears a quiet conversation going on somewhere in the house. He gets up, stretching, and follows the sound into the family office, just next to his parents' bedroom. Well, his mom's bedroom now, he thinks. Dev and Marion are sitting in chairs facing each other, the sides of the arms against the wall of the office, with a small table between them holding tea.

Oak smiles when he sees Marion is here. They both turn and look at him seriously. His smile begins to fade as their eyes pierce into him. "It's time to go," Dev says, setting down a teacup. "Your grandmother canceled her entire day at work to come with us."

He looks to Marion, who is wearing a long black open robe with the sleeves pushed up past her elbows. He can smell the faint tinge of various oils and incense coming off her. "Where are we going?"

"To see Hyacinth, dear," his grandmother answers, cleaning her hands with a napkin. Oak wonders if Marion knows about his parents' situation. He assumes she does, as he just woke up from a nap and they looked pretty settled in when he interrupted their tea. She must have arrived just shortly after he fell asleep, he guesses.

It is still early in the day since Oak got expelled before lunch, so the sun is shining high in the sky as they get into the car to head to Divinity. On the way, Oak asks Marion if his grandpa is still in Peru, trying to strike up any sort of conversation. Pepe travels the world programming old machines that are no longer in production, one of five people in the world that still knows how to do the job. "No, honey, he was in Peru a few months ago. He's in Greece now." The conversation ends there.

They arrive at the store and head inside, the opening of the front entrance letting off a tiny chime. Dev is the first to notice the cardboard book display resting at the right of the checkout. She looks at Marion. "The book of affirmations? Has she lost her mind?"

"OH! My dears, hello hello!" Hyacinth pops out from a back storage room after hearing the door alert her to customers. "Marion! My love, long time!" She opens her arms to hug Oak's grandma, her many bangles clanking and tinging like wind chimes, her endless necklaces rattling.

Marion embraces her. "Mrs. Clove, how wonderful to see you."

"Please, Marion, Miss Clove. I haven't gone by Mrs. since Lulu passed away." Hyacinth's fingers search through a tangle of metal until she holds out a small charm that appears to contain ashes.

"My apologies, dear, though your wife was so wonderful, it's as if her energy never left this place."

Embarrassed by her mother's lapse of memory, Dev interrupts and changes the subject. "Hyacinth, why on earth are you selling the book of affirmations?"

Hyacinth turns bright pink, a color that appears to be quite complementary to the streak in her hair. "This thing sells off the shelf faster than I can keep it in stock. We all know it's a total sham and not one coven member has purchased it, but the talk-show host who hyped it up has everyone believing in the occult and it's helping me keep this place open. Even if they are silly enough to think a witch's bottle filled with hair and rusty nails is used to ward away witchcraft, the very thing they claim to be practicing!"

"So, it's a cash grab," Oak says, smirking.

Marion reaches around Dev and slaps Oak upside the head.

"Ha! I love this kid. Come here, you are my favorite." Hyacinth jingles over to Oak and wraps her arm around him, innocently smushing his face into her large bosom. Now Oak is as red as she was. "What can I get you today? I just received a shipment of dragon's blood resin."

"We are here for something a bit more serious than that," Dev explains.

Hyacinth becomes straight-faced as Dev speak. She may have a large personality but she knows a thing or two about the occult and if anyone has answers, it's her. Dev tells her about the boutonnière

Oak and Marion created to contain his energy. How she believes it is working but somehow his power is leaking out. She tells Hyacinth about Oak's random outbursts and strange behavior and that she believes it may have something to do with him being the firstborn male.

Hyacinth glances at the magical pin on Oak's shirt. "Is it safe for me to touch?"

"Yes, you just won't be able to unlatch it."

She reaches down and holds the pin, looking it over. "It appears very well made, clearly strong and accurate in its design. I see no reason for anything to leak from this. Perhaps you are right; this may have something to do with him being male. Let's check the ancestry of your line." She goes behind the counter and rummages around underneath.

"Our coven's last-known firstborn son was over two hundred and fifty years ago so, we really know nothing about this," Dev says, leaning around the counter.

Hyacinth pops up holding an antique-looking key. She heads to the front door of the store and flips the sign from 'open' to 'closed' and locks it. Then she motions for them to follow her to the far end of the store, to a shelf riddled with various magical items. Standing on the side of the shelf, she steadies her shoulder against it. She pushes it and it slides easily to the side and out of the way, revealing a large dark wood, arched door. Hyacinth places the antique key into the intricately designed iron lock and jiggles it until the door pops open, revealing a long dark downward staircase. She starts walking down the pitch-black stairs, metal snake sconces barely visible on the walls.

Hyacinth swoops her hand in an upward motion, using the wind she creates to light each sconce as she makes her way down. Dev, Marion, and Oak follow her. Oak blows on each fire as he walks down the stairs, changing the color of the flames from orange and red to blue and green.

They make their way down until the stairs open up to a large damp cellar filled to the brim with books. Aisles of shelves hold books that appear to be so old and tattered you can't even tell how they are being held together.

"Now, this is the tricky part," Hyacinth says, wiping sweat from her forehead that formed while traipsing down the stairwell. "A coven's lineage is often lost and forgotten due to the majority of the occult being women. They marry and change their last names and over time it can be almost impossible to trace it back."

Marion ponders the thought for a moment and then speaks up. "I believe I can make the books we need reveal themselves, but we need a lock of hair."

Hyacinth goes to a wall of drawers by the entrance to the staircase and removes a pair of scissors. "Whose?" she says.

"Mother, you are the crone, our oldest living of the coven; you have the heaviest ties to the rest of the ancestry," Dev says.

Marion tugs on a lock of her hair and holds it out for Hyacinth to cut. Hyacinth gently snips off the lock of hair. She faces the aisles of books. "I need all of you to focus your magic on the books."

Oak has wandered away from the group and has flipped to a passage from a book titled *Free Will and Compulsion*.

It is falsely believed that witches take on a single animal known as a 'familiar' to respect as an equal. While witches can and do take on various animals as pets, the true nature of the rumor is that they have the power to compel any animal to do as they please. The animal has to be of sound mind and willing to accept the compulsion to follow the will of the witch. The more stubborn or aggressive animals are much more difficult, if not impossible, to utilize, such as alligators, bears, and mountain lions. A scared animal will also break from compulsion even if it is in the middle of following. A good example of this, known throughout history, would be carrier pigeons. They were first willed by witches to deliver messages and letters to people as early as three thousand years ago to declare the winners of the ancient Olympics.

Oak pages through a couple more paragraphs until he realizes Hyacinth is calling for him. As he arrives, Hyacinth and Dev steady their feet to the width of their shoulders and hold both hands out in front of themselves like claws. Oak mimics this stance and they concentrate their powers on all the paper and leather in the chamber. Marion holds her palm up toward her face, the lock of her hair placed in it. The books on every shelf slowly begin to vibrate and shake, the sound of them moving getting louder and louder. Marion hesitates, waiting for the perfect moment.

They concentrate their power on the books harder and harder until the sound of the vibrations is deafening to the point where you can't even hear yourself think. Marion blows hard on her palm, sending the loose hairs flying around the room. They swirl and travel around every aisle and book, searching for the books that call out to them. A few seconds later, fifty books of various shapes, sizes, colors, and locations shoot out from the shelves and onto the floor, the shaking ceasing immediately after.

"Well, that narrows it down," Hyacinth says, returning to a normal standing position.

"Let's get to work," Marion tells everyone, as they go down the aisles gathering all the records of their coven lineage. Dev stands in an aisle, browsing page by page, looking for anything mentioning a male witch. Marion is seated at a desk in the corner of the giant cellar, her pile of books on the floor beside her. Oak sits on the cold floor of an aisle of books, his collection scattered all around him, learning about his family's heritage. Hyacinth reads two books at a time, glancing back and forth between each, searching for something of relevance.

After hunting for almost two hours, Dev calls the group over. "Come here, I think I found something." Everyone makes a note of where they are in their own search and goes to where Dev is standing. "Listen to this," she says. "Walt Fiches, born to Jeffrey Fiches and Cynthia Toothaker, was the first child born to the couple and was the only firstborn male child ever recorded in the history of the occult." She continues, "Although mythology reports tales of any firstborn child being male to be the most powerful witch any coven would ever know, Walt showed little to no signs of having had any abilities at all. His power appeared to be significantly inferior to any occult-involved first child, born a female."

They stand in silence momentarily.

"So, none of this has anything to do with me being a boy?" Oak asks.

"It appears not," Marion says. Dev looks disappointed.

Hyacinth holds up her hand. "Wait, what was the mother's name again?"

Dev scans the book once more. "Cynthia Toothaker."

"Toothaker. I read something in my pile of books about a Toothaker," she says, hobbling off to where she was reading. Oak and Marion peer over Dev's shoulder, scanning a few pages themselves, hoping for some more answers. "YES! YES! OH YES! PRAISE SATAN, I'VE FOUND IT!" Hyacinth yells from a few aisles over.

Oak giggles and feels appreciative that there is an adult in his life that can be a little silly like him in times that are meant to be serious.

Hyacinth comes barreling around the aisle with a book opened about midway through. "Listen, listen," she huffs, nearly out of breath from her short jog around the corner. "Although Cynthia Toothaker eventually wed Jeffrey Fiches and conceived a child, little is known about her previous teenage affair with a farmer's son named Edmund Nowell. The former couple conceived a child that was born prematurely at twenty-three weeks, and died an hour after birth. However, due to the Toothaker family's wealth, Cynthia's pregnancy was hidden and never recorded." She claps the book shut dramatically.

"That means Walt Fiches was not the firstborn!" Dev exclaims.

"And the premature baby was the one who siphoned Cynthia's magic but died after she was born. So when Walt was born, he was a second-born with hardly any powers. The family hid the original birth and pretended that the legend of a son being born first as the most powerful witch of the occult was all a myth," Marion adds.

They all turn their heads and stare at Oak in awe. Oak takes a step back, feeling uncomfortable.

"You are the very first male to ever be born as a first child in the history of witches!" Hyacinth yells.

"Which means, we need to begin researching the prophecies and legends surrounding the first male witch," Dev says.

Hyacinth claps her hands together. "That is a little easier than tracing your coven's lineage. Those types of books are over here, all in the same place." She begins to walk down the aisle and around the corner, two more aisles over.

Dev and Marion follow, Oak stays behind. He stands in the aisle in shock as all this information begins to sink in. He has always known he's a witch. He was born and raised in the occult just as anyone is raised with other beliefs. He knew he was the first son born as a first child in a very long time, but now he has just found out he is the first, ever. He's never had a huge interest in learning magic or studying it. He likes to play with simple tricks here and there but since his mother was raised in a time that barely needed magic, he needs it even less. But now, everything has changed. There are prophetic books about him. Mythological bindings and scriptures that talk about him as if he is one of the ethereal beings of the universe.

Every witch has powers that need to be suppressed until around the age of ten or twelve, and some late bloomers don't gain control until thirteen. He's on the cusp of turning fifteen and still can't live day-to-day without suppression. Now he knows why. Oak has so many answers. He also has so many new questions.

His vision is blurred in the dim lighting of the dank basement as he stares off at nothing, his mind swirling. His family is moments away from discovering exactly how powerful he really is, and how to handle all the missing links of his magic. This is why he was able to so easily understand transmutation circles without any experience and why he was able to create his brooch without any major flaws or holes or problems. He begins to sway, as he feels lightheaded. He falls backwards into the bookshelf behind him.

"Oak!" Dev yells, two aisles over.

"I'm okay! Sorry!" he says, responding to the books falling off the other side of the shelf. "Coming!" he yells, moving to the next aisle to put back the books that dropped. He shakes his head clear of the twisting ideas filling his mind. He works his way over to where the three witches are standing and researching, going up and down each aisle, his fingers tracing gently over each book he passes. He has a whole new appreciation for being a witch. For having magic. For being powerful. He wants to learn more. He wants to learn it all. Oak comes around to the ladies who are holding a few books and looking for more.

"Here, take these for now," Dev says, handing him three heavy books.

They search the shelves for any information they can find about the firstborn male witch. None of the books are based on fact, just speculation, because there has never been a male witch before. This makes things a little more complicated; no one knows what to believe from the books. It's all theory. After a while they gather the few extra books they find on the shelves and all head back up the stairs into the shop.

Oak lags behind turning all the sconce flames purple and pink, an homage to Hyacinth's face and hair when she's embarrassed. Hyacinth turns to him at the top of the stairs and says, "O powerful being, will you extinguish the glistening flames as my power is too inferior to accomplish the task?" Giggling, she heads to the front door of the shop.

Oak turns at the door atop the stairs. He narrows his eyes hard and concentrates on the flames. Just then, the iron snakes shaped into each sconce turn and bite out the flame from each torch. Pleased with himself, he closes the large wooden door and moves the shelf of merchandise back into place. Hyacinth is reopening the store, unlocking the door, and flipping the sign back to 'open.'

"I think we are about to have a long night ahead of us," Dev says to the girls, while Oak is wandering the store.

"I would love to come help after I close up shop," Hyacinth offers, adjusting her necklaces that have twisted around in all sorts of manners from going up and down the stairs.

"That would be delightful. We must meet at my house. I have far more references than you, Dev, and an entire apothecary to boot," Marion offers.

"I would much prefer not to stay at home tonight," Dev confesses. Her eyes sadden at the sudden reminder that her husband will not be sharing a bed with her tonight.

"Then it is done. We all meet at seven p.m. and study the prophecies."

They nod in agreement and call for Oak to join them in the car.

When they get home, Marion goes to her car and tells them she will see them at seven. Dev and Oak go inside and decide it's best to get a nap in before it is time to go. They know they will be spending most of the night researching.

Chapter 5

Dev and Oak pull up into Marion's driveway. Hyacinth's car isn't here yet. It's dark outside and the temperature has dropped. They knock on the plum door with the lion head. The door whisks open, and in the distance they can see Marion across the house in the living room, putting her arm down from opening the door for them by use of magic. They both walk inside, carrying overnight bags.

Marion has her glasses on, and she is already deep in study. "You won't be needing those bags; we shan't be sleeping tonight," she tells them, never looking up from her book, the glow of flames behind her roaring from the fireplace crackling through her words.

"Hello to you too, Mother," Dev snarks.

They make their way into the living room, passing the den and the kitchen on the right. Just past the hallway to the apothecary on the left is a closet, placed under the staircase. Dev opens the closet and places her bag inside. She reaches out to Oak and takes his as well.

Oak heads toward his grandmother, looking around the room. The fireplace is going and is never a boring view.

It's made of various sizes of stones and rocks and serpents its way to the ceiling without ever creating a straight line. The windows are all open, allowing the breeze in, and the wind pushes the steam from the spout of the boiling tea kettle sitting on the raw wood coffee table that looks like an entire log. Candles placed around the room flicker and dance in the breeze. A few candelabras with intricate metalwork to replicate bats sit on either side of the mantel. Vases filled with various types of flowers detail the room. There are ornate decorative pillows strewn across the floor. Marion means business tonight.

"Grandma, why do you have the windows open with the fireplace lit?" Oak asks.

Marion finally looks up from her book and gazes at Oak through the top of her glasses. "Sweetheart, we have learned miraculous things about you today. We need our magic to be at peak performance tonight. The elements will always strengthen our abilities and tonight, we are calling upon all four. Fire from the fireplace, wind from the windows, earth from the flowers, and water from our tea. We are a family of witches and it's time we started acting like it!" she says triumphantly.

Oak can't help but find her sentiment a bit over-the-top, but she knows more about this kind of thing than he does and with his newfound interest in the craft, he is not going to argue.

"Tonight, we have white tea enchanted by all four elements to offer us clarity of mind and the ability to focus," she tells him. He has never seen her so motivated or excited before; she beams with pride.

Dev comes into the room from the kitchen. "And some sauvignon blanc for parent/child relationship strengthening and success!" she says, carrying a couple stemless wineglasses and a bottle, shaking her hips into the room. Oak's mouth curves into a deep, cheesy smile.

"Dev, of all the times I tried to teach you witchcraft and you remember the properties of wine? There is no question, you are my daughter." Everyone laughs as there is a knock at the door. "Oak dear, please get that." He takes a step toward the door and is unable to lift his other foot. "Ah ah ah. Craft. Like I did to welcome you and your mom." Marion puts her hand down, releasing the energy holding his foot in place.

Oak takes a deep breath and focuses on the door. It's pretty far away and he hasn't tried any type of magic at this distance before. He considers his best options. Magic cannot be created out of nothing; it must use the sources around it. He can't open the door without exchanging the energy of something else to use for the strength to allow the visitor inside.

"Oak, all four elements are in the house. Use them."

Oak snaps out of his concentration and simply wills the door open. The entrance opens, revealing a robust silhouette sparkling in the doorway. It steps forward into the house, the light washing over the frame, revealing Hyacinth with her jewelry filled arms full of various snacks. She takes in a deep breath, closing her eyes as she enters the living room. "Ah, all four elements at play. Beautiful touch, Marion," she says, setting the snacks down on the log-style coffee table.

Dev pours the wine into two glasses and hands one to Hyacinth. "Liquid witchcraft!" Hyacinth exclaims and clinks her glass with Dev.

Marion claps her hands twice. "Settle down, children, let's get to work. Everyone grab a book. We all need to educate ourselves on what we are dealing with. I'm sure a few of these books will have slight contradictions to each other because it is all speculation. However, if anyone comes across an important bit of information, just read it out loud so we can take in as much information as we can." She goes back to the page she was on before everyone arrived. Dev and Hyacinth step over and around pillows until they agree on a spot to sit together. Oak grabs a book from the floor and sits right where he is, other books within reach.

They study into the night, flipping through various pages of books. Some are about nothing except the firstborn child of a mother in a coven. Some are only about the firstborn child being a male. Others simply discuss occult mythology, tales, and prophecy. Wind swirls through the room periodically, letting in a cool breeze which feels nice against the heat of the flames from the fire and candles around the room.

Marion looks up from the book she has been studying. She reaches for her tea and takes a sip. Flipping the pages backward toward the front, she stops and clears her throat. "I am ready to share a bit of information I found," she announces to the room, everyone shifting in their seats to focus on her. "It says here, a mother of a coven, birthing a male as her first child, shall pass on through her birthing canal the inherited title of 'the Divine.' The Divine is the only being which is able to achieve true divinity. The Divine may go his entire life never achieving divinity; however, at the time he does so, he then becomes head of the coven of which he was born to, surpassing every witch in line, including the crone."

Oak marks the spot where he was reading with a finger. "So, I'm the head of our coven now?"

Hyacinth chuckles, feeling the wine.

"No," Dev responds. "You will *become* head of the coven if you ever achieve true divinity."

"What is divinity? Isn't that the name of your shop?" he says, looking to Hyacinth.

Her face is turning pink and flushed from the alcohol. "Yes, honey, I named my shop after the highest form of enlightenment a witch can achieve."

"But, no one ever has," Marion interrupts. "Witches have gotten close. Very close. But true divinity is unquestionably apparent, and no witch has ever been able to prove it has happened." Oak looks to his mother for further explanation. "It's when your body is at its full peak of power, surpassing all the energy in the universe. You're washed over with unbridled euphoria and your mind completely clears of all things."

"So, how does that happen?" he asks.

Hyacinth sets down her glass, tapping it at Dev for a refill. "You have to be on the brink of death," she says. "It's a witch's last resort in magic. On the edge of passing, your magic will uncontrollably burst to the surface in order to attempt to keep you alive. Without reaching true divinity though, it will fail and you will die. No one has lived; thus, it has never been achieved."

"Also," Marion adds, flipping forward a few pages. "It says, the Divine's powers must be suppressed indefinitely, unlike that of female witches who may begin to wean off suppression between ages ten and thirteen. The only time a Divine can stop suppression is by completing the feat of divinity."

Oak's eyes begin to widen as she reads, but he soon realizes none of these books can provide proof of their claims. Plus, taking himself to the brink of death seems far too extreme to chance on a literary rumor. The room is a bit tense; they all know what Oak is thinking. Dev leans over to the coffee table and takes a few cheese cubes from the table of snacks Hyacinth has provided.

They all begin to get back to their research except for Oak, who excuses himself to use the bathroom. He locks the door behind him and leans on the sink, sighing outwardly. He looks at himself in the mirror. He is tall and kind of skinny. His dark, dirty-blonde hair is long on top and flopped to one side but shaved close on the back and sides. He has dark circles under his eyes that appear to look seemingly normal for the complexion of his skin against his blue eyes.

He pulls away from the mirror and peeks behind the shower curtain. Reaching in, he turns on the shower and lets the water heat. There is a small frosted glass window that he opens to allow the breeze in. He's learning to appreciate the elements and how they play against each other so beautifully. He unpins his brooch from his T-shirt and pins it into his hair. Undressing, he sticks his foot into the shower to check the water. It is warm against his skin and quickly cools from the breeze outside the window.

Oak gets into the shower and draws the curtain closed, then he puts his back to the running water and allows it to soak his hair and trickle down the rest of his body. He stands there, still and quiet with his head down and eyes closed. Time passes and the water begins to run cool. He washes his hair and soaps up his body with the only items available, his grandmother's homemade cosmetics. Rinsing the ginseng-infused shampoo and charcoal-enhanced soap off himself, the water begins to run ice-cold.

He hurries and steps out of the shower, grabbing a nearby towel, wrapping it around his waist, and closing the window before turning off the water. The mirror has started to defog from the lack of heat in the room and he looks at himself once more. He runs his fingers through his hair. Everywhere his fingers touch, the hair turns strawberry red. He passes his hands through his hair and appreciates the fact that even though he hasn't gotten the answers he was wanting today, he can still have fun. He towels himself dry and puts his clothes back on, heading out into the kitchen for some water before returning to the living room.

Dev is distracted from her book by Oak's return. "Feeling better?"

"Yes," he says, sitting back down in front of the pile of books with his glass of water.

Hyacinth clears her throat and turns a page. "This says that the Divine is the only witch who can transfer magic to non-occult-born individuals in order to grow his coven."

Marion lifts her face from her reading. "So, he can turn non-witches into witches?"

"Hold on." Dev raises a finger. "This book says something similar." She flips through chunks of pages at a time, to a few pages with the corner folded up. "Here. The Divine may transfer magic to non-magic individuals only upon the time frame of being in love."

"Oh, that's a bit different than the other one says," Marion responds.

"Can the magic only be given to the person he is in love with, or to anyone, so long as he is currently in love?"

Dev flips a few pages over. "It's not that specific."

Oak reaches out to the coffee table, taking a piece of prosciutto from the snack options. He folds it into his mouth and continues on the page he left before his shower. *The Divine is the only entity recognized by every culture of witchcraft as the supreme being.* He reads to himself, then asks out loud what that sentence means.

Dev is the one to deliver the answer. "It means, every form of witchcraft, every coven, all over the world, will agree that you are the most powerful witch and the only person able to achieve his full potential."

"Yes, all over the world, covens believe in a witch that is born as the head of all witches and though the title of that witch may vary from culture to culture, he is the same being, regardless of where he hails from," Hyacinth states, downing her third glass.

"But," Marion interrupts. "Until achieving full divinity, the chances of anyone actually believing you are the Divine will be slim, Oak. Even then, unless the entire world is there to witness the event occur, they will question you. Yes, you can prove you are a male who has the powers of a witch, but people are inherently skeptical of everything, so you are not going to be hailed as a head of the hierarchy by anyone except your own coven."

Oak nods.

"Why is your hair red?" Hyacinth questions. They all look at him.

Embarrassed, he shakes his head, flicking his hair back to its original color. "Sorry, I was just messing around."

They all smile and Dev turns to Marion. "Mom, something has been bothering me."

"Yes, dear?"

"The Toothaker girl, Cynthia. She gave birth to a premature baby that died after delivery."

"Yes," Marion confirms.

"But, a baby born to a coven pulls its powers from the mother through the birth canal. So, wouldn't that give the baby enough energy to survive, even if born prematurely?"

Marion ponders the idea as if she had thought the very same thing. "You know, I have never heard of a coven-born baby passing away after birth, regardless of prematurity. You're right."

Just then, a candle from the coffee table falls into the open book on Oak's lap and ignites the entire thing on fire. Oak yells. He grabs the candle from the pages and blows it out, throwing it aside. He tries patting out the fire with his hands but nothing is happening other than scalding his skin. So he pushes the book out of his lap and stands, frantically running to the couch and grabbing a throw blanket. Everyone is staring at him. He tosses the throw blanket over the book and snuffs out the flames. On his knees with both hands over the blanket, panting and out of breath, he sees everyone watching him.

"What ... was that?" Hyacinth asks, snorting.

"What?" Oak says between breaths. "The book caught fire."

"No it didn't, honey," Marion says, biting the end of her glasses.

"This is what has been happening," Dev tells them. "And none of these books are addressing it."

Confused, Oak pulls back the throw blanket and sees the book entirely intact, in the same condition it was before anything happened. He looks at his hands. They are fine. "The candle from the table fell and lit the book!" he exclaims. "It did!"

"There are no candles on the table," Hyacinth says.

"That's it. We need to talk to Toothaker. She might have the answers we need," Marion says, standing up.

Dev looks up at her mother. "A séance?"

"Precisely."

Oak calms slightly. "We're going to summon a dead person?"

Hyacinth claps her hands, her jewelry rattling. Marion lifts a finger and states, "That's exactly what we're going to do." Moving around the furniture, she exits the living room to the apothecary. They hear her shuffling around until she pokes her head out and yells, "Do you have your ceremonials and brooms?" She's referring to the long black garbs and pointed brimmed hats that witches are traditionally seen as wearing.

"In the car!" Hyacinth exclaims, hoisting herself up and sprinting out of the room.

Dev and Oak look at each other. Every coven member owns ceremonials and brooms, but they're hardly ever used.

Marion comes into the room, her arms full of materials. "Cynthia is not going to want to present herself to us if she cannot recognize us as witches," she says, laying the items in a pile on the floor.

"It is four a.m., so the sun will be rising very soon. And if we don't do it now, we'll have to wait until tomorrow night," Dev responds. "Well, Alan should be up, getting ready for work now. He could bring us—" She stops her sentence, looking down. She realizes that Alan is not at home.

"He can stop at the house and bring everything over," Oak responds. "I'll call him." He leaves the room, touching his mother on the shoulder before he goes.

Trying to divert her attention from the realization of her separation from her husband, Marion motions to the coffee table. "Help me move this out of the way to clear the floor," she says, bending at one end of the log. They hoist it up and move it out of the way. Together they push furniture to the sides of the room and kick the pillows from the floor.

Hyacinth comes back inside with a bag of garments and her broom. She holds it up at them. "Great!" Marion says.

Oak reenters the room. "Twenty minutes," he says, smiling at Dev.

"We have to be extremely careful here. We are about to open the spirit realm and call upon one of our ancestors. However, any opening is an invitation for unwanted essences to breach through to our world. We must have protections in place." Marion hands Dev a bottle of sea salt. Dev begins pouring the salt around the center of the room in a large circle.

"Oak, please grab the flowers from the vases and pull the life out of them. We want something representative of death to offer the dead. They shy away from the living most of the time, so the flowers will draw her to us." Marion motions to the various vases around the room currently being used to keep the air clear and protected. They will have an additional use tonight.

Oak pulls flowers out of the vases and causes them to wither and dry in his hands. After about ten or so, Marion instructs him to place them around the inside of the circle of salt Dev created. Marion herself grabs all the white pillar candles from around the room and places groups of them at directional polarity points north, south, east, and west. She asks Oak to go to the apothecary and find three incense cones of frankincense. As he does so, Hyacinth appears, fully garbed as a witch. She's wearing a long black cloak with a pointed black hat. Holding her broom in her hands, she smiles widely as she glides into the room, her cloak billowing behind her. She waves her hand like Miss America at no one in particular.

There is a knock at the door. Dev, wide-eyed, looks at Marion.

"I got it!" Oak yells from the other room, jogging to the front door. Relieved, Dev slinks into a corner of the room so as not to be seen.

Oak opens the door with a huge smile. "Hi, Dad!" he says, lunging toward his father, ignoring his hands being full.

Alan wraps his double-broom-wielding hand around Oak and then hands them to him after the embrace. He sets them on the floor, reaching out for the hats and cloaks. "Magical night tonight?" Alan asks. He looks above Oak and focuses on Marion and Hyacinth in the far back of the house. He waves a hand at them, glancing around for Dev. They wave back. Dev closes her eyes and ignores the interaction.

"You wanna stay and watch?" Oak asks, excited.

"No, bud, I have to get to work," he says. Oak gives him another hug and begins to close the door. "Tell your mother I said hello."

"I will," Oak says as the door clasps shut. He turns the lock and returns to the living room. He pulls from his pocket the three frankincense-scented cones and hands them to his mom. "Dad says hi."

She takes the cones from him and goes to the kitchen, ignoring the message.

"Honey, go change. We must do this before the sun begins to rise," Marion tells him. He sets out all the clothes, hats, and shoes and grabs everything that belongs to him and heads to the bathroom.

Dev comes out of the kitchen with the incense sitting in a neat triangle on a saucer and places it in the center of the salt circle. She notices her outfit set out for her. She runs her fingers over her cloak and hat, picking up a high-heeled black leather lace-up boot and bringing it to her face. "It has been so long since I needed these."

"When did you need them last?" Hyacinth says, filling another glass of wine, swaying to music that isn't playing.

"My wedding," Dev says, staring at the beautifully worn boots.

Marion walks to her, placing a hand around her waist and guiding her to the couch to sit. "What a beautifully magical bride you were that night."

It's tradition for witches to marry their husbands wearing their ceremonials during their wedding. They must marry under a full moon, indicating that the man they are to wed fully understands the implications of marrying a witch. Dev's wedding was under the harvest moon. The last full moon nearest to the autumnal equinox. It included a handfasting ceremony during which she and Alan lit a unity candle, binding them together.

"I was so young. How could I be so naive to think it would last?" Dev says, breaking into tears.

Hyacinth watches, her face turning sympathetic and shedding a tear, thinking of Lulu. Marion gently wipes Dev's tears away as Oak comes out of the bathroom. He walks in with short-heeled leather black boots with a multitude of buckles and zips, finishing the top with a laced bow. His cloak is thick and sturdy, the sleeves reaching just past his elbows, and a hood hanging against his back. Simple and sleek, it has no buttons or clasps to close it. Atop his head is a bent conical hat, slightly lopsided from being in storage, and a broom is in his hand. He has never worn ceremonials before; they were only initially provided to him as a status symbol.

Dev looks up from her tears and cups her hands over her mouth at the sight of her son. Hyacinth, smiling from ear to ear and utterly drunk, topples backwards off the arm of the chair. She plops into the cushion, an endless array of chimes filling the room from her excessive jewelry.

Dev stands and walks over to Oak, tears flowing freshly again at the vision of him. She squeezes him in her arms. "You are so stunning."

He is a bit nervous at his mother's crying. "Did I miss something?" he says over her shoulder, looking to Marion and Hyacinth.

"You are just so perfect," Dev says, releasing her tight grip and wiping the tears from her face, smearing them all over. She gathers her outfit from the room and heads off to change.

"What was that?" Oak asks, targeting his question toward Marion.

"This is all just a lot for everyone, not just you," she explains, opening his eyes to the idea that everything he is going through is affecting everyone in the room right now.

"I'm sorry," he says, feeling embarrassed.

"Nothing to be sorry about, just pointing it out," she tells him. Hyacinth begins to snore loudly. Oak looks at his grandmother. "We will deal with her later," Marion says, waving dismissively. "I shall go change and we will finish setting up," she says, making her way upstairs to her bedroom.

Dev emerges from the bathroom shyly with her hands clasped together in front of her. Her long, strawberry-blonde hair flows out from the bottom of her alewife hat. The freckles across her nose appear deeper now than they did before. Ceremonials tend to bring out the most in a witch, even if they have no enchantments. She gets her broom from the front door and walks back to where Oak is standing. She notices Hyacinth, asleep in the chair. "Someone overdid it."

Oak smiles as they listen to Marion's footsteps heading down the stairs. She gets to the bottom of the staircase and opens the closet underneath to retrieve her broom. She closes the door and meets her family.

"Are we flying?" Oak asks, trying to comprehend how that would even work. Marion and Dev both smile.

"No, as great as we have always found it that people think we can fly on brooms, we don't," Dev answers him and Oak masks his disappointment.

"They're for our protection!" Marion explains, trying to lighten his mood. "You see here, the top end and the bottom end of the handle both have the same sigil carved into them. All our brooms have this."

"What is it for?" Oak asks, turning the handle of his broom around to see all the details.

"Well, a coven's magic is stronger in numbers. These sigils represent our connection to each other, and when held from end to end, creating an unbroken circle, they can protect us from almost anything," Marion explains, livening up Oak's perception of the brooms.

"So, we need this for the séance?" he asks.

"Yes, to keep us protected from any unwanted visitors," Dev answers. In unison, they all turn to Hyacinth, crumpled on the chair next to the fireplace.

"We need her, unfortunately," Marion explains.

Dev walks over to her and holds out her broom, bristles first, and hits her with it. "WAKE UP!" she screams. Hyacinth is startled awake and starts to scream and jiggle in her chair. Dev screams back at her. Oak screams. Marion screams. They're all screaming loudly, mocking the shop owner.

Hyacinth starts flailing her arms to get them to stop. "Okay! I GET IT!" she yells. "Okay, I'm ready, I'm ready. Shut up!" Everyone stops screaming and laughs at her. She wipes her forehead and stands up, stretching out. "Good. Now remember, no matter what happens, we must not break the circle our brooms make. We have salt down as a first defense. If anything happens to that salt, increase your grip on your brooms. We cannot let a specter out of our circle. Cynthia should not be violent or unwilling; it is others seizing the chance to break the boundaries that I'm worried about."

They all nod in understanding. Hyacinth rubs her eyes and shakes away the drunken feeling.

Marion moves to the candles she has placed. She leans in and gently blows on the center flame at each directional point. North-side flames turn green. South-side flames turn red. East-side flames turn yellow. West-side flames turn blue. They set their brooms down end to end in a circle outside of the salt ring. Dev leans in and lights the triangle of incense.

"Everybody ready?" Marion asks.

Oak's heart is pounding out of his chest. He has no idea what he is about to experience. Everyone eventually nods and they all bend together and slowly lift their brooms, wrapping their fingers at the ends where they meet, locking a circle. The smell of frankincense begins to infiltrate everyone's nose, the smoke swirling and dancing among the rest of the candle mist.

"I, Marion Melt, member of the occult, summon my ancestor Cynthia Toothaker to heed the presence of my calling. We offer a gift of flowers we have sent to your death realm as proof of our sincere intentions. With me are my family, Dev Black, Oak Black, and our coven sister Hyacinth Clove. Show yourself so that we may inquire about our family lineage with you."

The lights in the house flicker as the wind from the open window picks up. The flames on the candles bend at the wind but do not extinguish. The colored flames at the key points of the circle shine brighter.

Dev begins to speak. "Cynthia Toothaker, we summon you to speak with us regarding your family. We are in dire need of having questions answered."

Smoke begins to plume upwards heavily from the incense in the center of the ring. The research books around the room begin to blow open, the hard leather covers making a thud on the hardwood floor, the pages spiraling through the books quickly. The wind kicks up any dust in the room and swirls it around.

Hyacinth speaks. "Cynthia Toothaker, we bring with us the firstborn male of a coven mother. We have questions about the Divine."

The curtains hung by the window blow forward as everyone's cloaks begin to billow, the points on their hats bending against the wind. Amidst the dust particles and rising smoke in the room, a light blue essence begins to appear above the séance circle. Oak's eyes widen as he notices the shifting plumes of dust slightly revealing the image of a woman fading and reforming as the mist reshapes on its way upward. The curtains lower and the cloaks drop, the wind calming to a slight breeze.

A blue face, periodically showing from the spray of tiny debris, appears. "I am Cynthia Toothaker. I have answered your summoning." A gentle, soft feminine voice speaks, the volume of it changing, warbling from sounding far to sounding close, as their magic fights to keep the portal open.

Chapter 6

The corporeal being stands still against the particles in the air.

"We thank you for answering our call and accepting our gifts, Cynthia," Marion says.

The blue being in the air turns to her. "What questions have you?" Her voice is haunting.

Oak's heart is about to explode in his chest; he thinks it can be heard by everyone it is beating so loudly in his own ears.

"We need to ask you about your child," Dev states, the gentle breeze catching everyone's hair. The books on the floor slowly turn their pages in the draft.

"Oh, my sweet Walt. Such a sweet boy, but such a temper. We never could really control it." The end of Cynthia's sentence drifts away as if she is leaving the room, turning her gaze to the window. A mild gust, sweeping up into the protective circle, highlights her sad blue presence.

"No, not Walt," Dev replies. "Your premature firstborn." Cynthia's face darts quickly to look at Dev. She does not respond. "Cynthia, we mean no disrespect but your firstborn was recorded in a book about our lineage. We come with questions about her death. How did your baby pass away after birth? Your magic should have empowered her to survive."

Cynthia calmly swirls around and drifts to Marion from inside the circle. "Yes, it should have. My precious baby. They told me it would never work. They warned me, but I didn't listen." She tips her head to the side, visibly upset at the mention of her loss.

"Who warned you?" Hyacinth chimes.

"My parents, the coven; they all told me it wouldn't work. I was so young and so stupid." Cynthia begins to cry. Her sobs echo through the living room in a haunting vibration.

Marion and Hyacinth adjust their grip on their brooms, ensuring the circle is kept closed. Oak's knuckles are white from holding on so tightly in panic.

Cynthia slowly spins around the circle, taking in the view of the room. Her focus locks on Oak. "You. You are the true Divine," she says, floating toward him with her arm reaching out toward his face. She attempts to caress him but he is beyond the circle of protection and her hand stops. "You will bring great respect to our coven and establish reign over all things magic."

"Cynthia, we need to know why your baby died," Dev says sternly.

A bit of wind billows into the room, lifting one of the dried flower petals up toward Cynthia's hand. She motions her fingers around it, studying its beauty. "Edmund is why."

"Edmund killed your baby?" asks Hyacinth.

Cynthia holds her pale blue palm out, as if holding the floating flower petal. She seems enamored by the gift. "Edmund was a descendant of a line of witch hunters. He loved me anyway." The petal floats up into the air, high above the séance. The witches all look at each other in shock.

"A baby born to a witch and witch hunter will be born with an internal conflict, the hunter side wanting to destroy the magic side. My baby killed herself internally as a result of the conflict from within her being too great. Nobody told me that a witch hunter is born of magic. The magic to sense a witch, the magic to need to destroy. I thought it was all a ruse to make us fear the hunters. That the hunters simply hunted in prejudice, not magical instinct. I was wrong."

She floats upwards, over their heads and spins, her transparent death dress flowing. "That's why I had to hide her existence. No one could know that I attempted to birth the child of a witch hunter. That's why I had to raise Walt as the Divine. They thought he was my first child." She starts drifting back down, stopping at eye level with the witches.

"How did you explain his lack of power?" Hyacinth asks.

"No one has ever known a Divine to exist. The strength of power was just an assumption. An assumption that I corrected. I told them this was my baby, the Divine, and the books were wrong because he had no powers. I explained to them that his powers would only awaken after reaching divinity, and since that would never happen, I never had to explain further." She gently bumps the edges of the circle, testing the strength, studying the craft involved.

Dev asks, "Did you study literature about the Divine?"

"Yes."

"Are you familiar with outbursts of power, even during suppression? Our Divine, Oak, is experiencing unexplained phenomena."

The smoke from the incense and candles continue to fuel the imagery of the spirit's form, turning blue wherever it touches her. She spins to Oak. "His problem is unrelated to being the Divine. It's far more serious than that."

Oak's eyes grow big as Cynthia's warning makes his stomach sink. "W-what is it, then?"

A strong gust of wind blows through the room, snuffing out the flames of all the candles and the embers to the incense. Cynthia's blue particles waft away on the breeze. There is silence as all the smoke dissipates out of the room.

"Cynthia?" Dev calls.

Nothing. They ease the grip on their brooms.

"Is she gone?" Oak asks.

A deep rumble forms in the distance. The vases and candelabras on the mantel begin to shake. Soon, every item in the room is vibrating and the floor beneath them starts to creak.

"Hold your ground!" Marion yells forcefully.

They tighten their grip on the brooms so much their hands hurt. The wind picks up again, lifting every small, loose object in the room. The objects float in the air as their pointed hats are all blown off their heads.

"NO!" They hear Cynthia scream as there is a sickening boom from inside the séance circle.

The lights flicker as the wind whips in the room, swirling all the objects around them slowly like a tornado. A deafening voice penetrates the center of the protection circle. "YOU WITCHES DARE TO BASTARDIZE MY NAME?" it shrieks.

Dev swallows hard and looks for something, anything to connect the voice to. Marion is breathing heavily. "Be gone, unwanted spirit. We did not summon you here!"

The voice booms once more. "OH, BUT YOU DID SUMMON MY MOTHER, TO TAKE AWAY MY TITLE AS THE DIVINE! YOU WILL REGRET THIS VERY DAY!"

His mother? Oak's eyes widen as he comes to the realization.

"It's Walt Fiches!" Oak screams over the chaotic sounds.

"We cannot take away a title you never had, Walt!" Marion yells at the angered poltergeist.

"YOU THINK YOU CAN CHANGE HISTORY? DENY MY PLACE AS THE DIVINE MALE WITCH?"

Some of the books floating around the room begin to slam into the edges of large objects, causing chairs and couches to slide around. They cannot place where Walt is in the circle since there is no smoke or debris to reveal his form. Walt screams as the floor booms, sending the salt protection flying outwards, dissolving their first defense. The witches struggle to remain steady on their feet. He strikes the side of the broom circle between Oak and Marion. It catches them off guard but they remain strong.

"We need to be able to see him!" Marion yells.

Oak considers the options. With his hands confined to holding the brooms tightly, he ponders what he can say to convince the spirit to show himself.

"I am the Divine, Walt! I order you to stand down and return to the land of the dead!" Oak yells at him, his hair whipping around his face so violently he can barely see. They all look around the inside of the circle, trying to place where he is. An occasional speck catching blue gives them nothing but the knowledge that Walt is there.

"YOU WILL NOT RUIN ME!"

In a moment of clarity, Hyacinth releases her grip on the broom to her right, knowing Marion can handle it for a moment on her own. She reaches up and digs into her necklaces upon her chest. She tugs at the vial of Lulu's ashes and tears it away from herself, snapping the clasp keeping it on her. She kisses the vial and throws it hard at the ground into the séance circle.

"Show yourself, coward!" she screams, the glass vial bursting with a small explosion of ashes, immediately lifting up in the wind, revealing Walt's spiritual form. His face is aimed at Oak, snarling. He wants nothing more than to have him destroyed so that his legacy of being the Divine remains untouched. He flails around from within the circle, promising death to each and every one of them. A few of the objects flying around the room begin to hit into the witches. A vase knocks into Dev's shoulder as a candle hits Oak in the back of the head.

"Go back to where you hail from, demon spirit!" Marion yells to him.

"Be gone from this realm!" Dev adds.

The ghost of Walt searches for a weak point in the sealed structure. He floats high and low, frantically looking for a way out. He slams into the points where the brooms meet, trying to dislodge their grip.

"Our coven banishes you back to the spirit world!" Hyacinth screams. A teacup smashes into Marion's arm, causing her to grunt. She remains focused.

Walt turns to Hyacinth, "YOU ARE NOT OF THIS LINEAGE, COVEN SISTER. DO NOT MEDDLE IN FAMILY AFFAIRS!" he taunts, noticing one of her shining necklaces glistening at him, hanging over her broom handle, *inside* the séance circle. Oak realizes what is about to happen and screams for Hyacinth to pull back but it is too late. Both Marion and Dev's jaws drop open, mouthing 'no' as Walt furiously grabs hold of the charm dangling in his territory. He pulls it downward, causing Hyacinth to topple forward, breaking the circle of brooms and falling onto the ashes of burnt incense.

In a flash, the blue disappears from the donated ashes in the air and everything swirling around in the room comes crashing down onto the floor, breakables shattering. Marion tosses her broom aside. Following her lead, Dev and Oak do the same. She kneels beside Hyacinth to check if she is all right. She pounds her fist on the ground. "Dammit!" Oak and Dev each grab an arm and help her to her feet. She brushes off the used incense, tidying her ceremonials.

"Where is he? Did he get away?" Oak asks, barely able to catch his breath. Marion's eyes drift upwards, searching the house. A faint maniacal laugh makes its way through the air.

"He escaped," Dev answers, helping to pat some of the ash from Hyacinth's clothes.

"But, he won't be able to leave the house," Marion explains.

"What? Why?" Hyacinth inquires.

"I have wards set up all over the house, to keep unwanted beings out. Fortunately, they also work in reverse. So, he is stuck in here, for now." They shuffle through the broken shards of vases and dented candles, trying to find anything out of the ordinary.

"We need to be able to see him," Marion says. "I believe I have enough sage to cleanse the entire second floor of the house. That should force him down here with us, at least." She brings Oak with her into the apothecary.

Dev and Hyacinth go into the kitchen, cautiously checking around every corner. The lights flicker and they jump; all the cabinet doors slam open and shut. "He's in here!" Hyacinth screams, huddling next to Dev, both of them defenseless to do anything at the moment. Suddenly, all the contents of the cabinets begin to fly out of the cupboards. They shield themselves as they are violently pummeled by pots and pans and china, cups and bowls. The ceramics burst across their arms, shattering into their hair, a few pieces cutting into their skin.

"Leave this house, Walt! Go back to where you came from!" Dev screams. They can hear Marion's footsteps upstairs, cleansing the second floor.

Oak rushes into the kitchen with a scrying mirror. "Grandma said to bring you this!"

"We can't force him to look into it if we can't see him!" Dev shouts, a tea saucer bursting on her shoulder. Oak holds his arm up as a bowl whizzes past him. Everything plummets to the ground. The cabinets swing back and forth gently, their slamming and knocking coming to a halt. They slowly lower their arms.

"Out of here, quick," Dev tells them, as Marion enters the kitchen.

"Follow me," Marion says. They follow her back into the living room. "Upstairs has five bundles of burning sage; there shouldn't be an inch un-cleansed. Walt is stuck down here with us. We need to get him to look at himself in the scrying mirror to force him back since he's not going willingly. We need to force him back into the circle. Grab your brooms."

They search around the mess and Oak has an idea. "We need to see him. We need to kick up as much debris as possible so that we can follow where he is to get him back into the circle."

There is a crash in the other room, and a lot of banging. They can hear roaring anger along the bottom floor of the house, but Walt is clearly not in the living room. Perplexed, they pick up their brooms as they find them. There is a slew of chaotic noises coming from each room of the bottom floor.

"It sounds like he is fighting someone away, but we are all here," Dev points out.

"YOU WILL DIE TONIGHT!" A strong spiral gust sweeps them off their feet and onto the floor, shifting everything a few inches.

"He's here!" Marion yells.

Dev starts sweeping the floor with her broom in fast, swift motions so everything is tossed into the air. Oak heads to the fireplace and begins throwing soot and ash upwards around the room.

They notice a few glimpses of blue sweep out of the room through a wall. There is more crashing and sounds of destruction going on in the other rooms. They continue to lift particles into the air, puzzled at the sounds of Walt trashing rooms no one is in. Hyacinth starts setting up and lighting the candles once again to get more smoke into the room. Finally, whirring and swirling into the room, the smoke and soot cover a blue essence in the room. It looks to be twice the size it once was, a blur as it flies across their field of vision.

"There's two of them!" Oak yells, his younger eyes able to decipher exactly what buzzed by.

"What!" Dev screams. They watch through the smog of dirt as the two spirits twist and entwine with each other, a battle of the paranormal.

Hyacinth's eyes begin to well up and shine as she watches the entities battle against each other. Dev looks to Hyacinth, noticing her distress. She then looks at the specters and connects the dots. "It's Lulu."

"Throwing her ashes into the séance circle summoned her; she's helping us!" Dev exclaims, running to Marion.

"Go to the kitchen. There should be more salt in there somewhere," Marion tells Oak. "Hyacinth, tell Lulu to keep Walt in a corner of the room!"

Oak runs across the living room, crunching over large pieces of broken everything. He gets to the kitchen and rummages around the items all strewn about the room. He can hear the struggle between light and dark in the other room. Trying not to be distracted, he searches for anything that looks like a container of salt. He lifts pots and pans, ignoring the banging against the walls and ceiling of the other room. The lights still flicker as he flips everything over, searching. Finally, under the lip of a cabinet he spots a navy-blue canister of salt. He grabs it and runs into the living room where the war rages on.

Hyacinth is with Marion and Dev now and they are attempting to force the battle into a corner. "Lulu, sweetheart, hold him over there as long as you can!" Hyacinth calls out as Oak reaches the group.

"Douse the room. Cover as much as you can. Leave them no space to escape," Marion tells him.

Oak starts shaking the canister of salt all around the room, walking backwards. The spirits can't go up through the ceiling because of the sage and they can't go out the walls to the outside because of the wards. They all follow him as he dumps lines of salt everywhere. Lulu is keeping Walt subdued; she has the upper hand at the moment. Dev and Marion hold their brooms up and begin to close in on the struggle.

"I want to do this," Hyacinth says, cutting in with her broom. Marion backs off. Dev and Hyacinth create a V-shape with their brooms, grasping them tightly at the meeting ends.

Oak continues to work backwards, spraying the salt. "I'm running out!"

Lulu seems to have a pretty good hold of Walt, as they have not moved from the corner for a good while. Lulu manages to get her face free of the exchange and turns to Hyacinth. Oak empties the rest of the salt onto the floor. "Do it now!" Lulu says, turning Walt to face them.

Hyacinth and Dev run at the corner of the room, gripping the brooms, hitting the ends up against the wall where Lulu has presented him to them. Trapping him with her in a square of protection. Marion throws the scrying mirror. "Oak!"

He turns to see it flying at him. He catches it in his hands and turns to the angry ghost, forcing Walt to stare at himself in the stark black face of the surface. Walt releases a wailing howl as all the blue-colored debris forming his shape turns back to black from within the square and falls to the ground, the sound of dirt and dust raining down.

THE COVEN'S SON

Hyacinth gets one last look at Lulu before her particles crumble and she returns to the spirit realm. "Thank you," Hyacinth says, a tear dropping down her cheek.

"I love you," Lulu mouths to her. They slowly remove the brooms from the corner and check around the room to make sure it's clear. Oak lies flat on his back on the floor like a starfish, pointed fragments all over his back. He is breathing heavily.

Hyacinth is crying in the corner and Dev has her arm around her, comforting her. Marion is stepping over the mess on the floor, looking around, taking in her destroyed house. The sun is beginning to rise and light is trying to poke into the windows of the house. She takes herself upstairs and collects the plates of burning sage from every room. The second floor has been spared from any damage. She brings the sage down to the bottom floor of the house, placing it in every room. The house needs to be cleansed of any leftover negative energies Walt may have managed to leave behind. She inspects the other rooms as she places the sage down. Some knocked-over pictures and wall hangings, a few broken knickknacks, but nothing as bad as what went on in the living room and kitchen.

Marion tidies up the few rooms that seem manageable by herself, allowing herself a moment of privacy to unwind. She has remained strong and knowledgeable in front of her family but this is more than anything she could have ever imagined possible. She begins to cry as she picks up large pieces of a broken palmistry figurine off the floor of her spare bedroom, the one where Oak usually sleeps when he is not passed out in the apothecary. She sits on the edge of the bed, taking in everything that happened tonight.

Back in the living room, Dev has comforted Hyacinth to the point where she is able to handle herself once more. She finds her broom and begins to sweep up all the soot and glass, ceramic and salt strewn everywhere. Hyacinth does the same.

Oak's breathing has regulated and he stands up and heads to the kitchen to clean up in there. He sifts through the mess, trying to salvage any unbroken plates, bowls, and cups. He stacks the pots and pans and sets them on the counter. As he is cleaning, he thinks about his best friend Kyle-Ray. He would have thought tonight was so cool. He would have said, "My best friend is a badass!" and cheered them on as they took down Walt Fiches.

Oak has no one his age to talk to about this kind of thing. All the witches he knows are adults and all the people who know he is a witch are adults. They love him, sure, but being able to joke around and be a witch around someone his own age sounds like a dream.

He is startled when a pan shifts from the pile he has made on the counter. Realizing he was staring off into space, he gets back to organizing the mess in the kitchen.

Dev can hear Oak cleaning up but wonders where her mother has gone. She sets down a trash bag she has been scooping up broken items into and walks around the house. She checks the den, noticing a few small things lying across the floor. She moves around and checks the bathroom and the formal dining room. Finally she creaks open the spare bedroom door, gently knocking to alert of her presence. Marion is fast asleep on the guest bed, next to the pile of broken palmistry fingers.

Dev enters the room and gathers the pieces from the bed, leaning in and kissing her mother on the cheek. She wonders how her mom got to be so old, staring at the deep wrinkles and sunspots that caress her face. She is certainly a wise old crone. Dev thinks about what she would have done if she was not here to help them through all this. Dev is not sure she could have done it without her. Hyacinth has been a huge help, but it seems to Dev, looking back, that Marion really commanded everything that happened tonight. She deserves to rest, so Dev leaves the room and slowly glides the door shut, hearing a faint click as it latches.

She heads into the kitchen to throw away the broken pieces and check on Oak. Most of the mess is cleaned up. He is just restocking a few of the last items. "You did an incredible job holding yourself together tonight," she says to him encouragingly. "A lesser witch would have run right out of this house with his tail between his legs."

He smiles at her. "Pretty good for someone named after a cabinet," he jokes.

"I know I joke with you about that, but let me tell you a story. When that cabinet fell when I was giving birth to you, your delivery nurse tried lifting it off the other nurse's foot. She pulled as hard as she could, but it was too heavy and completely immovable. When she asked what it was made of, the doctor said oak. And I knew at that moment that my baby would be strong, hardheaded, bold, and impossible to push around. *That's* why that is your name."

She tosses the chunks of plaster into the garbage and he gives her a hug. "Thank you for not giving up on me."

She pulls away from the hug and steadies her hands on his shoulders, looking him directly in the eye. "I will *never* give up on you. We will figure out what this is, no matter what." She pats his shoulder and leaves the room.

He wants to believe her but the last few days have been more chaotic, more terrifying, and more stressful than anything he can think of, and it's still not over. She gave up on his dad, after all. Oak finishes putting away the last of the kitchen items and, feeling extremely alone, goes out into the living room.

They gather the last of the garbage and haul it into the kitchen, setting up a pile to take care of later. They all slide the furniture back into place and wipe their hands together to pat off the dust. Marion appears, walking groggily into the room from her short-lived nap. They all turn to her and meet her at the threshold of the room; quietly, they all hug each other. They take a seat in various places around the living room, pushing aside the hats and brooms for space.

"I've got to go get the shop open," Hyacinth says, exasperated.

"You're staying awake? Dear, let me help you." Struggling to lift herself from the chair, Marion goes into the apothecary and looks the room up and down. It's in perfect condition, just the way it was before the attack. It is the only room she has with its own wards in place to prevent anyone from accessing her magical items. She pulls some orange oil and peppermint oil from her collection and a marker from the desk. She leaves the room and catches Hyacinth packing her things into her car.

Marion waits at the front door for her to come back. "Give me the back of your neck. This will help give you energy."

Hyacinth turns around and adjusts her shirt so it reveals the base of her neck. Marion uses the marker to draw a circle, another circle inside, open on the bottom, and another circle with a line horizontally through the center. She strikes a line above the smallest circle, through the one that she left open on the bottom. She connects three upward-angled lines from the center of the middle circle, then rubs a mixture of the orange and peppermint oil all around the inside of the outer circle. Hyacinth feels immediately refreshed.

"This should hold until you get home tonight," Marion says, putting Hyacinth's shirt back in place and patting where she drew her sigil. "We appreciate everything you have done for us tonight."

"Thank you, Marion. I will always be there for my coven." Hyacinth gives her a quick side hug and heads to her car. Marion waves as she closes the front door. She turns to see Dev and Oak gathering their things and pulling their bags from the closet underneath the staircase.

"Are you okay to drive home?" she asks Dev.

"Yes, I'll be fine."

Oak stuffs his ceremonials into his bag and attempts to fit his boots inside as well. They say goodbye to Marion and head to the car. "Get some sleep, Mom," Dev says.

Marion trudges up the stairs, the smell of sage overwhelming the entire home. She can rest easy knowing nothing would dare come in here today. She changes out of her ceremonials and slips on an oversized nightshirt before climbing under the covers of her bed, freshly made from the day before. The sun is shining brightly into the room from the window, birds chirping as morning peaks. She contemplates for a moment before closing her eyes to sleep. "I think we may need to call Mallie."

She wills the curtains to close themselves and block out the light of the morning. She sends the birds that would interrupt her sleep away to perch on another tree. As she drifts off to sleep, she wonders if dream walking could provide any answers to solving Oak's problem. Soon, she is fast asleep and snoring loudly as the events from earlier catch up to her and put her into one of the deepest sleeps she has ever experienced.

Chapter 7

THUD THUD THUD.

Oak rolls over in bed, groaning. A moment passes.

THUD THUD THUD.

He pulls the blanket over his head before realizing there's someone at the door. He rubs his eyes and sets his feet on the floor. In his pajamas, he heads to the front door, stepping over old pieces of paper from his transmutation attempts.

THUD THU—He opens the door and Kyle-Ray finishes knocking on his forehead. Oak winces and steps back. "Oh, hey."

"Happy birthday!" Kyle-Ray yells, holding up a wrapped gift.

"What?" Oak says, taken aback. He realizes now, after everything that has been going on, that today is his birthday and he had completely forgotten.

"Happy, uh, birthday?" Kyle-Ray responds, shaking the gift at him. Oak yawns and smiles, scratching his head, waving Kyle-Ray to come inside. "Were you sleeping? It's one in the afternoon."

"Yeah, I was up late with my parents. We celebrated last night since my dad works so late," he lies.

"Oh, cool. Here." Kyle-Ray hands him his birthday gift. It's wrapped with old holiday paper, covered in a mistletoe pattern. The most ironic choice ever, Oak thinks.

Oak takes the gift from him and they go into a small seating area just off to the side of the front door. It looks like it's meant to be a foyer but Oak never calls it that because he has no idea what a foyer even is. They sit on the couch and Oak rattles his gift to his ear.

"Just open it," Kyle-Ray prods.

Oak begins to pull and tear the paper off. It's wrapped poorly and the seams where it's taped pop up and open anyway, making it easier to manage. He tears into the package to reveal a long rectangular white box. He crumples the paper into a ball and tosses it onto the floor.

Dev pokes her head in and yells, "Happy birthday, my favorite wi—" She sees Kyle-Ray and immediately changes what she was going to say, elongating it and making it weird. "W-i-i-i-i-nner!"

Kyle-Ray gives Dev a strange look. "Yeah, I won the game we were playing for my birthday last night," Oak explains. Kyle-Ray accepts that answer and turns his focus back to Oak opening the gift.

"I didn't realize we had a visitor," Dev says. "I'm about to make a quick lunch. Would you like anything, Kyle-Ray?"

"Sure, whatever you're making is fine."

She smiles and makes her way to the kitchen, tapping her nails along the wall the entire way.

"Open it!" Kyle-Ray says impatiently, stomping his feet on the floor.

"Okay, calm down!" Oak lifts the lid off the unmarked white box. There is some tissue paper, covering something tubular that fits perfectly into the box. To the side, there is a small bundle of incense sticks. Oak has never kept his love for incense a secret, especially since he likes to use it to enchant his mood. No one knows that part but his family, though. He pulls the incense from the box and inspects it.

"So, the white sticks are birthday-cake-scented and the brown sticks are bubbly soda," Kyle-Ray tells him.

Oak fakes his appreciation of his scent choices. There is nothing he can do with these in the craft. Nothing calls for cake- or soda-scented enchantment. "Mmmm, yum," he says, bringing them to his nose. They do smell really good; they just don't have anything else to provide him. He realizes most people use incense just for the smell and that he has gone his whole life never really appreciating that. "Mmmmm," he says again, rolling his eyes in the back of his head and fluttering his lashes out of sync with each other.

Kyle-Ray punches his shoulder, "Ew, stop being weird." They laugh and Oak hands Kyle-Ray the incense to hold while he unwraps the tube-like object under the tissue paper. Tugging the glittery tissue out from underneath the gift he unveils a wooden incense holder, a tube shape that stands upright with a removable base. When you place incense into the base, you cover it with the wooden cylinder. The outside of it is covered in clay and painted to look like an ancient wizard. There's a hole where his mouth is, to allow smoke out while the incense is burning.

"Whoa, did you make this?" Oak asks, turning it to inspect the details.

"No, I got it in Puerto Rico on our cruise."

"This is amazing, thank you."

Kyle-Ray clasps his hands in his lap and sits back, pleased.

"Food's ready!" Dev shouts from the kitchen.

Oak takes the incense from Kyle-Ray and trades him for the wrapping paper and box. "Toss this in the garbage in the kitchen. I'm going to run this to my room," Oak says, hopping up and taking his gift away.

Kyle-Ray meets Dev in the kitchen and holds up the discarded wrappings. "Trash?" She holds her hand out to toss it. "Have a seat. Yours is on the farther end," she tells him.

Oak enters from putting away his present and takes the other seat. A simple sandwich and chips. A little plain for his birthday, considering he has always been an adventurous eater. But, his dad always takes him for a nice dinner. He gets off work early and everything. Oak scoots up to the table and grabs his sandwich. Dev leans over the table to pour them some iced tea. Kyle-Ray has already begun eating his sandwich, his hair pulled back into a ponytail so that he doesn't munch on it along with his food.

Oak takes a bite and chews slowly. Something is not right. He is crunching down on a weird texture. His tongue begins to burn. The overwhelming urge to spit out what's in his mouth gets the best of him and he spits out the mouthful. Kyle-Ray is now staring at him. Dev is working in the kitchen, wiping down dishes as if nothing is happening.

He sifts his fingers through the chewed bite of food left on his plate and uncovers a clove of garlic. "Garlic, are you kidding me? What the hell, Mom!" he says angrily as he wipes his mouth and begins to chug the iced tea in front of him.

Kyle-Ray sits perfectly still, his eyes moving from Oak to Dev. He has never seen anything like this. Why would his mom shove an entire clove of garlic into his food? Is this some sort of a birthday prank?

Oak stands up rapidly, knocking his chair over backwards. "Are you serious?"

She puts both her hands on the kitchen counter, her back to them both, elbows locked. Leaning on her palms and her head down, she says, "I wanted to see if it worked."

"If it worked? That spiri—" Oak stops himself, glancing at Kyle-Ray who is now just trying to avoid this entire confrontation. "That ... Cynthia already said this is NOT the problem!"

Dev turns around to face him, pulling a kitchen rag off the counter and beginning to dry her hands with it. "You were fine before you stopped the garlic. I just wanted to see."

Oak shakes his head in disbelief and storms out of the kitchen and out the front door, slamming it as he exits. Kyle-Ray jumps out of his seat, grabs a chip, and goes after Oak, awkwardly thanking Dev for lunch as he follows his friend. He shuts the door gently behind him and searches the area for a sign of which direction he went. He walks out past the driveway, and peers down the sidewalk. He spots Oak power-walking in the distance. "WAIT!"

Oak turns and sees Kyle-Ray jogging after him. He slows his pace so he can catch up. Winded, Kyle-Ray asks him what that was all about. Why did his mom feed him a raw clove of garlic? Why did he get so mad about it? Oak waves him off, ignoring his inquiry, and continues to walk angrily to nowhere.

"Dude, you can't just have an entire episode like that in front of me and not tell me what's going on."

Oak is gathering his thoughts on how he is going to explain himself. He considers for a moment just telling Kyle-Ray that he is a witch and that he used to use garlic to suppress his powers from bursting out of him uncontrollably but he made a magical amulet to control the problem. Before he can finish the thought, he realizes how insane that would sound and says instead, "My mom is a little bit of an over-the-top health freak. She read somewhere about some crazy health benefits garlic offers and has been forcing me to eat it."

Kyle-Ray looks like a deer in headlights, not knowing how to respond. "Is that why you—" Oak's side-eye pierces daggers into Kyle-Ray's soul and he stops the question.

"She let me stop a little while ago. I thought we were done with that part of my life. Boy, she really chose a good day to do this. Happy birthday to me."

Kyle-Ray rubs Oak's shoulder. "Where are we rage walking to?" Kyle-Ray asks.

"There is something special I wanted to do with my mom today. She's no longer invited, so now it's me and you," Oak explains, not sure if he can manage to have his special day without revealing himself to Kyle-Ray as a witch. He is so angry that he doesn't care if he figures it out, though he believes he can pass the activity off as some unexplained phenomenon. "We're going to the nature trail in the city park."

Kyle-Ray raises an eyebrow at his chosen location and shrugs his shoulders in agreeance. It's Oak's day and with his mood, Kyle-Ray isn't going to argue. They walk briskly through the neighborhood of houses along his street, turning down roads leading to the exit. Walking along the sidewalk of the main road just outside of the community, cars fly by, gusting them with wind. It's already a breezy day but the extra gust feels good and prevent them from breaking a sweat because of the pace of their walk. Their walk is mostly quiet, the sound of the cars passing by noisily prevents either of them from attempting to strike up a conversation.

About halfway to the park, Kyle-Ray decides to break the silence and say, "You know, I think your mom meant well."

"I know," Oak concedes, letting out a breath that seemed to be dwelling inside him as he uses the quiet walking time to think.

They walk for what seems an eternity but is only about three miles—though, three miles is a long way to walk unexpectedly and unprepared. They manage to walk around the large red brick wall that borders the edge of the property to the large brown sign with white letters that reads 'City Park' and continue past it, making their way in. Though they are inside the vicinity of the park, they still have a ways to go before they reach the nature trail. They pass by picnic tables, and families celebrating. There are a few baseball fields to the left as they are passed by skateboarders. A huge pond lies to the right, a few people fishing as a water skier zooms by in the distance, being pulled by a motorboat. There is a playground just up ahead that borders the start of a large golf course.

As they continue on, they feel the ground shifting up and down as the land rises and falls, the hilly nature of the park interrupting their steady pace. They pass by some tennis courts, listening to the grunts of the players as they serve a bright yellow ball back and forth to each other, the hollow thunk of the sphere echoing across the square as they go by. Eventually, as their calves burn, they make their way up a steep hill and at the top resides the entrance to the nature trail.

"Finally," Kyle-Ray puffs.

"Well…" Oak says.

"Don't tell me."

Oak looks past the sign that says 'Nature Center and Trail Entrance' and sees nothing in the distance other than a road with a grouping of trees on either side. "The actual trail is about half a mile in."

Kyle-Ray places his fists below the bottom of his chin and opens his hands, wiggling his fingers, indicating his head has exploded at the idea of continuing to walk any farther. Oak grabs him by the arm and tugs him unwillingly down the dirt road entrance to the trail. "I hate you," Kyle-Ray says, pouting.

Oak walks along the side of the road, kicking small rocks and stones as they go. He knocks a rock in front of Kyle-Ray's feet. He smirks and kicks the rock back. They go to and fro with the rock, playing a makeshift game until the rock falls off the edge of the path and into a tall grassy area, ending their competition.

Oak thinks how nice it is to be able to spend time with Kyle-Ray outside of school. They have visited each other's houses a few times before but never really hang out on their own time.

"Hey?" Kyle-Ray asks, breaking the silence.

Oak turns and looks at him.

"The day you left school. How did you know the sprinklers were about to go off?"

Oak chokes on his words at the abrupt question and tries to come up with an excuse on the spot.

"Oh. Um. I. There were some kids in the hall as I was leaving the office. They were planning a prank. They were talking about setting them off."

Kyle-Ray hesitates for a moment before accepting Oak's answer.

The breeze is gone as the nature center becomes visible in the distance. They can just barely make out the massive wooden porch that surrounds the building as they walk.

They make their way through the parking lot, Kyle-Ray realizing the road they took was intended for cars, not pedestrians. Reaching a set of wooden stairs connected to the big wraparound porch, they walk up to the front door of the conservation area and head inside. The cool air immediately strikes their faces, cooling them after the long walk.

"Sanctuary!" Kyle-Ray yells, not noticing the other people quietly perusing the museum of plants and animals. Someone shushes him and he turns a ruddy complexion, sinking his head into his shoulders and sidling up next to Oak.

Oak leads them into a room full of drawers on every wall. Made of a light-colored wood with matte silver handles, Oak pulls one of the drawers open and gazes inside. Atop the drawer is a clear covering of plexiglass creating a display case for cleanly skeletonized animal bones. Inside the exhibit is a deer mouse, a fox squirrel, a western pocket gopher, and a white-tailed prairie dog. Oak peers across the array of rodents, studying each one. He likes to remember the lives of the animals these once were. He could be here all day just looking through the various drawers offered in this wing of the center.

Kyle-Ray is opening drawers at a faster pace, peeking at them then closing them and moving on to the next. At this, Oak decides they should move on as Kyle-Ray appears to be anxious. "Come on," he says, and moves to the exit of the skeletal display room and heads to an exit door in the back of the building. Kyle-Ray follows behind as Oak heads down the stairs at the rear of the raw wood deck.

At the bottom of the stairs there's a butterfly garden, lantanas and echinacea lining the walkway that leads to the entrance of the nature trail. Various butterflies enjoy pollen over the array of oranges, pinks, and yellows. Oak can identify only a tiger swallowtail and a monarch as it flutters up and flits past his face as if saying hello. The monarch is Dev's favorite butterfly. He starts to feel guilty at how he reacted to her earlier. He shakes off the feeling, continuing on. Kyle-Ray is lagging behind, enjoying the butterflies even though he can't identify any of them.

Oak comes to a sign-in post at the entrance to the nature trail, stopping to sign them in, giving Kyle-Ray a chance to catch up. "What's this for?" Kyle-Ray asks, hovering over Oak's shoulder.

"It's so they know who is on the trail so they don't block off the entrance at closing time if we are still there." Oak signs both their names and sets the pencil down, noting that everyone that has signed in has signed out, meaning they have the trail to themselves, for now.

Entering the beginning of the trail, following the paved concrete path, there are small posts set up to educate patrons on the various vegetation and wildlife they could encounter. A picture and small description adorn each post. The trail leads through a gathering of forest trees bordering each side of the path. The grass between the trees is tall and unkempt, a perfect habitat for insects and snakes. The trees themselves are old and haggard, stretching many feet into the air. A canopy of entangled, dried moss hangs among the various branches, casting speckled shadows on the ground below.

    As they walk, they can see large spiderwebs woven between bushes and trees, creating a delicate silky net that shimmers against the sunlight when the breeze makes it through the brush. They watch a box turtle with its black and yellow patterns lazily cross their path, climbing over the trail and onto the other side, into the woods. Cicadas rattle their buggy tune all around them, nearly drowning out the sounds of the boys' footsteps. As they come to a turn in the path, the corner edge of the trail has been turned into a man-made lookout for wildlife. There is a viewing area at the edge of a small drop-off where animals are commonly seen.

    The viewing area has a few wooden benches, covered by a worn splintered roof with a stationary telescope. Kyle-Ray darts to the telescope and peeks into it, turning it side to side. He searches for animals diligently and Oak takes a seat on one of the wooden benches. They relax for a while, listening to the throaty caws of a raven in a tree nearby. Kyle-Ray finishes playing with the telescope and gives it a hearty spin as he leaves it to sit with Oak. "Why did you want to spend your birthday here?"

"You'll see," Oak says.

Recalling the passage from *Free Will and Compulsion*, Oak reaches his arm out around the back side of the bench and turns his neck to see the raven. The large crow dives from its perch among the trees and swoops up at the last minute, landing on Oak's arm. Kyle-Ray jumps up and backs away. "Dude!"

Oak slowly pulls his arm from the bench and positions it in front of himself. "Well, hello," he says to the raven. The charcoal-black bird responds with a scratchy version of the word hello, mimicking Oak's speech. Oak holds his arm out for Kyle-Ray to pet the raven.

Kyle-Ray is a little concerned but reaches his fingers out slowly to pet the mystical creature. He scratches its neck and it nuzzles its head against his knuckles, closing its eyes. "This is amazing," he says in wonder.

Oak stands and walks around the bench and out of the viewing area. He steps back onto the paved walkway and raises his arm, allowing the raven to fly back up into the trees.

"How did you do that?" Kyle-Ray asks in astonishment.

"I've been coming here for years." He hopes the vague reply is enough to quench Kyle-Ray's thirst for answers. He has never been one to think too deep into things.

"Dang," Kyle-Ray says, confirming the nonchalant explanation worked.

They continue on, taking the path. They dodge and weave their feet around tree roots in the ground that have burrowed under the concrete and lifted it from the earth, Kyle-Ray's foot gets stuck in one of the large cracks that couldn't sustain the pressure from the tree's mighty force. He kneels down, both hands on his shoe, trying to dislodge it.

"Shh," Oak says as Kyle-Ray pops his shoe from the hard surface. He looks up from the ground to see Oak slowly walking the path, knees bent. Up ahead are two deer peeking their heads through the forest, into view. Kyle-Ray slowly stands up, Oak's hand warning him to stay there as he reaches his other hand out toward the deer. This is why they came here. It's what Oak had planned to do with Dev, until she upset him. The two deer twitch their black, wet noses at the oncoming human. They appear to be male, as they both have antlers. The bigger of the two cautiously takes a step back as Oak approaches.

Kyle-Ray stands still, watching. The younger buck steps forward, sniffing into the air, attempting to get Oak's scent. His ears perk up as he is willed by the magic resonating within the witchy human. He steps forward onto the path, the larger one watching with concern, not yet willed by Oak's scent as he approaches. They approach each other warily, and meet face-to-face. Oak stands about eye level with the highest point of the deer's antlers, looking down at him with his hand out. He places his hand on the side of the animal's face and carefully scratches. The deer leans into his touch and allows himself to be petted.

Oak leads his hand away from the deer, in the direction of where Kyle-Ray is standing, and the deer follows the command and walks over to Oak's star-struck friend. Oak now puts his attention on the stag, still hiding in the trees. Reaching out an arm toward the gentle creature, he uses his other hand to conjure some wind, wafting the smell of himself to the slick nostrils of the wild beast. The scent catches and the deer steps onto the path, curious.

Kyle-Ray watches as the deer Oak sent his way trots over and nuzzles his shirt. He sets his hand down on top of the animal's head, between his small antlers. He shifts his sight to Oak to see he is now petting the larger, more intimidating deer. "You ready?" Oak asks.

"For what?"

Oak reaches over the back of the deer and grabs onto the base of his antlers with his other hand, swinging his leg around and mounting the animal like a horse.

"Are you nuts?" Kyle-Ray shouts, scaring his deer from compulsion, so it darts into the thicket about fifty feet and then turns back to stare.

Oak rides his mount over to Kyle-Ray, teasing, "You wanna try again, with your mouth shut?"

Kyle-Ray nods and Oak rides into the forest to the smaller deer and brings him back over to the path. Oak offers his hand and helps his friend get on the unusual steed. They head off the path and into the woods, trotting along side by side. They watch dragonflies swoop around tall plants and buzz by them as they go deeper into the forest. A few small rodents are disturbed by the hooves and escape into the overgrown grass, only their tails seen through the brush.

Oak leans forward on the majestic animal and rubs it, laying his cheek on its warm furry neck. He closes his eyes and listens to it breathe as he is calmed by the bumping motion of the deer walking along the forest floor. The sun shines through the canopy of branches and moss, shooting beams of light down through the dark shadows cast from the looming trees.

Oak feels a sudden thud by his leg into the side of the animal. He opens his eyes and sees the tail end of an arrow, lodged in the deer's ribs. The stag bucks upwards, rolling Oak off and throwing him into the ground as it runs off. "No!" he yells as he scrambles to stand up and help the animal.

Kyle-Ray jumps off his deer to assist Oak and it runs off to be with its injured partner.

"What happened, what's wrong?" Kyle-Ray asks.

"An arrow! Someone shot the deer!"

Kyle-Ray looks around the dense gathering of trees, a long ways from the intended path. "From where?"

"My left. It stuck right into his ribs. I have to help it!" Oak says frantically.

"Oak ... I was right beside you on the left."

Oak stares at him.

Kyle-Ray is looking for the deer now, pointing in the distance. "Look, he's fine. There's nothing there."

Oak follows Kyle-Ray's hand in the direction he's pointing and sees the animal in the distance, not a single thing wrong with it. Oak holds his head. "What is wrong with me?"

"Your eyes were closed. You probably fell asleep, into a dream or something."

Kyle-Ray's observation makes sense, but things like this keep happening. Oak agrees with his simplification of the events that just transpired but knows it's not correct.

Kyle-Ray brushes leaves and small sticks off Oak's back, patting him clean. "Let's head back. The sun will just be going down by the time we get home if we leave now."

Oak agrees and they start heading back in the direction they came from, leaving the deer uncompelled and free to run wild. As they get back to the trail's original path, Kyle-Ray smacks a mosquito on his arm. "So, do the animals just get used to you coming here so much?"

"Yeah, my mom and I have been visiting here for years." It's a half lie. Obviously, the wild animals have not become tame from his and Dev's frequent visits, but they did used to visit often, when he was little. They wind around the serpentine path of the trail until finally, they can see the conservation center up ahead, marking their exit. They reach the edge of the forest and the sky opens to a bright orange-and- pink sky. The exit log sits atop a tall wooden post with two uniformed staff members inspecting it.

The boys walk to the exit log and the staff members greet them. "Are you Oak and Kyle-Ray?" one asks.

"Yep."

They point to the logbook. "Go ahead and sign yourselves out. We were just about to come check on you. We're getting ready to close," one man says, giving a friendly smile.

They sign the log and apologize for being there until closing time. They head up the stairs along the porch and follow it around to the front of the building, the nature center now locked for the evening. They go down the stairs at the front of the building and into the parking lot, dreading the idea that they now have to walk that entire dirt path, the entire city park, and all the way home.

As they get to the end of the parking lot, slogging along with their shoulders drooped and exhausted, a car honks. Oak ignores it as a security system locking a car but Kyle-Ray looks toward the sound. "It's your mom," he says, tugging on Oak's sleeve.

He turns around to see his mother there to pick them up. She knew exactly where he would have gone. Relieved that they don't have to walk another step, the boys climb into the car and slump down.

Chapter 8

Mallie holds her hands inches away from the woman's limbs. The heat between her palms and the client's body gathers intensely. With slow, graceful movements she moves her hands up and down the length of the woman, stopping to concentrate on areas that feel warmer than others. Calm music playing light chimes and gongs sings in the background as incense fills the room to control the mood.

Mallie quietly opens a drawer and removes a bar of handmade soap wrapped in brown paper and tied in hemp rope, a small tag indicating its ingredients, and a tiny sample of body cream. She pulls a towel off a shelf and makes a presentation of the items on a tray. Whispering, she says, "Okay, my sweet, I am leaving you some items on this tray; your service is complete. Before you get dressed, I would like you to shower with this soap made by Marion, our owner. Then, rub the cream into your skin after you dry off. These items will prolong your healing." She squeezes her client's shoulder and exits the room quietly. Marion is passing by in the hall as Mallie closes the door behind her.

"All finished for the day?" Marion asks. She's holding a basket of used towels, the same type that Mallie has just given her client to shower.

"Yes, I just need to get her paid and rescheduled," Mallie responds. A warm smile that seems to always be there naturally complements her collarbone-length auburn hair with subtle hints of red that catch the light.

"Great, I have a favor to ask of you. See me after?" Marion requests as she reaches for a sliding door that leads to a washing machine and dryer.

"Sure."

Mallie Jeanine has always been soft-spoken and kind. The type of person that will get cut in front of at the store and stay silent, or loan money to a stranger and never get paid back. Her full cheeks are flushed with baby pink tones and her considerate medium-gray eyes sparkle next to her dark black eyelashes. She unties an apron from her back, pulling the loop that loosens the bow behind her. She slips the apron up over her head and hangs it on a hook on the wall, just around the corner from the front desk checkout area.

Behind the counter, she types away on the computer as her guest comes out from the treatment room to pay for her service. "Okay, Lisa. The effects of your cosmetics should prolong your treatment and the effects will start wearing off in about three weeks, so I suggest we schedule for a month."

Lisa folds her hands in front of her face, gratitude pouring from every inch of her. "I feel so much better, thank you so so much. A month will be perfect."

Mallie types away on the computer to mark the appointment and reaches out to Lisa, taking her hands into hers. "You are so very welcome, my sweet. That is why we are here. I will bag and label your soap from today for your next visit." Lisa pulls Mallie's hands to her lips and lays a kiss on them, releasing her to pay for the healing.

"If the effects begin to wear off prematurely to our next appointment, we sell the soap and body cream here in the studio," Mallie informs Lisa as she leaves.

Marion comes to the front, a bin of unwrapped soap in her hands. "Help me wrap and tag these while we chat," Marion says.

Mallie locks the front door of the studio and flips the 'open' sign, then follows Marion to the back where the wrapping supplies are. Marion hands her a tube of brown paper and a spool of hemp rope. She pulls a box of tags from a shelf and they head to a table toward the back to work. "What do you need to talk to me about?" Mallie asks.

Marion unrolls the paper wrapping and slices down the length against the table. "I need to talk to you about my grandson. I need to know if you can help provide us with some answers."

Mallie looks concerned as she begins to cut strips of the rope. They spend the next two hours packaging cosmetics, Marion explaining Oak's outbursts to her trusted partner. She goes into detail about the Divine and tells her everything she knows. Mallie listens intently, not missing a single word. Her heart aches for the family; she is a strong empath. Her evenings are spent cleansing her body of the healings she performed earlier that day. She absorbs everyone's ailments and accepts them as her own until she gets home at the end of a shift and expels them from her body with meditation and the help of a healing-spell candle marked with the caduceus.

"I know you do not do this often, my dear, but do you think dream walking with Oak would tell us anything?"

Mallie can see the desperation in the old crone's eyes. "I think ..." she begins. "I think it will lead us in the direction he needs to go, but I do not believe it will give any answers. His problem seems to be a problem of his mind. Dream walking can lead us to answers of the body, but a human's mind is generally locked tightly from outsiders. The magic within him will be a conscious entity inside a dream and will be able to lead us to the next step required for helping him, but it will not be able to directly tell us anything."

Marion considers her words for a moment before she heeds a warning.

"But Mare," Mallie says, "It's dangerous to dream walk. Especially on a child that is still suppressing."

"I know. That is why I did not come to you first. He will always be in suppression as the Divine. We have no other options."

Mallie puts her hand on Marion's, stopping her from finishing the last soap. "We're coven sisters. I want to help him. He is my coven brother. I will dream walk with him."

A tear rolls down Marion's face and she hugs Mallie.

***

Marion stocks the newly made products in the treatment rooms and out front as Mallie cleans up and puts away the supplies. They'll fold towels in the morning. The lights cut off and they head out the back, leaving M&M Healing Studio dark and silent for the night.

On the drive home, Marion's mind is a mess of emotions and thoughts. She isn't sure if she wants to risk putting Oak in danger to get answers. She knows he can't continue to live with these outbursts; they are going to get him into trouble, and Cynthia's haunting warning has scared them from trying to mask the problem. Mallie hasn't dream walked in years. The last one was with a very famous celebrity singer. One so famous and well-known, she didn't have a last name. She paid M&M Healing Studios fifty thousand dollars for Mallie to dream walk into the artist's mind and discover her body was fighting fibromyalgia.

On her way home, Mallie decides she needs to make a pit stop to talk to Dev about the idea. She detours from the apartment and arrives at the Blacks' house. Dev greets her at the door. "Mallie, is everything all right?"

Mallie shuffles her feet. "Yes. Has Marion told you her idea?"

Dev looks at her inquisitively. "No, I don't think so. Come inside."

Mallie steps through the threshold and stops. "I can only stay for a moment. Can Oak be here for this?"

"No, I'm sorry, Mal, he's at dinner with his father. What's wrong?"

Mallie explains Marion's idea to dream walk. Dev listens intently for a moment before reacting. "I agree with Marion. We can't just let this go."

Mallie feels relieved that Dev is on board. "May I at least write Oak a letter? That way I know for sure he has all the necessary information I wish him to have."

Dev gets her a pen and paper, along with an envelope. "Of course."

Mallie jots down a letter to Oak, including some details about the process of dream walking. She thanks Dev for her time, seals the letter into the envelope, and hands it to Dev on her way out the front door. She gets back into her car and makes her way back in the direction of her apartment.

Once home, she goes to her balcony and pours a circle of black salt on the cold concrete. She lights her caduceus candle, sitting in the center of the circle. Her entire body hurts from the ailments she's healed today. Heartburn, tennis elbow, carpal tunnel, and Lisa's bone-on-bone arthritis.

She puts herself into a deep trance, meditating peacefully as a breeze cools her face through the screen. All of her pain begins to melt away slowly after just a few minutes. She is so accustomed to this routine, it doesn't take her long to recover. After about fifteen minutes, she breaks the seal on the black salt circle and snuffs out her spell candle.

She considers the risks involved in helping Oak, but when your coven needs you, you must come forward, risking your life if necessary. She has a combination of extremely old and ratty books locked away in a faux book safe in the apartment that she studies before every dream walk. The safe contains a book on astral projection, one on dream interpretation, and a small booklet of handwritten potions. Mallie spins the numbers on the lock of the book safe and removes its contents. She tosses the three items onto her bed and runs the shower.

After her shower she slips into a silky black robe, one that makes her feel like a sultry sorceress. She crawls into bed and studies, preparing herself for dream walking with Oak. She falls asleep, the book slipping out of her hand and onto the floor. The best way to retain the process of dream walking is to fall asleep learning it.

***

After getting home from dropping off Kyle-Ray, Oak gets dressed for dinner. His dad should be over soon to take him out for his birthday. Dev is sitting in the kitchen, adjusting settings on the camera she uses for capturing spirit orbs. Orbs are the physical manifestation of lost spirits trying to find their way. They are often around people or places they were familiar with during their lives. Dev's camera has enhancements that allow the photos to release the spirits to the other side when you snap a photo. She uses the photography as a hobby and has an album dedicated to all the souls she's released.

Oak comes out of his bedroom to show Dev his outfit. He's decided to wear his ceremonial boots and pin his protection charm through the top of the leather. He walks into the kitchen and they look at each other. Oak is still upset about earlier but there is a silent apology floating in the air, not needing to be spoken. "Why your boots?"

"I've never had a reason to wear them and they're comfy."

Dev nods and turns a dial on the camera. "I think I need to recharge the selenite in this camera. I'll have to check for the next full moon." She opens a compartment that releases a three-inch stick of translucent white crystal.

"What's wrong with it?" Oak asks, pulling up a chair and sitting next to Dev at the table.

"I think it's lost its charge; it hasn't released the last two orbs I captured to the spirit realm."

Oak leans over and takes the selenite from her, squeezing it in his palm.

Dev adjusts the focus on the zoom and peers inside. Oak can feel heat forming around the crystal in his hand, a slight vibration beginning to build. He feels the ability to recharge the crystal overwhelm him. Instead of fighting it, he lets the power take over.

Dev turns the camera around and inspects the sigils carved into the glass around the outside of the lens, not realizing what Oak is doing. There is a knock at the door. "Your father's here. Go have fun."

Oak's hand is nearly numb from the intense internal vibration of the now fully charged crystal. He hands it over to Dev as he stands up and walks out of the kitchen. "There ya go," he says casually, and heads out the front door.

Dev looks at the crystal in her hand. She can feel it has been recharged completely. She looks in disbelief in the direction Oak left. He is figuring out more and more of the craft every day.

***

Oak hugs his dad and they walk to his car. "Where we going?" Alan asks, starting the engine.

"There's that new place that only serves deconstructed dishes," Oak tells him, buckling his seat belt.

"Yes, I remember seeing them building it," Alan says, pulling out of the neighborhood and onto the main road.

"It's expensive," Oak tells him, remembering the walk he and Kyle-Ray took earlier that day, as Alan drives down the same path. They are going so much faster in the car than when they walked.

"It's you. I expect nothing but expensive," Alan jokes at Oak's high-end taste. Then he adds, "Your mother told me about earlier." Oak just puts his head down. "You had every right to be upset, but please don't take off like that again, okay?" He nods, looking at the floor. Alan puts his hand on Oak's leg and shakes it. "You know how easy it is to scare your mother."

Shortly, they pull into the parking lot of the newly designed building. It has a minimalistic approach to the exterior. A plain white building, shaped in a small rectangle with the panels of the front entrance covered in ivy, not an inch of building exposed. They get out of the car and head to the front door, pulling open the glass door by the perfectly square metal 'knob.'

"Welcome, guys. What name is your reservation under?" the hostess inquires as they stand at the podium.

"Oh, you're reservation only?" Alan asks.

"Yes, sir, I'm so sorry," she says, pointing at a small plaque at the front of the podium that explains.

"It's under Alan Black," Oak says to her. Alan looks at him. They just chose to go here a few minutes ago; he knows they don't have a reservation.

The hostess looks to her list of names and traces down it with a single finger. "Black, Black, Black, Black," she says, searching. Oak smirks at Alan. "I'm sorry, I don't see that name on our list."

Oak peers over her podium and points at 'Please sign in here.' "There we are," he says confidently.

She reads 'Alan Black.' "Oh my goodness! If it were a snake it would've bitten me." Compulsion on humans only really works with the simplest of tasks. Getting the hostess to read 'Please sign in here' as 'Alan Black' was simple enough to do after paging through the book back at Divinity. The woman turns and takes

THE COVEN'S SON

two menus and motions for them to follow her. Alan hits Oak on the shoulder.

Oak turns, ready to be scolded. "Nice," Alan says instead, giving him a fist bump.

Both Oak and Alan smirk slyly as they are seated at their table. The server pours them water and allows them to browse the menu. The menu is clear plastic with inked words printed on it; they are practically invisible while holding it. Only when you set the menu down on the white cloth of the table do you see enough to read it.

Oak lives for silly, trendy places like this. It reminds him of witchcraft, and how everything has to work together to create a cohesive experience. He's browsing the appetizers when Alan says, "We need to talk about some things."

It's Oak's birthday and he doesn't want to interrupt it with whatever Alan needs to talk about. "Not tonight, Dad, please." Oak reads about deconstructed mozzarella sticks. It's two fried mozzarella pieces placed directly on a skillet of breadcrumbs then each topped with a crushed steamed cherry tomato.

"We have to tonight, bud. You know I work too much to do this any other time."

The server comes by. "Any drinks or appetizers for you two gentlemen tonight?" Alan requests a soda with a wedge of lime and Oak orders iced tea and the cheese sticks.

Oak sighs. "Fine, what?" He pushes the edge of the menu hanging off the table onto the white cloth so he can see.

"What are your plans for school? We're trying to be understanding of the possible expulsion, but do you have any idea where you would want to enroll?"

Oak hasn't considered school for a single second since he was escorted out. He reads the entrees listed on each half of the menu. "I have no idea," he says bluntly.

"Well, while I don't like the idea, your mother has suggested you stay home. Practice witchcraft as a form of homeschooling with your grandmother."

This pulls Oak's concentration from the food. "What? She said that?"

The server drops by and sets down their drinks. Alan reaches for his glass. "Yes, I think you should be in school, but she explained how hard this all must be for you. I want what makes you happy. Would you consider that plan?" He sips his soda, the lime wedge touching his lip as he sips.

Oak didn't think staying home would even be an option. Studying the occult, spells, potions, and learning more about the craft would have sounded terribly boring up until recently. Now that he's realized he knows so little about himself and where he's come from, how important he is to the world of magic, it sounds like the perfect idea. "I guess. I don't know." Oak stirs his iced tea, swirling the warm tea from the bottom to flow through the ice at the top.

"Well, I just want you doing *something*. So, I can agree to this if the other option is to do nothing."

Oak isn't quite sure why Alan thinks the alternative to studying at home is absolutely nothing, but he assumes he and Dev have had private conversations with Principal Santora about being bullied and they think he will refuse to go to any school. "I guess that's fine," he tells his dad.

Oak sips his iced tea, looking around at the décor of the restaurant. There are big square hand-painted canvases of vegetables lining the stark white walls. The tables are covered and the chairs are a light silver metal. He decides he is going to order the 'molecular gastronomy sampler.' It consists of three different two-bite meals that are broken down scientifically and created into different textures with the same flavors as the traditional version of the meal would be. It reminds Oak of alchemy and how much he impressed everyone when he turned his pin to iron.

The server comes by and drops off the appetizer. "Are we ready to order?"

Oak points to the sampler and Alan orders a plain version of some sort of steak. He is not as adventurous in eating as Oak is.

"The steak normally comes with a reduced balsamic vinegar foam. Is that all right?"

Alan stares at the server then looks at Oak. "You pick weird restaurants." He turns back to the server. "Can that be on the side?" The server assures him it can, stifling a giggle, and leaves to submit the order.

"How's work, Dad?" Oak asks, noticing no one really ever checks on him.

"Work is work. It's a lot." Alan changes the subject. "I'm going to be looking at condos soon. Would you want to come check them out with me?" he asks, reaching across the table for a mozzarella stick. "Maybe you can convince the realtor to lower the prices," Alan jokes, biting into the appetizer and making a face of disgust. "Oh, this is horrible." He tosses the rest of it back onto the plate.

Oak explains to his father that compulsion wouldn't work out so well with something like prices. The realtor gets a cut of whatever she sells, based on the price she sells it for. Her will would be too strong wanting to make a higher commission and compulsion would be a waste of energy.

Oak grabs his own portion of the appetizer and tastes it. It tastes fine. He looks at Alan like there is something wrong with him. "This is delicious. You're dramatic."

Alan dismisses him with a wave. "If you can't get me a good price on a condo, what good are ya?"

Oak holds his heart with his free hand, pretending to be shot and in pain. They both laugh and Oak finishes the appetizer by himself. They talk about this and that, reminiscing on memories and chatting about previous birthdays. Alan tells him a story about when he threw up all over the back seat of Dev's car from eating too much cake. Oak knows very well Alan changed the story about what made him vomit from alcohol to cake, to make it child-friendly. He plays along with it anyway, even though he's old enough to hear the real version of his dad's story.

The entrees come out and Oak devours his meal, making up for the lack of food he's eaten today.

"Hey, slow down, that's an eighty-nine-dollar snack you're eating." Alan says, mocking the eliteness of the restaurant. He picks at his own plate, barely tasting the vinegar foam, and decides he hates it. He eats his small portion of steak and pushes his plate away. "Well, that sucked."

Oak finishes every last morsel of his meal and notices a gathering of servers out of the corner of his eye. He spots the head server coming their way, shielding a candle with her hand. *No, no, no, please, no.*

All the servers huddle around the table and place a fancy dessert with a lit candle in front of him. "Happy happy birthday, from our staff and crew. We wish it were our birthday, so we could eat with you!" In unison they all clap and disperse, their server staying behind. Oak is beet red and uncomfortable. "Happy birthday! Can I get you drink refills?" They nod and Oak slumps down in his chair, embarrassed.

Alan takes a fork from his napkin and reaches over to the dessert plate and gets a big bite. "If you sit there pouting, I'm going to eat it all," he tells him, putting the fork into his mouth.

Oak straightens up in his chair and grabs the spoon presented to him on the plate. There is a drizzle of chocolate ganache on the plate, topped with three thin slices of cake rolled into small logs set in between shards of hard caramel candy nets, two scoops of ice cream, topped with dehydrated crunchy marshmallows. The red embarrassment dissipates from his cheeks and nose as he enjoys his dessert.

Alan keeps helping himself to bite after bite while Oak fights him off with his spoon, a fork and spoon battle developing between them. "This is the only thing that's good," Alan says, maneuvering his fork around Oak's spoon shield and capturing some cake.

Oak summons the craft and sends his dad's fork flying across the restaurant. Alan's head darts in the direction it went. Oak begins laughing at the sound of the fork clattering on the floor somewhere in the distance; he has no idea where. Alan can't believe he did that. He is speechless. Oak is in tears, his face completely red again, laughing so hard he can barely breathe.

A random server heard the fork and is staring at it from the bar. Alan is starting to be unable to control his laughter. Oak can't hold himself up in his chair anymore, he is so weak from laughing.

The server brings the check and sets it on the table. "Have a great birthday. Thank you all for coming."

Alan has regained his composure enough to pay the bill. Oak just keeps imagining the fork flying through the air, the sound of it clanging onto the ground so far away. It sends him immediately back into hysterics.

"Let's go before they kick you out," Alan laughs, standing and making his way out of the restaurant.

Oak follows behind him, holding his stomach, his abs sore. He wipes his tears away as he gets outside and into the car. Alan smiles at him. "I'm glad you obviously had a good time."

"Thanks, Dad," Oak says, and they drive off.

THE COVEN'S SON

Alan pulls up to the curb of Dev's house. "See ya, bud. Happy birthday." He gives Oak a fist bump.

Oak gets out of the car and waves goodbye to his dad, wishing he would come in with him. His parents are avoiding seeing each other and it's weird. Oak opens the front door as Alan drives away.

Oak enters the house and Dev is in the distance, standing on a couch with her camera pressed up against her face. "Dammit!" she says, looking from the camera to see Oak coming home.

"What are you doing?" Oak asks.

"I smelled my great grandpa's cigars and there's an orb in here I'm trying to free. I think he found me, but he's a tricky one to catch."

Oak goes into the living room where she is. "How do you see where he is?"

"They only show on camera, but if you photograph areas you notice have a different feeling to them, you'll usually cross over an orb and capture it on camera," she explains.

"A different feeling?"

She steps down off the couch.

"Go where I was, you'll see." He steps up onto the couch. "Smell up toward the ceiling." Oak gives her a weird look. "Just do it." He smells the air from on top of the couch. He *does* notice the faint lingering smell of a cigar in that area.

"Oh, oh okay, yeah!"

"I just don't think I can get the camera high enough." Dev aims from the ground at the area Oak is and snaps a picture. The flash goes off and there is a tiny spark in the air toward the ceiling. "Or I just wasn't aiming in the right spot."

"Was that it? That spark?" he asks, still looking in that area.

"Yup, I crossed him over. They can come whenever they want, but they have to be crossed over or they'll just float around." Dev gives Oak her hand and helps him down from the couch. "Mallie brought over something for you to read. We're going to try something."

"Mallie? Grandma's friend?" he asks.

"Yes, she is part of our coven. She met you as a baby but I don't know why you haven't seen her since. She's seen you grow up from Grandma's photos of you, but I guess sometimes things slip by. Did you have a good time with your dad?"

Oak takes his mistletoe pin from his boot and attaches it to his shirt, unzipping the boots and sliding them off. "Yes, it was great."

Dev sets her camera down on the coffee table. "Good. Go read what Mallie brought you. I'm going to bed." She kisses his head and disappears to her bedroom.

Oak goes to his room to change into pajamas and sees his room is completely clean. The final part of Dev's apology. He doesn't like it when she goes through his stuff, but he knows this is because of earlier. He takes the envelope off his bed and opens it, reading the letter that's inside.

> *Oak, it's Auntie Mal Mal. I'm so sorry we haven't been in touch over the years. I am,*

however, relieved to know you're reading this letter at an age where I know you will fully understand how hard Reiki is on my body. I've hardly been away from home or work in ten years.

Excuses aside, your grandma Marion has requested my assistance. I am willing to help, but I want you to be fully informed about what we are going to do. I am going to be dream walking into your mind and this can be dangerous. I have included on the next page the process and risks involved.

Along with the risks, there is a page of ingredients to be used for making a soak and a serum you need. I would create it for you, but I'm sure you are aware that making it yourself will be more to our advantage. Have it ready by the time I see you.

Love, Mallie.

Oak scans the second page. His breathing increases, reading what can happen. The third page contains two recipes. He has to decide if Cynthia's warning was dire enough to put his life on the line.

Chapter 9

"I'm going to bring Oak to my house so he can create the brews you need," Marion says to Mallie as she's dragging a large copper basin, covered in dust, from the back storage area of the studio.

Mallie wipes her forehead and stands straight. "Did you reschedule all the appointments for today?"

Marion flips the open sign to 'closed' and dims the lights in the reception area. "Yes, the studio is shut down for a day of 'maintenance.'" The sun is rising brightly into the sky, the warm golden colors of morning lighting up the world.

Mallie begins wiping the dust from the tub. "Make sure you don't help him; it'll be more compatible to his body if he does it all himself."

Marion dismisses her with a wave. "This isn't my first twirl around the maypole."

As Mallie scrubs down the bath, Marion leaves out the back door, her keys rattling as she locks the door behind her. Mallie arrived at the shop early to create the astral projection potion she needs for dream walking with Oak today. Marion called her extra early when she noticed they did not have many appointments scheduled today, thinking today was the perfect day. The next few weeks are booked full; this is their chance.

Marion pulls into the driveway of Dev's home and enters without knocking. She doesn't have to unlock the door, which she finds strange. She can hear someone rustling around in the kitchen. "Oak, honey, is that you?"

Dev peeks her head out with a cup of coffee. "No, Mom, it's me. But, Oak's awake."

"Why are you awake so early?" Marion inquires, walking into the kitchen.

"Why are you coming into my house without knocking?" Dev gives Marion a sly smile, bringing the coffee to her lips. "I'm up because Oak was up worrying about dream walking. I assume you're here this early for that?" She sits on the edge of a chair.

"I know we just considered this yesterday, but the day the studio was available happened to be today. Where is he?" Marion helps herself to some coffee.

Oak walks into the kitchen, drying his hair with a towel. He just got out of the shower. He sees his grandma and stops. "I have to decide now?" He frowns.

"Yes, dear. I'm sorry it's last-minute but it's important."

Dev mentioned how he woke her up, anxious about the decision. She does not know how many hours on top of that he rolled around in bed panicking before he decided to come to her.

Oak takes a deep breath. "I'm going to do it, but I want the option to opt out at any time between now and the moment we start the process."

Dev isn't surprised.

Marion studies him for a moment. "I can agree to that. Get in the car." She heads to the front door.

Dev's eyes widen. "Whoa, whoa, whoa, *now?*"

Marion turns around. "Not exactly. I have to take him home so he can brew the ingredients. Then, we go." She opens the front door.

"Mother, stop! I want to be there."

She turns on her heel. "Dev, relax. You will be there. Come to the studio. You'll know when."

Oak races by Dev. "Bye, Mom, love you."

Dev feels her forehead. She is getting hot. Stress is overwhelming her; this is too fast. Oak gets in the car and they are gone. Dev shuts the door, alone in the house.

***

On their way to Marion's house, she asks Oak, "Do you have your ingredient list?"

He reaches down and grabs the outside of his pants pocket, his mistletoe pinned to it. He pulls down the edge of the pocket, showing the list pinned securely into the inside of his pocket by the charm. Marion laughs and shakes her head. "You are a smart one." He continues to impress her, causing her to believe more and more that he actually is the Divine. Not that she didn't believe he was; it's just that the reality is hard to swallow and every day it becomes more apparent.

They pull up to Marion's house and head inside. The glittery plum door creaks open and on the other side Oak sees a six-foot-three tall, hefty-looking man, with gray hair on the sides of his bald head, a gray mustache, and glasses staring back at him. "Grandpa!" Oak yells, running to him for a hug.

"Easy, Big O, I'm a frail old man!"

Pepe arrived home from Greece late last night. Marion briefly explained the most recent discoveries in their family to him before going to sleep. He knows to make himself scarce, so he does not distract Oak from his craft today. "Good to see ya, kiddo! Now, I'm so tired from my nineteen-hour flight from Greece, I'm going back to bed." He ruffles Oak's hair and stomps up the stairs.

Oak smiles. He didn't expect to see his grandpa today, even if was only for a moment.

Marion had gone to the kitchen; she pops back out and tosses Oak a bottle of water. "Get in there and get to work," she says, pointing toward the apothecary.

He gets to the door and notices she hasn't moved. "Are you coming?" he asks, swinging the door back and forth.

"No, you're on your own for this one, dear." She turns and heads back into the kitchen.

His stomach flips. He's doing this alone? This could be a potentially life-ending day and he has to do it by himself. He shuts the door behind him quietly, unpins the ingredient list from his pocket, and sits at the table where he crafted his suppression charm. He unfolds the paper and chooses to do the serum first, going over the ingredients. *Valerian, honey, kava, belladonna, moon water.*

Marion knocks lightly and opens the door. "You'll need this." She plugs in an electric kettle and sets it on the edge of the desk, exiting the room backwards, waving with a big cheesy smile.

Oak looks at the kettle. "Wait, what?" He looks back at the ingredient list. "Belladonna? That's deadly nightshade." He puts his head in his hands, reconsidering the whole thing after seeing a poisonous ingredient. One wrong measurement and this could kill him.

Oak puffs his cheeks and lifts his head up, looking around the room. He goes to the wall of jars and searches for all the ingredients. There are bottles of water on a rolling cart by the window, individually labeled. *Wolf moon, Thunder moon, Harvest moon, Pink moon, Hunter's moon, Buck moon, Flower moon.* He stares at them. The list doesn't specify which to use; he didn't know there were choices.

His eye is drawn to the spine of a book on one of the bookshelves beside him. *Mystical Properties of the Various Moons.* He snags the book off the shelf and flips through it, scanning pages quickly as he goes through. He flips back and forth between a few pages, reading the meanings behind the moons he has water for. He reaches for the Buck moon and notices his finger is holding a place in the book he hasn't looked at. He opens to the page;

it's about the Flower moon. He reads through the page and feels his shoulders loosen. This must be the right answer. He has to go with his gut.

He grabs hold of the Flower moon water and unscrews the cap. Taking it over to the kettle he pours it in, turning it on to boil. He turns to find a small black iron cauldron at the bottom of the rolling cart. He brings it to the desk. He sets down the jars of herbs he pulled from the wall and turns around to find the last ingredient, honey.

His eyes scan the room until they stop on a clear plastic bin filled with miscellaneous items. Digging through the bin, he pulls out a jar of honey. Bringing it to the desk, he sits down and starts adding ingredients. He adds the valerian, then the kava to the tiny cauldron. It can only hold about two cups of ingredients. Then the belladonna. Oak adds slowly since there are no measurements on a lot of witches' potions.

He listens to his body, his internal magic, his ancestors. As soon as he feels relaxed, he stops adding. He spoons honey into the pot and pours a small amount of moon water in. The mixture begins to swirl on its own and a small whirlpool forms in the center. Oak smiles widely as the ingredients begin to mix themselves. He is not using his magic to stir it; he knows he did it properly. He finds a glass tube in a basket of empty containers underneath the desk. He pulls the cork off and pours the piping hot mixture in, replacing the cork. The mixture is a greenish brown and smells like dirty grass.

Oak sets the serum aside, grabs the water Marion tossed him earlier, and begins to gulp it down. He sits back in the chair, taking a moment to breathe. He is scared, and is in total control of this part of the process, which scares him more. He reaches over and grabs the ingredient list, pulling it to his face from his reclined position so he can see what is needed for the soak.

Epsom salts, ylang ylang oil, mugwort, crushed moonstone.

Oak leans up and unplugs the kettle.

Searching for where the moonstone would be, he finds a velvet drawstring bag full of rocks and crystals. He pours it out onto the floor and sifts through it. There are three moonstones in the bag. He takes the smallest one and replaces the others, tying the bag and placing it back where it came from.

The mortar and pestle sits on the side of the desk where he left it last. The moonstone gets tossed in and Oak begins crushing it down with force. It's difficult at first to crush the hard material, but once it gets started he soon has a gritty sand texture. He stands and grabs a jar of Epsom salts and mugwort. Looking through the vials of oil, he searches for ylang ylang. He plucks up the only bottle of oil that he can't read, the words smudging off it. Squinting, Oak decides it may have said ylang ylang once. He sits back down, opening the jar of Epsom salts. He mixes the salt in, shaking the mortar to stir. He then adds the mugwort, doing the same thing.

Pulling the top off the oil, Oak tips it over the herbal salt and stone mixture, shaking out enough drops until his nose opens and it feels right. He grabs another glass tube from the basket under the desk, pops the cork, and carefully pours the mixture in, filling the tube. Once the cork is back on, he shakes the whole thing until everything is sufficiently mixed. He sets this tube next to the first and looks at them.

Oak wants to run away. He wants to escape this world and never return. If he disappears now, maybe he can save himself. He imagines himself sneaking into a dark, thick forest, compelling another buck to ride far, far away where no one will find him. He imagines Cynthia's ghost telling him his problem is far more dire than being the Divine. She reaches out to touch his face and he snaps back to reality.

Then he chugs more water. He wants to reread the warning letter Mallie wrote him about the entire process. He was smart enough not to bring it, though, to not torture himself with it. Gathering the vials for dream walking, he leaves the apothecary and searches the bottom floor for Marion. After checking a few rooms, he hears movement upstairs. She must've gone up for something, maybe to visit with Pepe for a moment.

He comes out into the hall and around to the bottom of the staircase. Marion becomes visible from her bedroom and begins down the stairs. He holds the vials up.

"Are you ready?" she says, making her way carefully down the stairs.

"I ... I think so."

She holds her hand out to take the vials from him. Her glasses are dangling from her neck. She puts them on and inspects the concoctions. First, she views the serum by holding it up to the light and turning it against the brightness. It is a cloudy and unattractive color. "The belladonna is in here?"

Oak nods, recognizing that she understands his hesitation to add it.

"It won't work without it," she says, peering at him from above the frames of her spectacles.

"It's in there, I promise."

She accepts his answer and switches the serum vial for the bath soak. "I had moonstone?" she asks, seeing the iridescent grains of sand between the shiny salts.

"You had three."

She hands them back to Oak. "Wonderful job, dear. I am certain the walk will go just fine," she says smiling, stepping off the staircase. She grabs her broom from the closet under the stairs and heads to the front door. "Ready?"

"You're bringing your broom?" He looks around for his, forgetting that he took it home.

"Yes, to place protection at the doorway when you begin. Your mom is bringing yours; she's meeting us at the studio," she tells him, walking outside to the car. Oak follows behind her, shutting the door on his way out.

***

They pull into the rear of M&M Healing Studio and enter through the back. Mallie has everything set up in their biggest treatment room. Marion passes by and goes straight to the laundry room. Oak pokes his head in with Mallie, recognizing her from photos displayed in Marion's house. "Is my mom here yet?"

She turns around from a pile of ingredients on the counter next to the sink. "Yes, she's establishing a glamour on the front of the building. I'll be ready soon." She gives him a welcoming smile.

He thanks her and heads to the reception area at the front. He can see Dev outside the shop, spraying the area with something. Rosewater. She pulls a few stones of hematite from her purse and stacks a small pile on each corner of the building. She opens the door to the studio and comes inside. DING. The door alerts of a customer entering. Everyone's brooms are set by the door.

"What does that glamour do?" Oak asks Dev as she steps inside.

"Hi, honey, it will make the building appear to be gone, so no one tries to come." She sets her purse on the reception desk and takes a deep breath. "You ready?"

He looks her in the eye. "No."

She forces a smile. "You can still change your mind."

"It's okay."

She takes his hand and puts her other hand on top. "Mallie is a very skilled dream walker. She hasn't lost anyone."

"Yet," he replies cynically.

Mallie appears from the treatment room. "I'm ready."

Marion walks into the room with an armful of towels. Dev steps behind Oak and grabs his shoulders, leans in to his ear, and says, "I love you." She pats him on the back, giving him a gentle push toward the treatment room.

Mallie opens her arm to Oak, guiding him into the room as if he is one of her Reiki clients. He steps slowly into the room, taking it all in. The copper basin sitting in the middle of the room is filled with steaming hot water. Marion is tucking towels into a warmer. "We'll need these later," she says, shutting the warmer and heading to the entrance of the room.

Mallie steps inside, moving around a chair placed to the right of the tub with a cushion on the seat. She takes a bottle from the counter and sets it on the floor by the foot of the chair. Oak stands at the foot of the bath, waiting. "Oak, do you have your things? Release the soak into the water."

He pulls the glass tube of salts out of his pocket. It rattles in his hand as he pops the cork off and pours the contents into the basin. The water begins to bubble and stir on its own. Mallie smiles. "Perfect, honey. Looks like you did it right. Go ahead and strip down and get in."

He watches the bubbling as it calms down and looks at her. "Strip?"

"Oh, sweetie, if this were the 1800s you would've been raised to run naked through the forest with ten other people. Just your shirt, pants, shoes, and socks."

Dev is at the door, placing her broom down at the entrance, peeking inside a moment. Oak sighs, and pulls his shoes and socks off. His bare feet are cold on the tile floor of the studio. Marion comes to the door and sets her broom down on the floor, sealing the protective threshold. He unpins his mistletoe and clasps it into his hair. As he reaches for the button on his pants, he looks up at Mallie. She smirks, shields her eyes with one hand, and moves to the light switch on the wall. He removes his pants as Mallie dims the lights.

"Marion, can you cut the spa music? We have to be in silence," Mallie calls out. Oak takes off his shirt and walks around to the side of the tub. The music quiets to nothing. "Step in," Mallie says to him, gathering his clothes off the floor. He lifts his leg over the edge of the tub, slowly easing into the hot water. Mallie folds his clothes on the counter and removes the serum from his pants pocket. He slides down into the water, the copper cool on his back as he leans against it. The magic liquid reaches the top of his chest.

Mallie walks to the tub with the serum. She pulls the cork out and hands it to him. He pulls his hand out of the water and reaches for the potion, dripping onto the floor. "Once you ingest this, we cannot stop," she warns.

Oak's heart is rapidly knocking into his sternum, trying to escape. He downs the horrible-tasting liquid, scrunching his face as the flavors of muck and grime dance on his tongue, the sediment at the bottom nearly gagging him.

"So mote it be," Mallie says, nodding her head at his acceptance to continue. She peers out the doorway. "We are beginning, all hands on deck." Her voice echoes as she shuts the door quietly.

Mallie sits upon the cushion in the chair she staged for herself, picking up the astral projection drink from the floor and holding it in her lap. Oak begins to feel dizzy, the room tilting. His heartbeat slows drastically and his head slumps to the side, eyes closed.

Mallie brings the potion to her lips and swallows every last drop. She sets the empty bottle on the floor and stares off into the distance. Her sight becomes clouded as darkness sets in around the periphery of her vision. Her eyelids shut and there is complete silence in the room. The dream walk has begun.

Dev and Marion sit in the waiting area of the reception, playing cards. They are there to ensure things remain as quiet as possible, to protect Oak and Mallie from the risk of being woken up.

They do not usually perform dream walking at the studio because of the dangers involved, aside from a few high-profile exceptions willing to pay a steep fee. The dream walker must astral project themselves directly into someone's mind. If the dream walker's body is disturbed during the process and woken up, consciousness will be torn rapidly from the client's mind, causing severe shock and death. However, if the client is woken up, the dream walker will be trapped in the mind of the dreamer and pushed far back into the subconscious, leaving the body an empty living shell. The only way out is for the client to have a recurring dream of that moment, which could take years.

***

Mallie wakes up in a four-post bed with an elaborately designed lace canopy hanging down, blurring the outside view. She sits up wearing expensive silks and swings her feet to the edge of the bed. Moving the lace covering aside, she slides her feet into luxurious house slippers. She stands and hears the sound of her own voice echoing in her head. "You are asleep." Confused, she brushes off the idea; she has obviously just woken up.

One of the most difficult parts of dream walking is creating a lucid dream. You must muster the strength to convince yourself, while you are asleep, that you are dreaming. She leaves the bedroom and glides down a beautiful curved white marble staircase with golden handrails. "This is not your apartment," she hears, looking around for where the voice is coming from.

Irritated, she turns to a large decorative mirror on the wall of the grand foyer. She admires her reflection. "That is not you." Her reflection slowly changes from a rich, spoiled heiress of wealth, into her usual more recognizable self. The reflection speaks to her. "You're dreaming. Control it. It's time to find Oak."

The whole room spins and turns black as the Mallie in the dream's appearance now matches the reflection of her true self. She is wearing her M&M therapist uniform and apron. Now aware that she is dreaming, she squints her eyes in the dark emptiness. She can feel Oak's presence. His mind is calling to her. She walks through nothingness, following the pull of his energy. Her footsteps echo into the beyond until her eyes begin to water. She feels an overwhelming sense that she is outside. Wind is blowing and she can feel the sun.

Uncontrollably, her eyes clench shut and her mouth opens. She sneezes and feels a tap on her arm. When she opens her eyes, she is in a wonderful, endless flowery field. Oak is next to her, offering her a tissue. "Oak!" She successfully astral projected into Oak's dream, the flowery field representing the moon water he chose for his serum.

"Oak, you're dreaming. You have to accept that." He stares at her, still offering the tissue. She takes it from him and shoves it into a pocket. "Listen to me: we are dream walking. I made it here; you're asleep." He blinks a few times, as if he's fighting himself from within. "Come on, Oak. Come forward. You can do this."

He grabs his head and bends forward as if he was just struck by something. "Mallie?" he says, slowly standing back up, releasing his head. "Did we do it? Did it work?"

Mallie grabs Oak into a tight hug excitedly. "Yes! Yes, you did it! *We* did it. We are doing it, right now."

Oak looks around the infinite field. "What do we do now?" he asks, taking in the scenery.

"Now, we search. Your mind will warp our surroundings as a normal dream would, but magic should guide us to whatever it needs us to know." They begin to walk through the flowery field, looking high and low for any sign of something they may need.

Oak notices a small speck in the distance out of the corner of his eye. He turns that way. "There's something over there." Mallie turns and they both heard towards the object. As they traipse closer, it begins to focus into view. "Is that an elevator?" Oak asks, surprised.

"Looks like it. This is a dream; weird things are going to happen," Mallie answers.

The big, rectangular, brown box, a vintage elevator cab, sits in the middle of the field.

"Do we go in?" Oak asks, looking it up and down.

"Yep, we follow the path being laid out for us," Mallie says, pressing the only button.

DING.

The doors slide open. They step inside and turn around. The doors slide closed. They look for a panel of buttons, but there is nothing. Just as Oak is about to ask what to do, they feel the cage rattle and begin to move. They hold onto the rail along the walls to keep their balance.

DING.

The doors slide open and they step out of the elevator and into a neighborhood. They take it all in, centering themselves to their surroundings. The place feels odd. The front yards are all cemeteries with various tombstones lining the properties. The candy-colored houses create a feeling of whimsy among the darkness of the graveyard gardens. They walk around, trying to find things that seem out of place or which appear to be calling to them. There are no cars or people, the weather is overcast and the air is still.

Hunting for the next hint, Mallie weaves through headstones, hoping something will catch her eye. Oak jiggles the handles of the front doors of a few of the houses, but they're all locked. A loud clap of thunder booms and lightning streaks across the sky, pulsing light all around. The houses disappear and reappear in sync with the fulmination. In the distance, a metal clang is heard by both Oak and Marion. In unison they turn their heads to the sound.

"Over there?" Mallie points.

They walk about a block until they notice a rusty old shovel lying on the sidewalk to the left, near a pile of dirt that sits beside an open grave that's placed just off the front yard of a baby-blue block home. At the foot of the hole, Mallie takes Oak's hand and they lean forward to peer inside.

There is a plank of plywood lying inside, about six feet into the ground. A young girl lies on top, about Oak's age. Her skin is pale and her lips are gray; her eyes are sunken in, but they are closed. Her arms are folded across her chest and the only thing softening her gaunt appearance is her bright ginger hair. Oak begins to shake. His jaw drops open as he stares at the body of the girl before him.

"Do you recognize her?" Mallie says, noticing his reaction to the body below.

"It's … Kate Sumpter, the girl who unclasped my pin at school."

Mallie takes her gaze off Oak and studies the girl. "Your mind and your magic are working together to show their distaste for the girl's actions by presenting her to us like this."

Just then, there is a slight movement from Kate's chest, deep in the ground. A low hum is coming from her throat and exiting out of her mouth in a horrifying death rattle. Her lips hardly part, just enough for the excess air in her lungs to escape her body. "Gggggggrrrrrrrrrreen."

Mallie tilts her head at the sound. "Did she say green?"

Oak verifies that he heard the same thing. "What would green mean?" They look up and search the street. Among the various colored houses there are orange, blue, pink, purple.

"There," Mallie says, pointing. One street over, there is a green house. The only one in the entire neighborhood. They walk towards the house, acutely aware of their surroundings. Another boom of thunder and a streak of lightning lights up the sky. The houses flicker in and out of existence, except the green one. The green house remains solid. They search around the graveyard for a few minutes, making sure they aren't missing anything.

Oak walks up to the front door and tries the handle. It turns all the way, unlatching and opening. He calls Mallie from the cemetery to meet him at the door. They peer inside and cannot see anything. They step through the entry and the door slams behind them, causing them to jump. The area lights up into a grand ballroom, much too big for the house they just entered from. They step forward, hearing the sound of splashing water as they notice a feeling of wetness.

Looking down at their feet they can see they're standing in a few inches of water, and the entire ballroom is flooded. In the reflection of the water is a brilliant masquerade; men and women spinning and twirling in elaborate costumes and masks. It looks like the impression of the water is mirroring an elegant party going on in the ballroom, except the ballroom is empty. They swish through water, exploring the vacant venue, when Mal grabs her head.

Oak turns to her and notices her body flashing into transparency. "Mallie!" Oak cries, pushing through the water toward her. She is regaining her composure as her body turns solid once more. He puts his hand on her shoulder, halfway expecting it to go right through. His hand lands solidly on her. "What happened? Are you okay?"

She steadies her balance and regains herself. "I'm fine," she says quietly, a bit of confusion sweeping across her expression.

"Aunt Mal, something happened. It was like I could have walked right through you."

The masquerade continues on, completely unbothered by the change in mood from the empty floor above their soiree.

Mallie's face turns pale as she looks at Oak, the color draining rapidly from her cheeks. "I think our bodies are being disturbed," she says gravely.

Oak gasps and begins feeling his body, remembering the letter explaining what happens if either of them wake up. Other than scared, he feels fine. Mallie suddenly loses her balance as she begins to be pulled backwards by an unseen force. Her heels drag through water, creating a wave that shoots high into the air on either side of her feet. She is slammed full force into the wall at the end of the ballroom, where she collapses into the water.

Chapter 10

Dev and Marion sit in the reception waiting area, on two small couches by a table riddled with magazines. They've stopped playing their card game and are now quietly reading. Marion pages through a book as Dev flips the pages of one of the magazines. Everything is silent aside from some mild traffic sounds from the main road outside the studio.

Dev notices movement outside the shop from where she is sitting. She looks up from her magazine and notices a man walking toward the building. Marion sees something has grabbed Dev's attention and follows her eyes to the outside. "Who in the world is that?" Marion asks, setting her book on the table. It isn't a client she's ever worked on or recognizes. The man is bald, but has facial hair.

"It's Oak's principal," Dev says in surprise, watching him closely. They both watch, expecting him to bypass the building since the glamour they have in place should deter him from it. He walks straight to the front door. "Why is the glamour not working?"

"Well, they aren't one hundred percent effective, dear," Marion reminds her. "But, the glamour should be in full effect to a regular man without any abilities like Mr. Santora."

He puts his hands on the glass door, peering inside.

Dev goes to the door and points to the sign.

The man waves and yells through the glass, "I need to speak to Oak!" He doesn't have any reason to believe Oak is here, or to think that Dev would be here either.

"He's not here," she mouths, shaking her head.

"Please, let me in," he says, knocking on the glass.

"Shhh. Make him stop that!" Marion whispers firmly.

"I'm sorry," Dev says to him, just loud enough to be heard between the barrier. Mr. Santora's eyes narrow at her and he slams his fist into the door forcefully. Dev jumps back from the door, startled by the powerful sound.

"LET ME IN!" He bangs again, anger forming on his face.

"Dev, open the door. Make him stop; he's being too loud," Marion says, standing up now.

"Mom, look at him, he's enraged."

Mr. Santora begins banging on the door loudly, over and over.

Marion has had enough; his banging is going to interrupt the dream walk and get someone killed. She walks to the entrance and moves Dev aside. She unlocks the door and pushes it open slightly, sticking her face through the opening. "Mr. Santora, is it? Sir, I am afraid the studio has been bought out by a high-profile guest for the day and we're unable to accept any visitors, whether for business or personal matters. You will have to come back in the morning. Our guest requires complete silence and you are disturbing him."

Mr. Santora's arm juts out and he grabs hold of Marion by the throat. "I need to speak with Oak," he says through clenched teeth, cutting off Marion's breath. She gasps for air, stunned at the sudden turn of events.

Shocked, Dev tries to close the door on the man's arm as she pulls Marion back by her shoulder. Marion reaches up and grabs him by the wrist, her eyes pleading for air. Mr. Santora is unaffected by the door closing on him and he pushes himself forward, hauling Marion back and entering the studio. Marion now has both hands on his arm, hitting him in an attempt to release his grip.

DING.

The censor to the front door warns that there is a guest. "Shit," Dev says, glancing around the room. She runs to the front desk and takes her purse off the counter.

"Where is he?" Mr. Santora demands, strengthening his grip on Marion's throat. Her face is turning purple and her eyes are streaming tears. Dev swings her purse by the handles and knocks the man across the side of the head with it, sending him toppling to the side. Marion falls to the ground, his grip released from the blow.

"Adam, I'm calling the police," Dev says, kneeling to help her mother.

Mr. Santora props himself up on one knee. "I am not Adam," he hisses.

Dev sets Marion on the couch and stands to face him. "Who are you then?" she asks, looking him dead in the eye. His eyes peer back at her, ice blue.

"You know who I am. Your family took my soulmate and your magic took my baby!" He stands and stares at her.

"He's possessed," Marion manages to choke out, through the coughing. "His eyes—he's not Oak's principal."

Dev tightens her grip on her purse. "What baby? Who are you?" she demands. He lunges at her, his hand reaching out to choke her as he did Marion. Dev holds her purse up to shield her throat.

Something overcomes the man and he is forced to step back, confused. The anti-theft sigil burned into the leather of her bag protects Dev.

"My name is Edmund. My family hunted witches like you. I didn't want to hurt my daughter, but now I see why. Your horrible magic kills beautiful life. You must be destroyed. I will kill your child as you have killed mine," he seethes.

"It's Edmund Nowell, the witch hunter who Cynthia fell in love with," Marion chokes out, sliding back farther from Edmund.

"You will not touch a hair on my child's head!" Dev backs up next to Marion as he advances on them.

Marion bumps into a display of her soaps. "Get him outside; it's going to get too loud to fend him off in here," she whispers, reaching behind her and lobbing a bath bar at Edmund's head. It doesn't do much but she continues throwing soaps to distract him while Dev runs to the front door and pushes it open. She has an idea to trick Edmund.

DING.

She winces at the sound and yells outside, "Run, Oak! Don't stop!"

Edmund turns his attention from the barrage of soap to the sound of Oak's name and growls. He lunges at Dev, knocking her down and sending her purse sliding across the room. He runs outside of the studio, thinking Oak has somehow managed to escape the building.

DING.

Marion frantically signals Dev to get outside. Dev follows Edmund out of the building.

DING.

Marion sneaks away to the treatment room and peers inside, only opening the door a crack. Oak and Mallie both seem fine. Mallie is slightly moving, but is still asleep. Marion closes the door and heads back.

Outside, Dev is chasing down Edmund as he searches for Oak. "I'm going to kill your boy!" he roars.

Dev kneels down and gathers a handful of dirt, walking behind Edmund cautiously. In his search to find Oak, Edmund has lost interest in Dev and Marion, so it comes as a surprise when Dev is directly behind him when he turns around. She blows the handful of dirt directly into his eyes, infusing a bit of magic from her breath into the loose earth, temporarily blinding him. He screams as his hands fly up to cover his face. When he removes his hands, his ice-blue eyes begin to flicker brown.

"Adam!" Dev calls. "Adam, fight him!"

He blinks a few times and studies Dev. "Mrs. Black?"

Relieved, Dev puts her hand on Adam's shoulder. His eyes flicker back to icy blue and he knocks her down with a blunt swing of his arm. From the ground, Dev sees Marion open the door to the studio and throw Oak's broom.

DING.

Dev bolts toward the building. Edmund, regaining his control over Adam's body, rushes after her. She swoops the broom off the ground and turns to him, holding it at the base of the bristles. He stops as Dev hauls the broom back like a baseball bat and pummels the handle across his face. The protection symbols carved into the wood cause the blow to be ten times worse. His eyes flicker from blue to brown once more.

"Help me!" Adam Santora screams. Dev has the broom pulled back once more, ready to give him another face full of wood, then lowers the broom just as his eyes flicker back to blue. Edmund springs at her, taking advantage of her sympathy. Taking her by the throat, he pushes her forward toward the studio door. He menacingly taps on the glass to Marion inside, showing her he has her daughter by the throat.

Defeated, Marion goes to the door and as she gets there, bends down and rips the wire of the welcome censor out of the wall. She stands and unlocks the door, letting them inside. Edmund throws Dev onto the couch and motions for Marion to sit with her. "The only reason I am not killing you both right this instant is because I want you to watch your boy die, just like I had to watch my princess slip away." He glances between them. "WHERE IS HE?"

Marion and Dev both wince at the volume of his scream, worrying for the safety of the others. He looks around the room, sniffing the air. "He's here somewhere, isn't he?" He walks around the studio, searching and smelling the air.

"I can't get into your purse, Dev. Your camera. You can cross him over," Marion whispers.

Dev eyes her purse on the other side of the room and looks back at Edmund, walking the halls. As soon as he goes around a corner, Dev seizes the chance and darts across the reception area to her purse.

Edmund sees the treatment room Oak and Mallie are in, the protective barrier of brooms laid on the floor in front of the door gives away their location. He steps in close, and reaches for the handle but his hand cannot get past the wooden protection. He snarls and then whips his attention around to the sound of movement in the front of the studio.

"Dev," Marion whispers, on the lookout. Edmund comes running through the hallway. "Dev!"

Dev is about to open her purse when she feels a tight grip on her hair. She is yanked up to her feet, still holding onto her purse. "You're coming with me," Edmund says, reaching for the purse. He still can't manage to grab it so he takes his anger out on Dev, yanking her hair to position her in front of him. "Don't you move," he says, pointing at Marion. He forces Dev down the hallway, a bar of soap whizzing by as Marion protests.

They get to the door protected by carved brooms. Edmund pulls his hand back and flings Dev to the ground. She slides across the floor, hitting the brooms and pushing them with her across the hall, taking the room's protection with her.

* * *

Oak clutches at his head and screams. A searing pain runs through his brain as Mallie is torn violently across the ballroom. After it passes he runs to Mallie, splashing along the ground to find her slumped onto the floor, soaking wet. "What was that?" he asks, helping her to her feet.

"We have to hurry. I'm being torn from your mind. I think I'm being woken up," she says worriedly, wicking water from her outfit. The disturbance of the watery floor causes the ground to churn.

Oak and Mallie have to steady themselves as the water begins to swirl into a circle in the middle of the room, racing quickly across their feet, threatening to knock them off balance. The water spirals into a whirlpool, rising to nearly five times its volume. Oak tries desperately to keep his balance but is swept into the maelstrom, screaming. Mallie reaches out for him, but she, too, is pulled down and taken around the room. Various items from the masquerade float through water. A wig sails by Oak as he struggles to grab onto something.

Mallie splashes in the vortex and her hand hits a plague doctor mask. They are stuck swirling around and around, slowly being pulled toward the center of the room. A jester hat with tiny bells chimes past; a pair of white gloves collide into an elaborately decorated mask on a stick. Mallie tries to scream for Oak in a moment when they spin by each other. Oak reaches out to her and their fingertips graze but they are pulled apart, whirling in opposite directions. Oak has to remind himself that they are in a dream in order to avoid going into complete panic, and wonders if Mallie has to do the same. Stuck in a carousel of liquid, they're unable to stop.

Eventually, the water pulls them into the center of the tornado, swallowing them like a giant drain. Water rushes upwards across their bodies as they are sucked deeper and deeper, able to see nothing, submerged in the cold pitch-black fluid. The smooth-flowing water begins to feel grainy. Particles pass over their body as the wetness dries out and everything feels rough. They continue sinking, the water now replaced with dirt.

They gasp for breath and choke on soil as roots and pebbles push past them until they drop out onto the floor of an underground cavern. They groan as they attempt to stand, dirt stuck all over their wet bodies. Oak feels around on the ground to confirm the floor is solid as Mallie lifts herself to her feet by grabbing a root poking out from the cavern wall.

They look around, taking in their surroundings. They are underground, surrounded by sticks and roots jutting out at every angle around a low ceiling and tight walls. There appear to be skeleton bones also protruding from various parts of the cave. Mallie takes the lead and guides them toward an opening in the distance.

"Can we get hurt in a dream?" Oak asks, curious after nearly drowning.

"No. Everything feels real and it's extremely difficult to disconnect it from being awake, but nothing that happens here has any effect on your real body."

A short walk later, the cave opens into what appears to be a rundown western town. Still brushing dirt off themselves as it dries, they look upon the dimly lit underground town. While it initially seems there are people are standing around, upon closer inspection it turns out they're old animatronics. They are rough and tattered, some with their faces peeling off and others with their eyes hanging out of their sockets. They move stiffly in a rhythmic pattern, looping over and over again around town.

"We should be getting close to an answer," Mallie says, taking the lead as she heads into town, browsing the different buildings.

"How can you tell?" Oak says, following behind, stopping to watch a moldy-faced sheriff draw a fake pistol on repeat.

She flicks a piece of dirt away from her eye. "Very few dream walks contain more scenarios than this before your mind is able to provide help." She pushes through a set of batwing doors and into a saloon.

Oak stays outside and studies a robotic horse sipping water from a trough attached to a hitching post. An entire leg is torn off, exposing the wires and circuit boards inside. The town reminds him of one of his favorite theme park rides he used to love when he was younger. Loud music suddenly begins to play from the saloon, causing Oak to jump. An old-timey tune echoes through the cavern.

Mallie pops out of the saloon, her face red. "Didn't mean to do that," she says shyly, having somehow set off a player piano.

Oak laughs and they move on. They pass a man with no jaw repeatedly sipping out of a whiskey jug, and a cowgirl with pigtails waving with only three fingers. As they search, bones from the mixture of earth and roots surrounding them begin to drop to the ground from the walls and ceilings, clumps of dirt following. Oak looks up and his face is speckled with falling soil. His eyes open wide as it begins to rain femurs and phalanges, ribs and clavicles.

"Aunt Mal?" He reaches blindly around for her, keeping his gaze upwards at the falling debris.

Dirt starts pouring from everywhere, the clumps varying in size and shape. The floor rumbles, warning them of renewed danger.

"I think this cave is about to collapse," Oak says to Mallie, concerned. A skull plops right next to Mal and she agrees; it's time to move. Oak's stomach drops as Mallie grabs him by the arm and they begin racing through the town, narrowly avoiding pieces of the crumbling grotto.

Mallie loses her grip on Oak and falls, tripping on a thick, arched tree root in the ground. She hits the ground hard, turning transparent. Oak watches in horror as she lies still for a moment, not moving. Then she begins to re-solidify and comes to, jumping up and moving Oak along with a push.

"What is that? Why does that keep happening?" he yells over the rumble of the quivering ground, picking up speed as he runs. Not knowing where he is going, he turns to look at Mallie.

"I think we're trying to wake up," she says, yelling back, trying to keep up with his pace.

"We're about to hit a dead end!" he yells back at her. The rumbling intensifies and shakes away dirt from the wall in front of him, revealing an old wooden ladder stuck into it.

"Climb up!" she yells, pointing to the ladder.

They look up and see the ladder reaches all the way to the ceiling. Oak jumps at the wall and clings to the splintery wood. He climbs up a few notches and swings his hand down to catch Mallie as she scrambles on to the ladder behind him. His heart is racing, and he feels like this is what it must be like to be a stunt double in an action movie. As they climb, the dirt connected to the ladder shakes loose and soon they are climbing up an unsupported ladder that reaches all the way to the top of the cave. As they're scrambling, a rung below Oak's foot snaps and he loses his balance. Mallie catches his foot and helps push him back onto the ladder and they continue fighting their way up. They reach the top, stopping at the ceiling of earth.

"What now?" Oak yells down to her.

"Try digging up," Mallie tells him, looking at the long way down below.

He claws into the soil ceiling, scraping away at clumps of dirt. The turf is soft and Oak pushes his entire arm into the clod. "We can climb through!" he yells down to Mallie. He feels around and pulls himself up through the ceiling. He climbs up out of the ground and reaches back through, feeling for Mallie. She gives him her hand and he pulls her through as the ladder falls away, Oak falls back as Mallie is birthed through the surface of the dirt.

They stand up to see they are in the middle of a dark, abandoned shopping mall. The floor is now solid tile where they just emerged. All the stores around them are gated shut and there is construction debris strewn everywhere. The lights shine on, an electronic hum following the clicks of the bulbs popping with electricity. Oak feels his body getting wet and he looks down, patting his dry clothes.

"What's wrong?" Mallie asks.

"I feel wet but there's nothing there," he says, rubbing his clothes, trying to find where the sensation is coming from.

Her eyes go wide. "You're waking up. You're in the copper basin; you can feel the water. We have to go."

Oak shoots his gaze to her in panic. "How do we get out?"

"We have to die."

"WHAT?"

His heart beats faster as he looks around like he is going to somehow discover another option.

"You don't feel anything; you wake up from a dream when you're killed. It's the easiest and most controlled way out. As long as we wake up within a minute of each other, we both escape safely."

Oak can suddenly taste the horrible flavor of the serum he made. "Do it," he says, accepting that he is waking up now. Mallie browses the court and picks up a heavy metal pipe. They hear a clacking noise coming from a wing of the mall. "Hurry!" Oak says, feeling the cold, copper tub against his back.

Mallie rushes over to him, the clacking noise getting louder now. The lights flick off and on, buzzing. She hauls the pipe up over her head in front of Oak and he closes his eyes. The lights flicker more, now strobing. She brings down the pipe over the top of Oak's head and just as it strikes him, he is gone. The clacking is coming for her. She turns to see what it is. The lights pulsate like a nightclub.

From the wing of the mall where the sound echoes, a huge beast appears. It has hooves for feet, and the head of a bull. A massively muscular, human-like body is covered in fur. It has long, sharp, curved horns on top of its head and a large black, wet animal nose. Its bright red eyes peer at Mallie, pulling her into a trance. With less than a minute to get out, she decides she's going to let the Minotaur finish her. It stomps a hoof and swipes it against the tile floor. It is holding a long sword in one hand and an unknown item in the other. The lights continue to rapidly flash on and off. It charges toward Mallie at full speed, bellowing like a cow. She moves her attention to the item in the hand opposite of the sword.

Mallie stands her ground, welcoming the creature. It comes to an abrupt halt inches from her, showering her face in spittle as it breathes. From the hand opposite the sword, the human part of the beast holds a large white brick out to her, shimmering with a gold aura. This is it. This is the item Oak's magic has led them to.

Mallie only has about fifteen seconds left before she is lost in Oak's mind forever. The Minotaur pulls back its sword. She reaches out and grabs hold of the sturdy brick just as the sword pierces her gut.

**

Oak's eyes pop open and he gasps violently for air, splashing in the copper basin that is now filled with slushy ice water. Edmund bursts into the room, his eyes full of rage as he spots Oak. He lunges for him, ready to kill. Mallie takes a large gulp of air and opens her eyes to see Edmund launching himself at Oak. She stands from the chair and with all her force, she lifts her arm and slams the white brick across the side of Edmund's head just before he reaches the boy, tumbling to the ground.

Dev, on the floor just outside of the door, yells, "Mom, my purse!", and she shuffles into the room, climbing to her feet and throwing herself over Edmund's seizing host body. Marion grabs the purse from across the room and darts down the hall, stepping over various bars of soap, and runs into the treatment room, throwing the purse as soon as she enters.

Dev catches her bag and sits on top of Edmund, attempting to still his convulsions. She tears open her purse and removes the camera. She twists a dial and aims directly at Edmund's face, snapping the shutter once she can see his haunting blue eyes. There is a bright flash and a spark fizzles from each eye as they return to brown and Adam Santora passes out.

Oak shivers in the ice bath as he struggles to stand in the slippery tub. Marion rushes to the towel warmer and drapes hot towels over him as Mallie takes his hand to help Oak out of the basin. "Why did my water freeze?" he asks, stepping out of the tub.

"Ice is the direct path to a desired result in magic. The closer we came to the answer your magic was guiding us towards, the colder your water got. The ice means we retrieved what we needed."

Oak tugs on the corners of the hot towels, pulling them tighter around himself, his mistletoe pin dangling from a few hairs, loose from the excitement. "We didn't get anything, though. We had to leave."

Mal holds up the white brick. "*You* didn't get anything," she says, smiling.

"A brick?" Dev interrupts, crawling off Adam and shoving her camera back into her purse.

"Yeah …" Mallie says, looking at the confusing object.

"Well, it has to mean something. We can trust the magic," Marion says, using a towel to dry Oak's trembling legs.

Dev wraps her arms around Oak and nuzzles her face on his head. "Are you okay?"

"I'm fine. I died; it was awesome," he says through chattering teeth.

"I'm going to call an ambulance for Adam. He won't remember anything and we will tell them he came pounding on our door, bleeding, and that we don't know what happened," Dev says, walking out of the room to make the call.

Oak glances down to see his principal lying on the floor. Confused, he looks at Mallie.

She hands Oak his clothes. "Go dry off and change. We need to figure out what this brick is for." She picks it up from the ground. He takes the outfit from her and heads to another room. Marion tosses towels onto the floor to wipe up the overflow of water and places a towel over Oak's principal, still unconscious.

After placing the emergency call, Dev steps outside and removes the glamour from the building. The ambulance arrives, along with a few police officers to take statements. They cart Adam away, lifting him up on a gurney and applying an oxygen mask as they wheel him out of the studio. Dev explains to the cops that he came banging on the door asking for help and they offered him a room to lie down in, but he passed out before he got to the bed. With Oak's help, Mallie replaces the tub with a massage bed while Marion explains to the officers what happened, so the story matches.

The police investigate an area outside of the studio that appears to have contained some sort of struggle before Adam came knocking on their door. The fight between Dev and Edmund outside provides the perfect evidence for the police. They dismiss everyone as a suspect and thank them for the help.

They all gather in the lobby of the studio, studying the brick. It is off-white, rough all around, and dirty. It seems to have no apparent magical properties. Oak takes hold of it and inspects every inch, his mistletoe pin now back in place on his shirt. "Do you recognize it?" Mallie asks, perplexed.

"No, I have no idea what it is. How did you get it? You said you had to wake up within a minute of me."

She explains that the moment after he woke up, a beast rounded the corner of a wing of the mall and gave it to her. "It was a huge centaur. He had big black horns and just as he woke me up with his sword, I grabbed the brick."

"Hold on," Marion says, questioning. "Horns? Was it a centaur or a Minotaur?"

"What's the difference?" Oak asks, still turning the brick in his hand. He is a little disappointed that he didn't get to see this magnificent beast.

"A centaur has the body of a horse, all four legs, and his top half is a man, usually with pointed ears.

A Minotaur has the head of a bull with horns and the body is more man, with two legs and hooves."

Mallie ponders the difference for a moment. "Then, I guess it was definitely a Minotaur. His head was a bull and he grunted like a cow."

Dev looks at Marion. "The labyrinth," Marion whispers.

"Jazzy," Dev says. Marion's eyes widen as she makes the connection.

"Who is Jazzy?" Oak asks, finally setting the brick onto the table.

"Jazzy is the only member of our coven you have never met," Dev tells him.

"There are more members in the coven?" Oak asks.

Dev smiles. "Yes, there are six members altogether. Yourself, me, Grandma, Hyacinth, Mallie, and Jazzy. Jazzy runs the Hecate Health Institute about five hours north from here. She is only in her twenties but she inherited the resort from her parents. It is a resort for witches to go to hone their magic and learn to focus. Part of the resort includes a labyrinth. She will know what this is," Dev says, picking up the brick.

"Right, then." Marion stands up and hugs Mallie. "Thank you so much for your help. The coven is indebted to you," she says sincerely. Mallie smiles in appreciation. "We must get going if we want to solve this little mystery we have on our hands."

Dev gathers her things, handing the brick back to Oak. "Mom, go pick up Hyacinth. Make sure she brings her ceremonials; they are required for entry into the resort. We are going to go home to get ours. Meet us there. We will go together to get dinner and then hit the road. The resort opens at five a.m."

Oak slips outside by himself, brick in hand. He takes a deep breath and tries to keep himself composed. The endless barrage of obstacles is starting to become far more overwhelming than he expected and now they are suddenly leaving to go somewhere. He turns the brick around, inspecting it. *I hope this ends soon,* he thinks, wanting to just go home. He gathers his emotions and goes back into the studio.

Mallie has gathered their brooms and brought them to the group. "Be safe, everyone. I shall await your return," she says, wishing them well.

"You're not coming?" Oak asks, disappointed. They all turn their focus to her.

Mallie puts her head down. "Dream walking exerts so much energy and magic from my body, I won't be able to use the craft for about three days. I will be useless to you all."

Marion and Dev already knew this, but it is news to Oak. He springs at her with a hug. "Thank you, Aunt Mal Mal," he whispers into her ear, holding her tight. She squeezes him back, holding away tears.

"Mallie dear, get some rest and worry about this mess in the morning. We shall see you upon our return," Marion tells her, waving her hand at the chaos of the studio. They lock up the building and head to their respective vehicles.

***

Dev and Oak arrive home. They gather their full ceremonials and pack everything in the trunk, leaving room for Marion and Hyacinth to place their belongings as well. Marion rushes into her house, collecting her ceremonials, kissing Pepe on the cheek, and grabbing an emergency apothecary travel kit she has hidden away for such occasions. She picks up Hyacinth, dragging her out of her apartment half asleep.

They arrive at the Blacks' house where Dev and Oak are waiting outside, ready to go. They greet Hyacinth while Marion packs the rest of the trunk. As they drive along the highway in the dark, they pass a brightly lit billboard depicting a twenty-four-hour diner.

"FOOD," Oak grunts, tapping on the window.

"I think we should listen to the caveman back there," Hyacinth teases.

Dev agrees to stop for something to eat before the long drive. She drives down the next exit ramp and pulls into the parking lot of the diner. They head inside and wait to be seated. After a few moments, a lovely server named Chloe, with thinly plucked eyebrows and her hair cut into a blunt bob, seats them. She hands them menus and takes their drink order.

Marion notices Oak's bloodshot eyes. She nods to Dev and she notices as well. Dev puts her arm around Oak, allowing him to slump onto her shoulder and rest. Chloe returns with beverages and they order food. Oak groggily sips his drink, trying to stay awake.

They all enjoy this peaceful moment as they know it may be the last one they have for a while.

Their food arrives and Oak gains the strength to slap Hyacinth's hand away from stealing a French fry off his plate. Marion picks at a salad while the others indulge in a heavier meal. Chloe sets the bill on the table with a bright smile and wishes them well on their travels. They take a moment to sit in quiet, listening to the soft sound of music playing in the restaurant.

After paying, they head to the car, moving slowly on full stomachs. In the parking lot, Marion asks Dev to open the trunk. She pulls out her apothecary kit and adorns Dev with a waking sigil on the back of her neck, to keep her awake during the trip. They head onto the highway and make their way to the Hecate Health Institute.

Chapter 11

The trip is long, but smooth. Everyone is asleep aside from Dev, who is driving. Hyacinth is snoring in the passenger seat and Oak and Marion are quietly dozed off in the back. The radio fizzles in and out of signal as they cross through each city. Oak is jostled awake by a bump in the road. He opens his eyes and rubs them awake, searching the car to see what everyone else is doing. Looking over at Marion, he watches as a giant whip scorpion crawls up her shirt while she is fast asleep with her head leaning against the window. He stifles a scream to avoid startling the arachnid. It crawls onto her arm and up to her shoulder.

Oak sits straight up, hunting the car for something to hit it with. The book Marion was reading in the studio during the dream walk is lying between them. He grabs it and readies himself. The whip scorpion crawls onto Marion's neck and Oak reels back to strike as his nose is filled with the pungent scent of vinegar. The smell is so strong it makes him sneeze.

His sneeze grabs Dev's attention and she adjusts the rear-view mirror to focus on him while she drives.

"Honey, why do you look like you are you about to beat your grandmother with a book?"

He turns his attention to her and realizes there was never anything actually there. Embarrassed, he lowers the book and apologizes. Dev recognizes it as another one of his unexplained visions and reaches a free hand behind her seat to hold his. "Go back to sleep. We have a few hours yet."

She places her hand back on the steering wheel and Oak dozes off again, his heart slowing from the random encounter with nothing. When he wakes up again, it is because of the breeze he feels on his face from Dev opening her window. She turns down the volume of the softly playing music from the radio. They are pulling up to a brightly lit security booth that glows against the darkness of the night.

A man with short dark hair under a black bowler hat, with a name tag that says 'Chris,' greets them as they pull up. "Checking in?" the man asks.

"Not exactly," Dev responds. "We are here to see someone."

He steps outside the booth to talk to her. "I'm afraid I can't let in any visitors without a reservation at the resort."

She pulls out her driver's license from her purse and hands it to the security guard. "Please, I am here for Jazzy Pesce. She is a member of our coven. Please call her and tell her we are here."

The guard steps down off the curb and takes her license, returning to the booth. He places the call and looks back and forth between the car and the computer system while on the phone. Marion sits up and stretches at the sounds and sees they have arrived.

The guard drops the phone to his chin and leans out of the booth. "Are you equipped with ceremonials or does an associate need to bring you rentals when you park?"

Dev smiles. "We are fully prepared, thank you."

He speaks into the phone another moment before hanging up. He steps back out of the booth to Dev. "Sorry about the strange question. No one gets past security without ceremonials. You're free to go in. Have a great stay." He hands her back her license and the bar keeping their car from entering rises. Stepping back into the booth, he waves them through.

They drive through to a huge brass gate and stop, allowing it to open. It's adorned with 'Hecate Health Institute,' curving along the arches at the top. Vines of ivy hang gracefully along the designs of various magical herbs and plants designed into the metalwork. The caduceus symbol in the center splits in half as the gate opens, welcoming them inside. They drive forward, passing through an enchantment that plays audio through the car's speaker system.

A soft female voice speaks. "Hello, and welcome to the Hecate Health Institute, the premier relaxation resort for witches of the occult. Whether you are in a coven or practice the craft as a solitary witch, we thank you for choosing us."

They drive down a long, winding road lined in big bushy trees. Colorful glass bottles hang from the branches of the trees, twinkling in the light of the early morning. The voice continues. "We offer an array of options for you to choose from during your stay with us. You may choose to unwind and use your time here to relax with others just like you, or you may want to enhance your skills and learn more magic. Either way, there is no right or wrong way to enjoy your experience with us. As you approach parking, please note before entering, all guests of the Hecate Health Institute are required to wear traditional ceremonials in order to be identified as witches by anyone you encounter during your visit. We apologize for any inconvenience this may cause. We can't wait to see you!"

There is a magical chime and the audio stops. The pitch of the chime is enough to finally wake Hyacinth. She sits up and studies the surroundings. They reach the end of the road where it opens into a large parking lot with various cars. Dev pulls into a spot and they all get out of the car. She pops open the trunk and they all rummage through their bags, donning their ceremonials over their clothes. Dev pulls out the brooms and Hyacinth slams the trunk shut.

Everyone takes their brooms and Dev places the white brick in her purse and swings her bag over her shoulder. They look to the entrance of the resort. There are no buildings to be seen, just large overgrown trees, bushes, and plants. There is a small opening with two security guards and they all agree that is the entrance. Various wind chimes sound through the breeze of the early-morning air, some metal, some plastic, some bamboo. Every material you can think of rattles with the wind. They walk to the entrance, brooms in hand and cloaks flowing behind them.

The security guards watch them carefully as they approach. The guards check their eyes with flashlights. Ensuring none of them are possessed, they nod to each other and allow them to pass. "Merry meet. Enjoy your stay," one guard says as they walk past.

They travel down the path, passing small, quaint buildings along the way, spaced far enough apart to provide total privacy for whatever goes on inside each one. In the distance they see a short woman walking the path towards them, animatedly waving them down. As she gets closer, they can see she has black-framed glasses and thick eyebrows. A very short haircut pokes out from underneath her conical hat and under her cloak hides a red flannel shirt that distracts from her being quite chesty. She wears flat-heeled boots like Oak instead of the elegant stiletto heel the women generally wear. Oak assumes, based on how she walks, that she would stumble flat on her face if required to wear the heel.

"My coven arrives, unannounced, from five hours away. I assume this is not a visit for pleasure?" Jazzy asks, her face concerned, but her features friendly and welcoming.

"I'm afraid not," Dev answers, shamed that they are only here because they need something.

"Who is this?" Jazzy asks, reaching out to Oak for a handshake. Oak shakes her hand firmly.

"This is Oak. Dev's son," Marion explains.

"Jazzy," she says to him, introducing herself.

"Nice to meet you," he answers.

"He is the Divine," Marion says.

Jazzy stops and stands completely still, her face suddenly serious. "What?" She looks to Dev. "He's your firstborn?" Dev nods and Oak feels uncomfortable at the interaction. "No need to explain any further. Come to my office."

Jazzy turns on her heel and walks back in the direction which she came from. They all follow her down the path. She walks at a quick and steady pace, making small talk along the way about the activities that go on in all the small buildings strewn throughout the property and the different rituals and offerings they perform here daily.

They pass by a large fire, witches dancing around it completely naked. "This is the moon ritual we perform every morning to remove negative energy from the day," she explains to them. Dev reaches to Oak and covers his eyes. His cheeks get hot and his face turns red, embarrassed.

"Really, Dev, it's tradition," Marion scolds.

Jazzy turns around to see what Dev is doing. She laughs. "Going sky-clad is completely optional. We perform this ritual on the other side of the property in ceremonials for our more modern witches." Oak swipes his mother's hand from his face as they continue to walk.

Jazzy goes off the path to the left, walking through overgrown grass and plants. Gnats and other bugs fly away from the disturbance. "This building here is my office." She points toward a building that is slightly larger than the rest. All the buildings are relatively small, but this one looks about double the size. Oak wonders if there is anything larger than this in the resort.

They get to the front entrance and Jazzy opens the door, allowing everyone in first. The front office area takes up the space of about half the building; the other half unseen. "We generally start the morning with a traditional witches' brew. Anyone?"

Marion nods excitedly. "Oh, yes, please, dear. It's been ages." Dev passes and Hyacinth makes a face as if no one should ever drink that.

"What is it?" Oak asks.

"It's a magical brew of herbs that slightly enhances everything a witch has to offer. I don't remember everything but it has things like mustard seed, ivy, holly leaves, and buttercup flowers in it," she answers, pouring a steaming cup for Marion.

Hyacinth turns to him. "Yeah, and the part she doesn't remember is that it tastes like the fungus you find in between a dog's toes." Oak laughs but abruptly stops when Dev knocks him with her purse.

"Be polite," she warns Hyacinth angrily.

Jazzy hands the cup to Marion as steam lifts from it. "Can't hurt to try," she urges Oak.

"Okay, yes," he says hesitantly.

Marion takes a cautious sip and sighs. "Just like I remember." A smile spreads across her face.

"Please, everyone sit. We obviously have business to discuss," Jazzy says, pouring Oak a fresh cup as they all find chairs. She brings him his cup and takes a seat behind the desk at the back of the room.

"Jazzy, we are sorry for arriving unannounced but we are having some problems with Oak here," Dev explains. She goes on to tell her about the visions and the outbursts, the suppression charm and the séance, the dream walking and everything in between.

Jazzy listens intently, the seriousness of her face letting everyone know she is extremely interested in what is being said. After a long explanation of the events leading up to their visit, Dev pulls the white brick from her purse and sets it on the table. "We hoped you would know what this is."

Jazzy picks it up, inspecting it all around. "It looks like one of the stones from the labyrinth at the back of the resort," she says confidently. Marion sips her brew as Jazzy confirms her thoughts. "You pulled this from a dream walk? Where is Mallie, by the way?" Dev explains that it was best for Mallie to stay behind, but informs her that it was handed to her by a Minotaur.

Oak takes a sip of the brew. The hot, acrid liquid fills his mouth with an unexplained spiciness that contradicts the initial bitter taste that ends in a puckering sour effect on the sides of his tongue. He tries to maintain a neutral face as he does not want to offend Jazzy the way Hyacinth had no qualms over doing.

Jazzy sets the brick back down onto the desk. "I have no doubt that your trip here was not wasted. The labyrinth is exactly the place Oak's magic was trying to send him."

Dev smiles and lets out a large sigh of relief. "We can head there now, if you like. I can explain how it works along the way," Jazzy says, standing, prodding them to agree to leave right away. Oak takes this as an opportunity to get rid of the witches' brew prematurely so he walks to the desk, sets his cup down, and picks up the brick.

Hyacinth stands, and soon everyone is heading out of the office, back onto the path that winds around the property. As they walk toward their destination, Jazzy begins to explain how the labyrinth will work. She tells them that everyone is called to the labyrinth in different ways and theirs was by this white brick. She lets them know that once they reach the center of the labyrinth, their questions will be answered.

"Is the maze complicated to navigate?" Oak asks, keeping up with her brisk pace.

"Oh no, a witches' labyrinth is not a maze as many people believe; it is a series of turns and curves that make a circular pattern, but it is one single path. You cannot get lost." Jazzy checks behind her to make sure everyone is keeping up.

"Can we go in with him?" Dev inquires.

"Yes. The labyrinth sends for particular individuals to find answers. It did not send for you, so you will not affect the outcome of Oak's search." They reach a huge open field that must be about five acres large. There is a giant, swirling circular pattern of white bricks sitting in the overgrown grass. "Your experience in the labyrinth will be unique to you. Unfortunately,

THE COVEN'S SON

because of that I cannot give you any suggestions on how to get through it smoothly."

Oak looks around at the large open field of single bricks in the ground. "I'm confused. Do I just walk around here?"

Jazzy points to an area that indicates the entrance of the labyrinth. It's missing a brick. "The labyrinth has called to you, Oak. Replace the missing brick if you're ready to start your journey."

He holds up the missing brick and looks at Dev, Marion, and Hyacinth.

"We're ready when you are, kid," Hyacinth says. Dev and Marion nod, smiling at him.

Dev puts her hand on her son's shoulder. "Let's finish this."

On the outside, Oak appears confident and ready, but he thinks about how different this will be from dream walking. He can get hurt here, and that really scares him.

Oak bends down to the gap in the pattern and places the brick on the ground. The ground rattles fiercely beneath them as the brick is placed back into its home. Every brick in the massive pattern on the ground begins to rise up into the air, revealing other bricks underneath. They emerge from the soil, shaking the ground like an earthquake. The dirt from the earth sticks to the rising walls of the labyrinth. The walls stretch high into the air, stopping at about the height of a two-story building. The rumbling slows, and they all watch in awe as the looming structure settles. Standing before them is a giant white-brick-walled labyrinth, the entrance right in front of them.

Jazzy motions for them to enter. "Good luck!" Oak leans forward, peering inside the massive structure. "Oh! I almost forgot," Jazzy says abruptly. "No magic. It interrupts the function of the labyrinth and will reject your request for answers. Only when you get to the center and your answer is presented can you use the craft."

Oak steps in slowly, taking in Jazzy's words, and starts to walk the route formed by the walls. Hyacinth goes next, as Dev and Marion trail behind, thanking Jazzy for everything. They are all in the labyrinth now, traveling the forced path. Oak trails his fingers along the wall, feeling the texture of the stone as they walk. Wisteria climbs up the sides of the path, stretching out into the distance. The overgrown grass makes it a bit of a struggle to navigate easily. They walk along the mostly empty path, navigating curves and rounding turns as needed. A breeze picks up through the winding trail.

"Boy, this wind is getting intense," Hyacinth says, breaking the silence of their peaceful walk. Their hats begin to bend as the breeze intensifies. Dev has her arm out in front of herself, blocking the flying dirt and leaves being blown against her. Oak's hat blows off but hits Marion and she catches it. She hands it back to him. The sound of the air whooshing by is so extreme that they can barely hear anything.

They push on, now being pummeled by dirt and sand. Vines of wisteria rip from the wall and whip back and forth, creating an obstacle to get past. It takes all their strength to move forward along the trail, leaning forward into the wind with all their weight. Marion trails behind, using the rest of her coven as a shield from the intense weather. Oak lifts his broom as he approaches the tunnel of botanical lashings. Dev and Hyacinth follow suit. Marion hides behind Hyacinth. They use the bristle ends of their brooms to block the violent attacks.

Hyacinth yells something to the group, but the sounds of her voice are muffled against the hurricane-strength winds and no one knows what she is saying. They push forward, forcing themselves to stay upright and keep their feet on the ground. Dev yells for Oak, but he can't hear her. He is leading the group and is oblivious to everything else around him. He wishes he had studied witchcraft more and decides he wants to be homeschooled so that he can be more proficient in magic. His powers usually come naturally, but not having more book knowledge makes him feel he is at a disadvantage here.

Dev continues to scream his name as Oak gains more distance from them. Finally, he catches the sound of her voice as it bounces off the wall, snapping him out of his deep thought. He turns around to see Dev far back behind him, tending to Hyacinth and Marion. They appear to have been captured against the bricks by the wisteria vines.

Turning his back on the wind, Oak is pushed forward and falls, the wind carrying him backwards uncontrollably until he rams the top of his broom handle into the ground as he gets to Dev. She is struggling to free Hyacinth and Marion from the vines trapping them against the structure. Oak uses the broom stuck in the earth to stand and steady himself against the powerful blasts of air. He starts to rip the plants from Marion's body as Dev tears the ones from Hyacinth.

Hyacinth is trying to yell something, but no one can hear her. They fight to get the vines off, but they are very strong and difficult to rip. Dev leans in to Hyacinth, trying to understand her words. "I have a box cutter in my pocket for package deliveries from the shop!" she screams into Dev's ear.

Dev feels her pockets and finds the blade, pulling it from her pants. She clicks off the safety switch and slices away at the wisteria. It shrivels and dies as she cuts. After a few seconds, Dev is able to free Hyacinth from her green restraints. Oak continues to struggle with removing Marion from the trap. Dev lends her landscaping skills and cuts Marion free, hugging her when she finally drops from the wall.

They point, using basic gestures since they can't speak to each other, to signal that they need to keep moving forward. There is a turn up ahead in the distance that they hope will be free of this fierce wind. They cling to each other and lock their arms around one another, using their combined strength to push around the corner.

When they finally make the turn, the wind dies and they feel ten times lighter, no longer using all their weight to move forward. The abrupt cessation in sound causes their ears to ring. Now out of the way of the windy obstacles, Dev and Oak inspect Hyacinth and Marion for injuries. Everyone appears to be okay and Dev puts the box cutter away in her purse. The stretch of passage ahead appears to be clear. They hold their breath as they resume their walk. Everything seems to be normal.

"Let's appreciate this break while we can. I have the feeling we won't get many of these," Dev says as she latches her purse shut. The sun shines brightly through the top of the labyrinth, beating down on the coven as they progress.

Oak raises his face to the sun and closes his eyes, enjoying the warmth.

"It tasted like dog feet, didn't it?" Hyacinth says abruptly, trying to lighten the mood. Without Jazzy there to take offense, Oak opens his eyes and laughs, agreeing with her description.

"Oh, hush," Marion says. "The daylong boost it gives your magic is worth it, and it is a flavorful delight," she adds.

"We all know Mom needs a boost for her soap-throwing arm," Dev teases.

Oak and Hyacinth are confused by the joke but Oak thinks it has something to do with all the soaps on the floor of the studio when he woke up from the dream walk. Marion uses her broom as a crutch to walk, the wind tunnel vexed her elderly body. Still, she trudges on, staying strong for her grandson. They walk for a good distance, staying cautious to anything that might spring up, but nothing does. They worry about the upcoming curve in the labyrinth, though.

"Did Jazzy say anything about the time frame of getting through this?" Oak asks, wondering if he wasn't paying enough attention and missed a detail.

"No, she said the journey is different for everyone. That probably included the time frame," Dev answers. Hyacinth responds by blowing air through her lips like a horse.

They reach the upcoming turn and stop. Oak leans his back against the wall and peers around the corner. The coast seems to be clear. They cautiously continue on winding and turning, walking stretch after stretch, checking each turn. Some paths have rocks strewn around; some have dead grass; others have more vines. They all vary. They come to another turn in the pattern and Oak walks around and peers down. It looks like there are spore pods growing from cracks in the walls, like the pincushions you get from a sewing kit.

Oak turns to the group. "It looks like the spore pod plants in the book Grandma gave me." Dev peers around the corner, seeing a puff of gray powder from one of the pods.

Hyacinth lets out a sigh and waves Oak forward. "Go on then, just be cautious." He steps around the turn and into the territory of all the pods intermittently puffing small bursts of pollen. The air is dry and barren of moisture, like a desert in Nevada.

Suddenly Oak clutches his throat and stumbles backwards and around the corner, falling onto his butt. He gasps for air. It wasn't the spores that affected him, he realizes; this is a trial that contains nothing to breathe. "There's no oxygen. We can't breathe there."

Dev looks stunned.

"That trail looks like it's a quarter mile long!" Hyacinth exclaims. Marion says nothing. She knows she will again be the weakest link in this challenge.

"If we just push it as hard as we can, I think we can do it," Oak says, trying to instill confidence in the group.

"Honey, you have youth and energy on your side on this one," Hyacinth points out.

"Hyacinth is right," Dev says. "This is going to be next to impossible and there's no way of knowing if it ends around the turn like the last one did."

Oak sits on the ground, feeling defeated. "So, what do we do then?"

"Should he go alone from here? Jazzy said this stuff was designed specifically for him," Hyacinth mentions.

"No," Dev responds. "I think we just push it as hard as we can."

Oak stands again. "Are you sure?" he asks.

"I'm not leaving you," she tells him.

Marion suggests that the plants on the wall may be charmed to remove all the oxygen from the air. They agree that seems to be what is happening. Oak wonders if they should destroy each pod as they go, releasing the pull of air, but his idea is quickly squashed by the fact that when they destroy a pod, the spores will pour out and they don't believe it is safe to breathe those, either.

"Come on, Mom, get on my back. You won't make it by yourself," Dev says. Hyacinth and Marion look at each other. "It's okay. Get on." Dev kneels down with her back to Marion.

Hesitating, Marion slowly climbs onto her daughter's back, securing herself as tightly as she can. Dev gets to her feet and hoists Marion up, grabbing onto her legs for support. "As hard as you can," Dev says, looking intently at Oak. He nods and looks at Hyacinth.

"As hard as you can," Hyacinth says to him, turning in the direction of the path they are about to take.

Oak takes a huge breath of air and takes off running at full speed, leaving the rest of them behind. Next up, Dev speaks to her mom behind her shoulders. "Deep breath, Mom." They both pull in as much air as they can and begin to run into the waterless sea. Hyacinth follows last, pushing her legs as fast as they will take her.

Oak blasts through, nearly at the halfway mark when he begins to feel the need to breathe. He passes by the largest pod clinging to the side of the wall as he starts to struggle. He sees his finish line ahead coming closer and closer. Dev runs, Marion bouncing on her back as she is carried along the airless path.

Oak's energy is running low as he attempts to gasp for air, with nothing to take in. Hyacinth brings up the tail end of the group, sweating profusely as there is no breeze to cool her. She hasn't reached the halfway mark and starts to struggle for air. Oak claws at his throat as his running slows. Dev just barely passes the halfway point and her face is bright red. She opens her mouth to breathe and is met with a lungful of emptiness.

Oak's eyes begin to roll into the back of his head and he tumbles forward, losing his balance from lack of oxygen. As he falls, his head just barely passes the end of the unbreathable path. His body thuds to the ground and he pulls in a massive gasp of oxygen, his head at the turn and his body still lying in the desert.

Dev catches a metaphorical second wind and forces herself to continue running, feeling Marion's grip begin to weaken. She begins to stumble in different directions, grazing the large plant on the wall. The pod shrivels and begins puffing a thick, blurry cloud of black powder behind Dev. It billows around the area like an octopus inking underwater. Oak pulls himself from the path and stands, bent over, hands on his knees, catching his breath.

About twenty feet from the turn, Dev falls to her knees. She begins to frantically crawl.

Oak peers around the corner and sees his mom and grandma struggling to make it. He takes in a lungful of air and darts back around the corner, running forward and pulling Marion from Dev's back. He turns around and races Marion to oxygen, laying her on the ground and going back for Dev, collecting a breath of air before returning. Hyacinth is trapped running through the murky, dark gray irritant. She cannot see anything and flails into the walls, losing her sense of direction.

Oak grabs Dev by her hands and drags her, running backwards until they are out of the life-threatening section of the labyrinth. Dev gasps for air so hard she begins coughing and she crawls to Marion, who is nearly passed out on the ground, trying to aid her as she catches her breath. Hyacinth has collapsed on the ground, completely unconscious.

Oak looks back around the corner and as the ink clears, sees Hyacinth on the ground. "Hyacinth has collapsed. I'm going back."

Dev leans back and looks down the path. "Oak, she's too far away. You can't make that." He darts onto the trail anyway, after Hyacinth.

"Oak, no!" Dev yells, holding Marion's hand.

Oak reaches Hyacinth and flips her onto her back, struggling to roll her over. He grabs her hands and starts to drag her along the path. She is much heavier than Dev and Marion and he fights to keep the momentum going as he pulls her along. He begins to doubt his ability to do this as Dev appears and reaches out to take hold of one of Hyacinth's hands. He fears they won't make it and he will die of asphyxiation.

I am the Divine, Oak reminds himself. He looks at Dev and they nod together, dragging Hyacinth as fast as they can. They get her over the threshold where the oxygen begins again.

Dev dives on top of Hyacinth and begins mouth to mouth, attempting to breathe life into her coven sister. Marion sits up, watching the devastating scene unfold. Oak reaches a hand out to Marion and she takes it as he helps her stand up. She holds Oak as they watch Dev fight to keep Hyacinth alive. A few moments go by and just as Dev is about to give up, Hyacinth inhales so hard her entire chest burns. Dev dives onto her, hugging her tightly. Marion begins to cry and Oak feels all his muscles relax.

They take a break, allowing Hyacinth to recover for a few moments, making sure she is okay. They help her to her feet and dust off the pollen, agreeing they are recovered enough to continue on. They walk the long distance, taking corners and turns, awaiting the next challenge. They proceed cautiously around each corner, but they don't run into any more obstacles. They spend their time mostly in silence. It feels as though they can't seem to get enough air after being deprived of it so severely.

They continue along for what feels like hours until they see a long stretch ahead of them ends in a large open area. "That's it! That's the center of the labyrinth!" Oak yells excitedly. A smile spreads across Dev's face.

Hyacinth screams, "ALL HAIL THE DARK LORD!" She throws her hands into the air. Marion cracks a smile at Hyacinth's dark humor.

"This could lead to an extremely difficult challenge," Dev warns.

"It's the center. Jazzy said the center will reveal the answers we're looking for," Oak says.

"That does not mean it doesn't come at a price," Marion warns. "Witchcraft is more complex than handing out simple answers to complicated questions, as you have seen," she adds.

Oak concedes that this may not be as easy as it looks. "I'm beginning to learn that," he says,

Dev puts her hand on his shoulder and rubs it. They walk forward, stopping just prior to the grand opening at the center of the labyrinth. They huddle close together. "No matter what happens, we are a coven. We are sisters and brothers of the occult. We must trust in our magic and let it guide us," Dev says, ending the pep talk with a group hug.

The unknown ahead horrifies Oak. He is about to get the answer he's been searching for. He stands tall as he feels a rush of adrenaline course through him.

Oak turns to the opening and walks into the center of the labyrinth. His coven follows right behind him.

Chapter 12

The labyrinth opens into a giant circular grassy plain. Lush green grass sways in the gentle breeze against the pinks and oranges coloring the sky as the sun begins to set. Oak walks forward, taking in the scene set for him. Dev, Marion, and Hyacinth come in behind him, as a unit. About twenty feet in, there is a large concentric circle of mushrooms gleaming in the twilight.

Oak takes in everything around him. Marion gasps and puts her hand over her mouth. Hyacinth breaks from the women and walks next to Oak. "What is it?" he asks her.

"A fae circle," she tells him.

Dev takes her place on Oak's other side. "It's the only way the fae have any interaction with our world," Dev says, the wind gently blowing her hair.

"Did you cross through a fae circle?" Marion asks from the background.

Oak turns around and looks at her, suddenly having a flashback of his weekend making his suppression charm. His mind has been fully cleared by the labyrinth and is able to recall things quite easily here. "Yes, at your house," he tells her.

She takes a step back, placing her hand on her chest. "At my house? But, how?"

He describes what happened. "When I went outside to get sap for the enchantment, I turned to walk back into the house and I fell. My foot didn't move when I tried to walk, so I tripped. When I turned over, my foot was stuck in the middle of a small circle of mushrooms. I had to use both hands to pull it out from the center." Oak realizes now, that was around the time weird things started happening.

Hyacinth comes to a realization. "It's the curse of illusions!"

There it is. The answer Oak's been searching for. His stomach tightens as his mind races with both fear and relief.

Marion's face tightens in dismay. "How did I not see it? How could I have been so foolish? I've put you in so much danger."

Dev turns to her mom. "This isn't your fault. The fae are notorious for being mischievous. This could have happened anywhere."

Marion gets louder. "But it didn't happen anywhere, it happened at my home!"

"Enough!" Hyacinth yells.

Oak looks at Hyacinth. "What is the curse of illusions?"

She turns to him. "The fae are horrible little creatures who love to torment witches. They were banned from entering our world and their only interaction with us is to create a circle of mushrooms. The circle is a small portal to their world and when you stepped into it to gather the sap, they had free rein over you in that moment. They put a curse on you. They are the reason you've been seeing things."

He turns to the huge circle of mushrooms in the labyrinth. "So, what do I do?"

Hyacinth turns him to her with her hands on his shoulders and looks directly at him. "Go to their world. You have to find their king and ask him to remove the curse."

"What if he won't?"

She puts her forehead against his. "Make him."

Oak's cloak billows in the breeze as it gets darker outside. "If the books are correct about every culture recognizing the Divine, the fae will, too. The king will not want to have a curse on you. He probably has no idea his minions did this," Dev says, following the path of mushrooms with her eyes.

His heart beats loudly and Hyacinth gives him a hug. He turns to Dev and she kisses him on the forehead and hugs him. Marion is still standing back. He turns and goes to her and gives her a hug. "I was supposed to keep you safe. You were supposed to be safe in my home," she says sadly into his chest as he hugs her.

"Grandma, it appeared overnight. It wasn't there the first time I collected the sap, and then after I crossed into it, your lawn crew mowed the grass. You had no way of ever knowing."

She looks up at him, relief washing over her face. She puts her hand on his cheek. "Be careful."

He turns and walks to the edge of the mushroom circle. He grips his broom by the handle, adjusts his hat, takes a deep breath, and marches into the realm of where the fae reside. When he crosses over the path of mushrooms, his body turns transparent. The deeper he walks into the center, the more of him dissipates into smoke, swirling away in the breeze until he is in the center and the wind carries away the rest of his transpicuous vapor.

"I guess we wait," Hyacinth says as she glances around the center of the labyrinth for a way out. They head over to the white brick wall perimeter of the field to sit.

***

As Oak enters into the realm of the fae, a white haze starts around the outer edges of his eyes and gradually spreads to the center, blinding him with white light until his vision clears the more he walks and begins to focus through a fog that fades away within seconds. He takes in his surroundings and confirms that he is, in fact, not in the labyrinth any more. All around him are multicolored luminous mushrooms and alien-looking plants that glow like they've been painted and lit under a blacklight. Quite a few of them are starting to rot or are already dead, no longer glowing in those areas. There is a feeling of filth around the area; the glowing plants are covered in dirt and muck.

He walks forward, trying to find anything beyond the plants and fungi. He passes by tall, skinny trees, most of which are broken in half or splintered. Some even appear to be burned. His feet begin to squish in the ground as it becomes softer and wet. The plants and trees open into a boggy, swamp-like area, the water struggling to glow a mystical sea-foam green against the bubbling sludge taking over its otherworldly properties. This is not the cabalistic world of fairies Oak had imagined it to be. He hops over areas of the swampland that appear to be deep and tries to find the safest path.

Oak makes it to the other side of the bog and continues through the unrecognizable dying plants. He begins to notice tiny hovering flecks of light appearing around the area he is walking through. They're about half the size of a lightning bug. He ignores them on his path but passes by one that is close enough to stir interest, so he stops to inspect the insect. He peers closely at it, squinting his eyes through its glow.

"You're not a bug!" he exclaims, stepping in closer for a better view. It hovers in front of him, its tiny human-like body only an inch long. This one is glowing a pale pink and has no discernible features like fingers, toes, bellybutton, hair, or even a face. It has only a head, chest, stomach, arms, legs, hands, feet, and tiny, smooth little pointed ears. It reminds Oak of a featureless mannequin you would find at a fancy department store, waving happily at him.

Oak laughs and stands up straight and waves at it, then continues walking. "I just saw a fairy," he says to himself, in awe of the magical being. He continues walking, inspecting the nature of this realm. He hadn't expected there to be so much ugliness among the beauty.

Feeling like he's being followed, he turns around. The tiny pink fae speck is hovering a few feet behind him. He smiles at it and continues on, stepping over a fallen tree blocking his path. As he walks, a few more fae rustle up from flowers or grass and begin to hover around him. They are all different mystical colors. He sees a baby blue one, more pink, some oranges, and purples. He walks with a little more purpose now, beginning to feel nervous as the fae follow him.

The more he walks, the more gather to see him. Oak stops and turns to look behind him. There must be about a thousand of them now, all gathered to watch him. It looks like they are all happily waving, same as the first one. Oak waves back and gives them a nervous smile, not knowing what to expect.

As soon as he gives them his attention, they swarm all over his body. They lift up the back of his cloak, pull on his pant legs, and float his hat up off his head so he has to reach up and grab it. They gather on his arms and pull and push. They tug on his boots, and force his knees up. Their tiny hands are so small they pinch into his flesh, wherever they grab. They pull Oak's hair and tug on his arms forcefully. They appear to be making him do a silly dance but it is starting to become painful; they are being very rough.

Tiny droplets of blood begin to drip from every bit of exposed flesh the fae have touched and Oak is getting a headache from the hair pulling. He tries pulling his arms away, yelling for them to stop, but together they are able to overpower him. They grab onto his face and pull at his cheeks and forehead, smushing and stretching. They try to lift him into the air, which is very uncomfortable, seeing as how he is too heavy for them and keeps dropping from the few inches they get him, landing hard on his feet.

Oak's face is streaming small rivers of blood and he musters the strength to pull away, flicking a few of the fae from his fingertips and shaking the majority of them off. They stop for a moment, registering his sudden violence.

Oak takes the moment to dart back in the direction he was originally going. He runs through the realm, stepping on mushrooms, jumping over branches, and ripping through vines as he makes his getaway. He runs over a tiny bridge that creates an overpass for a clean, teal, glowing brook. The fae dive into the water, splash him, and toss a few unearthly looking fish at him. Oak continues on, unfazed by the aquatic assault. He sees a clearing in the direction he is running and heads for it at full force.

A few of the chasing fae slam into passing trees, their glow flickering before they shake off the collision and go after Oak once more. He makes it to the opening of the phosphorescent forest and is bathed in moonlight, skidding to an unexpected halt as he comes face-to-face with the edge of a steep cliff. In the distance, beyond the drop-off he notices a large, beautiful, mansion-sized house, made from organic materials like moss, bark, feathers, and stones.

He spins around, holding his broom up like a weapon, his heels hanging off the edge of the crag. "I need—" He begins to explain why he is there, but the swarm of fae are too close for him to have time and they pummel into him, knocking him off balance. As he falls backwards, Oak shouts, "I'm looking for your king!"

***

Dev, Marion, and Hyacinth sit patiently against the cold wall of the labyrinth as they wait for Oak to return, curse-free. Hyacinth is half asleep, staring off into nothingness as Dev and Marion sit in silence, taking in the events leading them here. Dev shuffles her feet against the grass, anxious.

"Dev, will you stop that? You're driving me crazy!" Marion scolds, pulling Hyacinth from her partial doze, breaking the silence.

"I can't help it. I am so stressed out. I'm so worried about him. I can't stay still," Dev complains.

"Then go walk. Go do something," Marion tells her, waving her hand, shooing her away. Dev stands up, taking her hat off and pulling her hair back into a ponytail.

She replaces the hat on her head and says, "You know what? You're right. I'm going to go do something." She picks her broom up off the ground and runs into the fae circle, disappearing in a whirl of smoke.

Hyacinth straightens her back against the wall and her eyes widen. "Did she just—" Hyacinth blurts out.

Marion stands up in surprise and stares at where Dev once was. Using her broom to steady her balance, she goes after Dev. Stepping past the mushroom gateway, she's gone.

Hyacinth looks on, speechless. She looks around the empty labyrinth, as if searching for someone else who saw what just happened. "I'm … gonna stay here!" she shouts, wondering if they heard her. She wonders if she is abandoning her coven duties by staying behind, but no one asked her to come so she opts to sit and wait.

Dev steps through the fog, into the realm of the fae, searching her environment for clues as to what direction Oak went. Behind her comes Marion, working her way into the mystic domain slowly. Dev feels her entering and turns around. "Mom! Why did you follow me?"

"Because you know nothing of the fae. You're being reckless!"

"We don't have time for this. We need to find Oak," Dev says, ignoring her mother and moving deeper into the world. Dev follows a path of footprints she notices, thinking they might be from Oak's boots.

Marion shuffles behind Dev, taking in the devastation of the realm. "This is not right. This is not right at all. All this death and decay, the ugliness. Something is wrong here."

Dev spots a tiny hovering fae just past a fallen tree. She walks up to it, taking in its shape and form.

Her view is disrupted by the sight of broom bristles as Marion swats it away, sending it flying across the woods. "Horrible little creatures."

"What did you do that for?" Dev says in shock, now walking behind her mother.

"You give them any attention and they take it as an invitation to dance," Marion explains.

"Why is that a problem?" Dev asks, helping Marion pull her foot out of the mud.

"Dancing with fae is a bit more violent than dancing with people. Trust me, you don't want to."

They cautiously make their way through the bubbling, swampy bog and past the fallen tree in the path. Dev eyes something shiny pooled on a leaf on the ground next to a muddy footprint. She drops to her knees, wiping the wet spot with her fingers. She lifts her hand to her nose and confirms to Marion that it's blood. Her eyes well up with tears. "He's hurt."

They search for signs of Oak. They notice some smushed mushrooms and broken sticks that tell them he was here and they are on the right path. They continue walking on, Dev picking up the pace in a panic.

"Stay calm, Dev. It's a small amount of blood. He could have just cut himself on something."

They cross over a bridge and after a few minutes of slowing to a walk they spot a clearing in the distance. Marion brushes away a few stray fae with her broom, knocking them to the ground. She rubs Dev's back as they walk out of the wood and into the open, finding themselves on the edge of an empty cliff.

THE COVEN'S SON

***

The fae hear Oak's plea to find their king as he careens over the edge of the cliff. He lets go of his broom and it free-falls next to him. Screaming in horror, he plummets to the ground, thinking, *This is the end*! The fae are intrigued by his request to speak with the king and zoom down over the cliff with him, calling more to follow.

Watching the dark night sky as he falls, Oak sees the fae pouring over the edge of the drop toward him. He closes his eyes tightly and shields his face with his arms, fearing the worst from them. They surround his broom and soon it has a brightly glowing thick outline of fae attached to it, carrying it through the air. They bring the broom around Oak's back and in between his legs.

His frantic, trembling hands find the broom handle and they position it upright, leveling him to be parallel to the ground. His drop begins to slow as the fae raise the broom into the sky, carrying Oak's weight into the air. They carry him toward the giant mansion in the distance, keeping him steady in the sky.

"I'm flying!" Oak laughs, experiencing something witches usually only ever dream of. "I'm flying!" He bends forward into the wind, allowing the fae to soar him faster across the sky. He takes a deep breath of the moist night air and feels intense relief that the devilish creatures saved him. They fly him above the trees and toward the giant house he saw before he was pushed off the cliff.

Just before they arrive at the residence, the fae drop the broom and let Oak fall about twenty-five feet to the ground below, hearing the faint high-pitched sound of laugher as they skitter off into the sky.

Oak lands roughly on the ground, through some sparkling brambles that break his fall. Groaning, he picks himself up off the hard ground, picking twigs and thorns from his clothes, brushing his arms off as he looks for his broom. He shakes his head in frustration at the troublesome fairies when he finds his broom sticking out of the ground by the bush that he fell into. After pulling it out, he realizes he's a short walk from the earthen chateau which he believes is where the fae king resides.

He walks to the house and up the river-stone-lined stairs that lead to the front door. Knocking on the door, he admires the multicolored gems inlaid into the wood that make a pattern of a triangle with a swirl branching off at each point, encased within a circle.

The door swings open on its own. A bright light shines out, hurting Oak's eyes from the darkness of the outside. He can't see inside until he steps in and the door closes behind him. As his eyes adjust, he sees that the house appears to be made of one grand room. A beautiful spacious area seems to stretch on forever, looking much bigger than it did on the outside. A row of giant crystal chandeliers hang from the towering ceiling, lining the center of the home. Thick crown molding outlines the top and bottom of the walls, losing the organic feel from the outside. Yellow slabs of marble fill in the floor with brown and white hairline details.

At the very far end of the lavish house sits a large moss throne, mimicking a quilted cushion pattern along the back, each button point adorned with the cupule of an acorn. Along the top border of the throne is a combination of jutting twigs and colorful flowers. A stump coming out of the floor to the right of the royal seat acts as a side table, the entire display bringing the organic materials from the outside back in.

Oak steps a few feet into the room, when he hears the echo of slow clapping.

"Very impressive, my boy." A figure materializes on the botanical throne at the end of the chamber. "To make your way all the way here, dodging my every attempt to keep you away." The person crosses his leg over his knee, leaning back in the seat, his arms on the rests.

Long, pointed fingernails travel down the front of the chair arms as the person taps soundlessly on the moss. He has long shoulder-length pink hair that shimmers an iridescent shine, making it appear purple as it moves. The creature Oak presumes is the fae king tucks one side of his hair behind his ear, revealing a sharp, pointed elfin tip, with piercings down the helix. He adjusts the thin wired crown atop his head, adorned with the same jewels as the front door. His bright orange eyes are piercing and he is wearing a lace-patterned long green tunic lined with thick, corded button knots with long dangling sleeves, tied at the waist with what appears to be a natural rope made from braided vines stripped of their leaves.

The shirt underneath the see-through tunic appears to be black, giving depth to the entire ensemble. His pants are brown and capri length, with shattered edges along the bottom and stitching in various places, repairing holes and rips with patches made from leaves. His whole body glows pale green, although it is much weaker than the light of the tiny fae Oak encountered on his way here.

"Are ... Are you the fae king?" Oak asks, his voice echoing through the vast room.

"Indeed," he replies. "And you ... are the Divine."

The king stands and steps down from the throne, walking a few paces forward.

"What do you mean I dodged the attempt to keep me away? Your fae carried me here on my broom," Oak says.

"Haha, you dumb child. Those insignificant pawns are NOT what I am referring to." The king takes a few more steps forward. "You thwarted my apparition, Walt, during your little séance."

Oak's eyes widen and his heart begins to beat faster. "You summoned him?"

"Why yes, of course. He was the second-born child to Cynthia. He had no powers; he was simply the false witch. Why then, in death, would he have the ability to breach a summoning not meant for him?" Oak searches for something to say. "And my son, Edmund. Even gifting him a wonderful fleshly shell to possess wasn't enough to keep you away—you *and* your coven. Though, I have to thank you for having that little outburst in class. You left me a strong little magical trail that allowed me to direct Edmund straight to your school." Oak stares in disbelief at what he is hearing. "Even my little curse of illusions couldn't drive you mad enough to stop searching for me."

Oak takes a step back. "You ... are Edmund's father? How? Wouldn't that make you—"

The king smiles. "Half human? Yes, but even more so, half witch hunter." He laughs menacingly.

"You're half fae, half witch hunter?"

"Yes, boy, have a seat and I'll tell you a tale." The king waves his arm and Oak is thrown to the ground, forced to sit. Just then, Dev and Marion burst through the door of the palace.

Oak turns his head to them and screams, "He's a witch hunter! He is Edmund's father! Run!"

Their eyes go large and the king sways his arm once again, forcing Dev and Marion to the ground as the door shuts behind them, trapping them inside. "Join us, won't you?" he says, stepping forward more. "You see, back before the witches banished the fae to this world, we used to live together in peace. However, the witches were envious that they weren't the only ones able to use magic, so they banned us from your world and hexed us to be born a fraction of our original size because they knew we would find a way to dominate their powers otherwise. But, just before that, I was born Jasper Nowell. Because I am half human, I was allowed to choose which side to stay on. I chose your world until I got word that my mother had died and learned I would inherit the entire fae kingdom as my own. From that day forward, I became known as Loxias, king of the fae. Welcome to my beautiful kingdom."

Dev's face fills with anger. "Beautiful kingdom? Your kingdom is full of decay and rot; it is dying. It is dying because the witch hunter in you is toxic to magical realms!"

Marion adds, "And the fae weren't banned because of an envy of magic. The fae were banned because they wreaked havoc on our world and hurt people!"

Loxias scowls. "The fae hurt people? Tell the Divine, witch, why your women wear a spike-heeled boot."

Marion puts her head down. Dev responds for her. "It's only for the most extreme cases!"

Loxias puts a hand out, sliding Marion into the wall behind her. "TELL HIM!" She grunts as she fights to speak. She looks at Oak. "Witches wear the spiked heel because of blood. During rare sacrificial rituals, it usually flows freely onto the floor and doesn't get spread around as much during the event with a smaller surface area on the shoe."

Loxias focuses on Oak. "You see, boy? Who is the one that hurts people? Witches who make sacrifices with bloodshed and kill children who aren't full-blooded witch, or gentle and magical fae and witch hunters, who simply try to put an end to their reign of terror?"

Oak shuffles his feet on the ground uncomfortably. He knows Loxias is just trying to twist the truth, to take the life of a witch out of context.

"Our magic didn't kill your grandchild, *yours* did!" Dev screeches.

"QUIET!" the king screams, and he wiggles his fingers at her. Her lips begin to drip, a thick syrupy liquid coming off them. It burns and stings her mouth. It's a dense and sticky tree sap. It leaks all around her mouth, sealing it shut, quieting her.

"Please, I only came here to remove the curse. Remove it and we will be gone," Oak says, pleading.

"Oh no, boy. You see, you only came here because I couldn't kill you from your own world. We know I tried. Now that I have you here, what a great way to avenge my ancestors' hex, my son's broken heart, my GRANDSON'S LIFE. To KILL the witches' Divine." Loxias' voice wobbles, becoming crazed. He steps forward a few more inches.

Oak and Loxias are still about twenty feet apart in the large room. Oak swallows hard as he knows he is going to have to muster up all his power. He appreciates the fact that he decided to try witches' brew today. Marion crawls over to Dev, still forced low to the ground by Loxias' power. Oak fights with all his strength against the force pinning him down. He roars in frustration as he overpowers the magic and stands tall against the fae king.

Loxias looks impressed, but steps to the side and unblocks Oak's view of his throne. Trapped there, strapped down against the seat with vines and roots, sits Alan. Oak's eyes show shock and horror as his father screams out to him, "Oak! Please, don't let him kill me, please!"

Oak knows his father has no magic and cannot defend himself against any of this; if anything happens to him, Oak will only blame himself.

"DAD!" Oak screams, a tremor in his voice. Loxias smirks, pleased with himself.

"It's not real! Whatever you see, it's an illusion; there's nothing there!" Marion yells.

Loxias narrows his eyebrows at the reveal and swipes across the air as if smacking her. Marion's face whips to the side. A violent, slapping sound echoes and a red handprint appears on her cheek. She holds her face and slides back to the ground.

Oak balls his hands into fists, angry at the dirty trick and angry at the king harming his grandmother. He can feel magic coursing through him, fueled by the anger. He punches a fist forward at the fae king, a small spark pinging off the end of his fist. Nothing happens. The fae king stands, confused at the attack. He raises his arm to attack when suddenly, he hiccups. A loud gurgle can be heard in the room.

Oak smirks. A few drops of water drip from the king's pointed ears. His eyes begin to spill tears and saliva spews from his mouth. Within seconds, every orifice of Loxias' face is leaking with liquid. It begins to gush. His airways are blocked, a gurgling sound coming from him as he scurries around the room fighting to breathe. He holds his head, trying feverishly to wipe away the liquid suffocating him.

THE COVEN'S SON

Oak puffs up his chest, feeling brave and accomplished. He embraces the power encompassing him and allows it to help him defend himself and his family.

Loxias runs, hunched over and choking, to the stump that sits next to his throne. He stands in front of it and tree roots from the stump break through the marble floor and wrap around his feet. The roots drink the water from his body and there is a sudden line of rumbling in the floor that leads directly to Oak.

The ground starts to crack at Oak's feet and he turns toward the door and begins to run. Before he gets too far, thick, coiling tree roots branch out and grab him by his feet and legs, compressing around him so tightly his limbs go numb. He begins to feel weak as Loxias is in deep concentration.

Oak feels pulses of weakness all through his body until he realizes Loxias is pulling his power from him using the roots. Oak leans down to the roots and snaps his fingers just above the weakest, thinnest root. The tree's appendage ignites on fire, quickly catching the entire entanglement aflame and spreading under the ground; it roars over to Loxias, breaking open the floor completely as it reaches him, burning his feet and forcing him to release himself from the absorption of Oak's power.

Oak breaks out of the damaged and dead roots, crumbling them as he emerges. Oak begins to run at Loxias, deciding to face him head-on. The fae king has other plans. He summons water from the soil under the broken ground and soon the floor is flooded. Oak slips and falls on his back, winding him. Loxias walks briskly forward, raising his hand into the air, palm up. Marion and Dev watch helplessly, unable to move to help Oak.

Oak levitates. He swallows hard as he is lifted into the air. His mind sorts through ideas of what to do. Loxias raises him to the very height of the ceiling and motions downward, rushing Oak quickly and forcefully to the ground. Oak slams into the marble floor with a nauseating thud. His mind goes blank, all he can think about is pain. All the marble under him gives way, shattering.

Dev lets out a muffled scream through the sticky sap holding her mouth shut. She ignores the danger and forces herself, with all her strength, to crawl over to Oak. He is not breathing. As he lies there, lifeless, the fae king turns his back and walks slowly to his throne, looking satisfied.

Dev begins to cry as she shakes Oak's body over and over, trying to wake him. The king turns and takes a seat on his throne, prideful to be more powerful than the Divine. Dev's attention falls on Oak's mistletoe pin, suppressing his powers. She reaches for it and tries to unclasp the charm but can't budge it. She pushes so hard, her fingers begin to bleed, but the enchanted iron won't allow it to open. She looks around the room.

Marion kicks Dev's purse across the floor to her. Dev opens her purse, frantically searching. She finds Hyacinth's box cutter from the shop and she uses it to cut away the part of Oak's shirt that contains the boutonnière. She chucks the fabric-pinned brooch across the room.

"Get back!" Marion yells to Dev, knowing what is about to happen.

Dev kicks backwards, shuffling away from Oak as a white aura begins to emit from the perimeter of his exanimate body. All the debris of burned wood, marble, and water is pushed violently away from Oak's body, an energetic blast so intense that Dev is forcefully slammed backward and into Marion. Loxias learns forward in his chair, concerned. He releases his hold on Marion and Dev, allowing them to stand.

Oak's body lifts vertically, his feet on the ground, his spine stiff, and his head loosely hanging back until he is set on his toes, using the very tips of his boots. His head lifts and his eyes spring open. His irises and pupils are gone. His eyes are nothing but stark-white sclera.

The lights in the chandeliers flicker. Black snakes begin to fall from the molding woodwork at the top of the walls where the ceiling meets. The front door is violently swung open inwards and ripped off the hinges, soaring around the entire room, slamming into the perimeters of the house. The chandeliers from above sway and vibrate, flickering until they all come crashing down, strewing crystals and broken shards all over the floor. The room goes dark but is almost completely lit up by Oak's glowing white aura, casting shadows around the perimeter of the house.

"It's happening," Marion whispers.

From the tips of his boots, slowly, Oak begins to slide forward against the ground toward Loxias, grinning at him menacingly.

Loxias steps back. "Impossible!"

All the debris slides aside, making a path for Oak as he slides against the floor. Dev covers her sealed mouth and points up toward the ceiling of the room, as deities begin to manifest. Cernunnos materializes in the air, holding a torc. He's a Celtic being with antlers emerging from long, thick black hair and has fabric ornately draped over his otherwise naked body. Then, Faunus appears, a Roman deity with short spiked horns emerging from his temples and coarse animalistic fur growing over parts of his body.

"What is happening?" Dev asks, terrified.

Next, the blue-skinned Hindu entity Pashupati appears, folding his extra set of arms around himself. A tune can be heard as Pan, the half-man, half-goat Greek spirit comes into view, clacking his hooves together while playing a flute. Dev shrieks as the beings take shape around the room. Finally, English ghost Herne the Hunter takes shape in the back of the room, with long, jutting horns and a full beard. He has a fur pelt hanging off his shoulders and is holding a bow, wearing a quiver of arrows.

They all float majestically above the battle below.

"It's the five horned numen! A deity of every culture, here to recognize the Divine as he reaches true divinity," Marion says, in awe.

Snakes continue to fill the room as they drop from the walls. Oak reaches the throne. He thrusts his hand out, forcing Loxias toward him with his powers. Loxias fights the summons and holds onto his throne. "No!" he screams, his long nails cracking and breaking clean off as he is pulled from the chair into Oak's arms.

Oak grips the fae king by the shoulders and presses his forehead against Loxias. Loxias looks around the room frantically as he is lifted into the air with Oak and wind begins to swirl around the room. They hover in the center of the room as snakes, crystal shards, roots, marble, and a door all get picked up by the forceful wind and spin around them.

Oak grips the fae king so tightly that blood trickles down his body and catches in the wind, spraying blood all over the walls. Dev and Marion watch, holding each other, unharmed by the show of power. Oak smirks in the king's face and there is a boisterous clap of thunder.

The horned numen begin to chant deeply: "E pluribus unum, E pluribus unum, E pluribus unum." There is a deafening crack of lightning and everything goes white.

Chapter 13

Hyacinth is startled awake as Dev, Marion, and Oak are purged through the circle of mushrooms, and out of the fae realm. They land in the grass, thumping onto the ground in a pile. Dev scrambles to her knees and vomits on the ground, her mouth now freed. Marion paces herself, trying to stand. Oak is lying on the ground, not moving.

Dev gains control back over her body and looks to her son. "Oak!" she yells, kneeling beside him and checking for breathing. He is out, but he is alive. She cradles him in her arms as his eyes slowly begin to open.

"What happened?" Hyacinth asks, standing to greet her coven. Oak's eyes are still white until, after a few blinks, they return to normal, his pupils dilating. The moon is full and directly above them in the dark midnight sky.

Dev hugs Oak, crying on him. "You did it, baby, you did it!"

"Look!" Hyacinth exclaims, pointing to the center of the fae circle. They all turn their attention to it.

THE COVEN'S SON

Dev lifts Oak's head so he can see. A small plant is breaching the ground and rapidly growing. It turns slowly into a small tree and continues to swell. As it grows, like dominos, the mushrooms in the circle slowly die, one after another. The tree leaches its life from the circle of fungus as it begins to loom into the air, growing huge and mighty. The ring of dead mushrooms disappears and the only thing left standing before them is a sixty-five-foot oak tree, its grand, gnarled and twisted branches reaching toward the sky through the moonlight.

Oak notices something glistening on the lowest branch and finds the strength to get up from Dev's lap. He goes to the branch and pulls down a scrap of fabric with mistletoe pinned to it. A vision washes over Oak's eyes. He sees a forest filled with destruction and in the center, dilapidated ruins. Within the ruins sits a beautiful and lively throne made of moss, adorned with flowers and twigs. Next to it, a tree stump. On top of the stump sits a thinly wired crown adorned with gems.

Oak is snapped out of the vision by the rumbling sound of the labyrinth's walls receding back into the ground. A few moments later, the labyrinth is nothing but a pattern of bricks with a grand oak tree sitting majestically in the center.

Oak holds his head as the vision of the fae realm washes from his mind.

"Do you feel ill, dear?" Marion asks.

He nods at her, giving an exhausted smile. It's over.

They explain to Hyacinth everything that happened as they walk the trail out of the Hecate Health Institute.

Dev is not feeling well enough for them to try to find Jazzy in the vast resort, so they opt to leave a thank you note in her office on their way out. They get to the car, load their brooms, and change out of their ceremonials.

Dev throws up again just before getting in the car. Hyacinth decides to drive, putting Dev in the passenger's seat. Marion leans forward from the back seat and wipes away the awakening sigil from Dev's neck so she can get some rest.

As they hit the highway, Oak looks to Marion and asks, "Grandma, what were the horned numen chanting just before I destroyed the king?"

Marion smiles and looks at him. "E pluribus unum. It means *out of many, one*. They were confirming that you are the Divine in their eyes." Oak's face shines with pride. Being accepted isn't something he is used to.

The drive is long, but the three of them are exhausted and fall fast asleep. Hyacinth got plenty of sleep awaiting their return, so she makes the drive easily.

Hours later, Oak is startled awake by a bump in the road. He sits up defensively, thinking he is imagining things from the curse. He realizes they are almost home and that the visions are truly over. Relieved, he looks out the window and thinks about how strong he's become and how much he's changed.

They arrive at Dev's house first. Oak unloads the trunk while Hyacinth helps Marion get Dev out of the car. They walk her into the house and to her bedroom.

As Oak is bringing their things into the house, Marion finds him. "I'm calling your father to come stay with you until your mom's better. Hyacinth and I have businesses to run and someone needs to be here." He nods, not wanting to argue that he is old enough to take care of his mother himself because he wants to see his dad and visit Kyle-Ray without feeling guilty for leaving Dev alone at home.

The sun is just beginning to rise when Marion and Hyacinth head out, hugging Oak tightly as they go. Oak goes to his room and pulls out the fabric with the mistletoe on it. He looks at the tear in his shirt. Finally, he is free of having to suppress his powers, but the pin is a reminder of some very important time he spent with his grandmother, so he tucks it away in a small box in his closet for safekeeping. He heads to the kitchen and ransacks the pantry, shoving handfuls of sugar cereal into his mouth, spilling it onto the floor.

There is a knock and he sets the box down, kicking the spilled cereal under the stove, and answers the door. "Hey, bud," his dad greets as he swings the door open.

Oak jumps into his dad's arms, squeezing him like he never thought he would see him again. The illusion Loxias created of Alan strapped to his throne, helpless against his wrath, has been burned into his mind, and seeing his dad confirms it wasn't real.

"Whoa, easy there. Gettin' old. Can't take those tight squeezes," Alan jokes, unsure of why Oak is so emotional over seeing him. "Does she know I'm here?" he whispers in Oak's ear.

"No," he whispers back. "She's passed out in bed and shouldn't be up for a while. She's been throwing up."

Alan nods, understanding. He took some time off from work to stay with Dev because Marion called. He normally wouldn't have, but Marion doesn't generally ask for frivolous favors.

They watch TV for a short while until Oak notices the time.

"I'm getting tired. Do you care if I go lie down in my room?"

"Sure, your grandmother told me you had quite the adventure."

Oak leaves his dad and goes to his bedroom. He plops onto his bed, staring at the ceiling. His mind swirls with the thoughts of the events he just endured, filling him with emotions. He wants to tell someone. Anyone. It would be such an amazing story. He doesn't want to tell Alan because it will probably scare him. He wants to tell someone who will think it was cool. Kyle-Ray.

He thinks about all the ways he could reveal his secret. While quietly reciting different ways he could try to tell Kyle-Ray, Oak notices a glare from his window shining off the spine of one of his books. He sits up and squints, focusing through the glare. *Cognitive Transference.* He stands and pulls the book from the shelf. Lying back down, he casually flips through the pages as his mind periodically wanders off to process the past few days. After organizing his thoughts for a moment, he is able to focus on a few key elements of the book before falling asleep with it open on his chest.

***

The next morning, Oak awakens to the sound of the book falling onto the floor, not realizing he slept through half of yesterday and into the morning. He looks at his clock and realizes what happened. Groggily, he picks the book up and places it back on the shelf. He walks out into the living room to see Marion and Alan talking. They look like they are having a serious conversation, and Oak feels like he is interrupting something. They both stop and look at him.

"Perfect timing, dear," Marion says, standing to motion to him to take a seat. Alan pats the spot on the couch next to him. Oak seats himself, feeling anxious. "I've discovered a ritual that is going to speed up your mom's recovery. I want to try it as soon as possible, but I wanted you to be able to see her beforehand. It might take a while," Marion explains.

"Great! I'll go say hi, then we can start!" he says.

Marion holds up her hand. "Just me and your father."

"What?" He looks at Alan. "Dad? I'm confused."

Alan puts his hand on Oak's shoulder. "Trust your grandmother."

"But—"

"Oak! Do you want your mother to get better?" Marion interrupts.

"Yes, but—"

"Then go say good morning and allow me to perform my ritual."

Oak stands and huffs off to Dev's bedroom. He knocks lightly and opens the door.

"Hi, baby," Dev manages to say, through a heavy, wet cough.

"Hi, Mom," Oak says, sitting on the edge of the bed with her. "Do you need anything?"

"No, I'm fine," she says, forcing a smile and rubbing Oak's arm.

"Grandma says I can't help with the ritual to make you better, but she is letting Dad. He isn't even a witch."

"I don't know what the ritual is, but you should trust her. She is the crone of our coven. The wisest of the craft."

Oak puts his head down.

Dev pats his arm to shoo him out of the bedroom. "Go enjoy your day. You need a break more than all of us. I will be okay."

Oak leans over and kisses Dev on her cheek. He leaves the room and heads back to Marion and Alan. He stands at the entrance to the living room, saying nothing. They look at him.

"Finished?" Marion asks. Oak nods as Marion and Alan stand up. They walk by him as he lies down on the couch, turning on the TV.

Marion picks up a bag of supplies from the front door as they make their way into Dev's bedroom. Entering the room, Alan brushes his hands on his pants. Marion locks the door behind her and sets down her bag.

"Ready, dear?" she asks Dev.

Dev nods and adjusts herself into a comfortable position in bed. Alan looks at Marion, confused as to what he is supposed to contribute. Marion strips the blankets off Dev, leaving her exposed for the ritual in her nightgown. She pulls candles from her bag and sets them around the room, flicking her fingers and bringing them to life.

"Alan," she says. "I need you to stay at the foot of the bed, holding Dev's ankles tight. This ritual may cause her to rise into the air, but so long as you have her feet, she can't go anywhere."

Alan agrees cautiously. He has never witnessed any serious witchcraft. He's only seen simple tricks here and there. He kneels at the foot of the bed and grabs hold of Dev's ankles. Marion sprinkles an array of dried herbs all around Dev's body.

"Clear your mind, Dev," Marion says, placing a peeled clove of garlic into Dev's mouth. "Hold onto it so we can suppress your magic and it does not instinctually fight the ritual purging your sickness."

Dev takes a deep breath and exhales slowly, nodding.

Marion dims the lights, allowing the dance of the candle flames to paint the walls. She shuffles through her bag of supplies and pulls out a small box with holes in it. "This is the part that is going to make things a little intense," she says, focusing her words toward Alan.

A small series of squeals come from the box as Marion opens it and pulls out a guinea pig. Dev muffles her disapproval through a mouthful of garlic but is too weak to protest any further. "This is why I have not invited any of our coven to help me," Marion says, pulling a large four-inch sewing pushpin from her bag. She knows none of her sisters or Oak would approve of this ritual, but she is not risking her daughter getting any sicker.

"What are you doing with all that?" Alan asks nervously.

"We only do this in the most extreme cases," Marion says. "Close your eyes, Dev. We are beginning."

Alan tightens his grip on her ankles, sweating as Marion holds the guinea pig against Dev's chest. The candle flames begin to flicker and a low, whirring sound stirs in the air. The bed creaks through the sounds of the guinea pigs wheeks. She pulls the guinea pig into the air above Dev and plummets the sewing needle into its heart. Everything in the room rattles; pictures on the wall vibrate against the house.

Alan winces and turns his head as blood pours onto Dev, staining her nightgown a crimson red. Marion traces the animal over Dev's body, dripping its bright red ichor across her daughter. Suddenly, Dev arches her back toward the ceiling.

"Hold onto her, Alan!" Marion shouts over the rattling furniture.

Alan increases his grip as Dev's body rises into the air. She is lifting vertically, as if standing up, because of Alan's hold. Her eyes are closed and there is no reaction in her face.

Marion sets down the guinea pig's lifeless body and reaches for a tincture of mugwort oil. There is a pounding at the door.

"What's going on?" Oak yells.

"Not now, Oak!" Alan yells back.

Marion opens the tincture and pours the oil into her hand. She smears it across Dev's forehead.

"Open the door!" Oak screams in a panic.

Marion turns to the door and thrusts her hand toward it. Oak is knocked backward, away from the room. She turns back to Dev and begins mumbling a spell under her breath. Dev's nose begins to drip blood. Marion chants in a voice low and deep, slowly increasing in volume until she finally shouts, "PURGE THIS ILLNESS!"

Dev falls backward onto the bed. Everything in the room stands still and the whirring quiets. There is silence as they watch Dev's cheeks become flushed, healthy, and pink. She snaps her eyes open, breathing heavily. She spits the clove of garlic onto the floor. Marion nods at Alan and he releases Dev from his grip. They watch as Dev's body sinks into the bed, every muscle relaxing.

"Did it work?" Alan asks.

"It appears so," Marion responds, watching Dev fall into a deep sleep. "Let's allow her to rest. We will know more when she regains her strength," Marion says. She tosses a few of the ritual supplies back into her bag and Alan unlocks the door. They exit together, seeing Oak sitting on the floor where Marion knocked him down when he tried to get in.

He looks up at them with sad eyes. "Is everything okay?"

"Yes, but you could have tarnished the entire process. That was extremely reckless and dangerous of you," Marion scolds.

Alan offers Oak his hand. "I know, I got scared," Oak says, using Alan's strength to stand.

"You need to learn to trust your coven," Marion says to him. She runs her fingers through her messy hair, out of place from the intense activity.

"I'm sorry. Can I see her?"

"No, she is asleep. Give her time to recover."

"Hey, I have an idea. I have an appointment to see an apartment. Why don't you come with me? Get out of the house for a while," Alan suggests.

"That sounds like a splendid idea," Marion says. It will give her the opportunity to clean the bedroom while Dev sleeps.

"Okay." Oak perks up a little. He runs to his bedroom to change his clothes. Marion heads to the restroom to freshen herself up. Alan grabs his keys from the counter and waits for Oak.

"Ready to go?" he asks as Oak emerges from his room.

"Yep!" Oak says, excited to spend some time with his dad.

They drive past Kyle-Ray's house on their way out of the neighborhood. He is outside putting something in the mailbox. "Look, there's your friend," Alan says as they drive by.

Oak waves. His mind races with all his ideas of how to tell Kyle-Ray he's a witch. They drive into a gated apartment complex filled with brick-red and banana-yellow painted buildings. At the gate, Alan gives the pretty brunette security guard a wink as he hands her his driver's license. "I'm here to meet my realtor."

Oak sinks down in his seat, embarrassed at his dad's flirting.

The gate opens and Alan takes his license back from the guard. "I love your hair," he says to her. She ignores him and steps back for him to continue in.

"Ew! Dad! Just go!" Oak protests.

Alan shrugs and drives through the gate. He sees his realtor standing in front of the welcome center with her short platinum hair, in a frilly blouse and pencil skirt with a modest set of heels, waiting. He parks the car and greets her on the sidewalk.

"Patty, this is my son, Oak. Oak, Patty."

Oak smiles and shakes her hand.

"So nice to meet you, Oak. I've heard so many good things about you. Are you excited to see what I have to show you today?"

"Um, sure," he says.

She leads them to a building where they climb up the stairs to look at a three-bedroom apartment on the top floor of a beautiful complex. Patty lets them inside and they walk around the empty dwelling, checking closet space and bathrooms.

"This bedroom would be mine," Alan says, showing Oak the master. They walk to the other bedroom. "And this would be yours, for when you stay the weekend."

Oak looks around briefly and nods. "What do you need the third bedroom for?" he asks, walking out of his potential bedroom.

"Well," Alan says, walking to the third. He opens the door and shows him the blank, empty room. "This one would be for your apothecary."

Patty interrupts. "Here are your keys, Mr. Black. It was great meeting you."

Oak looks at his dad as the realtor leaves the apartment. "You already bought it?"

Alan smiles. "Yes, it's ours."

He hugs his dad again. Patty leaves and Oak explores the apartment in more detail now that she's gone. "We can put a TV here, and we can put a couch here, with a table. Oh, oh, SURROUND SOUND SYSTEM!"

Alan laughs as Oak excitedly bounces from room to room, deciding how they are going to decorate. He follows Oak into the would-be apothecary.

"So, I can decorate this however I want?" Oak asks.

"It's your apothecary, not mine."

Oak slides the window open and allows a warm, gentle breeze to enter the room. He stands at the center, motioning Alan to move aside.

Oak holds his hands out to the walls and releases the tingling sensation of his magic. Vines sprout from the seam in the carpets where they meet the walls and crawl up and across every corner of the room. They stretch and grow on every surface of the drywall until they reach the ceiling, blooming leaves as they climb.

"Okay, so no paint?" Alan asks.

Oak laughs as he lowers his arms and the growing vines crawl to a stop. "There," he says triumphantly.

"Come on, bud, let's go to the store and shop for some things to put in here," Alan says, leading Oak out of the apartment.

On their way to the store, they stop for a quick bite to eat inside a fast food restaurant.

"So, can we talk about your reaction to the security guard today?" Alan asks, biting into a burger.

"I'd rather not."

"You know, eventually I'm going to be dating. I hope you understand that."

The thought actually hadn't crossed Oak's mind. "I know, I guess. I just don't like it. I'm not ready to see that," he says, taking a sip of soda.

"I will respect that. We can talk about it in the future."

They finish their meals and get back on the road to the home décor store. Oak is talking excitedly about all the different things he needs for his apothecary as they park the car.

Once inside the store, Alan waves his hand to Oak, allowing him to take the lead. Oak peruses the aisles, looking at all the different things he can add to his new room. They reach an aisle filled with various types of jars. There are glass and plastic, tall and short, ones with cork tops and ones with screw-on caps. Some of the jars are tinted different colors and some of them are in fun shapes like hearts or genie bottles.

Oak starts gathering jars of different sizes and shapes into his arms as Alan follows behind him with a shopping cart. "I need all of these to fill with herbs," he tells Alan as he sets them down in the cart.

"Okay, get whatever you need," Alan tells him, though he is already gathering his second armful. Once Oak has about twenty or so jars in the cart, they move on to another aisle.

Next, they find an aisle full of bookends and statues. Oak browses through, looking at a bookend with a fleur-de-lis design and a wolf statue wearing a flower crown. He picks up a figure of a human skull and looks it over. "I think this will go great with that hourglass down there." He points to the end of the row of statues.

"What about this?" Alan says, picking up a figurine of a crying clown. They both laugh as they continue on.

Oak adds the hourglass with pale blue sand to his collection and notices a coin bank that looks like an eye. He grabs that, too. Around the corner, they find a supply of lamps and wind chimes.

Oak browses the lamps, picking them up and inspecting them, trying to find the right one. Finally, he chooses a lamp in the shape of a bat. Its wings light up to project light into the room. He also finds a salt lamp that can be used for his craft, so he adds that to his cart as well. They search the store for shelves, and a few other key items, such as small tables and storage containers.

"Nothing too big today. We will get the big stuff later," Alan tells him.

"Okay, and I can get the herbs and things I need from Hyacinth later, too."

They take everything to the checkout and pay. Once the trunk is loaded, they get into the car.

"Where to next?" Alan asks.

"Candles! I need so many candles."

"Candles, it is! Away we go!"

They pull on to the road and Oak begins to shift around in his seat. "Everything okay?" Alan asks him.

"What happened in there? With Mom."

"Oh."

"Tell me."

"Bud, I shouldn't."

"Dad, please."

Alan is silent as they drive to the next destination. He sighs and looks at Oak as he stops at a traffic light. "This has to stay between us, no matter how you feel about it."

Chapter 14

"Your grandmother killed an animal for the ritual."

"WHAT!"

"Your mom said no, but we were in the middle of the ritual; it wasn't about to stop."

"That's why she used you to help. None of us would have let that happen."

"I know. She mentioned that. Don't tell your grandmother I told you."

"I won't tell anyone. Promise."

The car ride the rest of the way to the next store is silent. Oak stews in anger at Marion for hiding that from him. After his encounter with Loxias and being blamed for sacrifices, Oak is furious that Marion decided to do that. But he can't be too angry because it helped Dev. He realizes that Dev would still be sick if Marion hadn't made that choice and is able to relax a little as they arrive at the store to find candles. They go inside as the scent of candles fills their noses, the overwhelming mix of every smell in the store bombarding their nostrils.

"What kind of candles are we looking for?" Alan asks.

"Well, unscented is always good, but certain scents can work for spells and things."

They check out all the shelves filled with candles of all shapes, sizes, and scents. Oak pulls down some plain tealights and a few candlesticks. "Oh!" Oak says, handing Alan the candles. He walks to an area of the store that has natural-scented candles. "These are what I need."

He collects an orange- and ginger-scented candle in a jar along with one scented as blue sage and another that's lavender and cedar. They find some thick black pillar candles and get those as well. Oak finds a few oils that he knows they don't sell at Divinity, so he grabs those, too.

"Okay, I've decided I'm broke now," Alan jokes, hinting at Oak to stop shopping. They take their purchases to the counter, pay, and leave.

On the way home, Oak plans out where all his new things are going to go. They pull into the driveway of Dev's house. "Let's leave everything in the car. I'll make a trip over to the apartment and drop it all off later," Alan says as they walk to the front door. They head inside and hear noise coming from the kitchen.

Oak investigates and finds Dev wiping down the refrigerator. "Mom! You're up!" He runs to her and gives her a hug. "How are you feeling?"

"I feel okay!" she says, hugging him back.

"You shouldn't be cleaning. Where's Grandma?"

"I've been cooped up in bed. I need something to do. Grandma left after I woke up; she had to work. She's coming over in the morning with a few teas and potions to help me stay healthy." She clears her throat and continues cleaning.

"Dad got me all kinds of stuff for his new apartment!"

"That's great, sweetie! Did you eat?"

"Yeah, we stopped for food. I'm going to go figure out where I'm putting all my new stuff." Oak heads to his bedroom. He passes Alan coming in, having heard Dev talking.

"Wow, you recover fast," Alan says.

"I'm sorry you had to see that," she apologizes, speaking about the ritual.

"It sure was ... something."

"Witches have a bad reputation for that kind of thing even though it generally hasn't been done for centuries. Does Oak know anything?"

"No," Alan lies. "I'm glad you're feeling okay. I have to head out and drop off some of the things I bought for Oak today. Where is Marion?"

"She will be back in the morning."

After an uncomfortable moment of silence, Alan works up the courage to say, "Dev, after I drop everything off, I would like to stay the night here until Marion arrives in the morning. Just to make sure you're okay."

Dev contemplates his offer. "Okay. For Oak's sake, I'll prepare the couch for you." Alan nods and sees himself out.

Dev finishes her cleaning and goes to Oak's bedroom. His door is open, so she walks inside, sitting next to him on his bed. He is drawing a blueprint of his new apothecary and planning where to put everything. This is the first time they have gotten to talk since the fae realm.

Oak explains to Dev what he is doing, where he wants everything to go, and tells her all the new things Alan let him get. She leans in to the paper and they spend time laughing and planning his weekend home's layout.

"Dad's going to spend the night on the couch until Grandma gets here in the morning," Dev tells him.

"Okay, good."

Dev coughs and excuses herself from the room to get something to drink.

Oak finishes his plans and realizes Dev never came back with her drink. He goes to the kitchen and finds that she is not there. He looks around the house for her and finally checks her bedroom. She is back in bed, fast asleep. "I knew she shouldn't have been cleaning," he says.

He goes to the living room and zones out in front of the TV, enjoying the makeshift bed Dev prepared for Alan before taking a nap. He enjoys the relaxation for a few hours until he is interrupted by the front door opening.

"I'm back," Alan says, coming into the house.

"Hey."

"Where's Mom?"

"She's asleep again."

"Wow. Well, she's earned it."

Alan joins Oak on the couch and they watch game shows, playing along until they are too tired to keep their eyes open.

Dev emerges late in the night from her bedroom and sees Alan and Oak asleep on the couch together. She smiles warmly at them until she is interrupted by the urge to cough loudly. She covers her mouth to silence the sound and escapes to the kitchen. Clearing her throat, she goes to the fridge for a bottle of water. She opens the bottle and gulps it down to soothe the tickle that is forcing her to cough. She fills a kettle with water and sets it on the stove, turning the heat to high.

"Some slippery elm bark tea should help," she says to herself, reaching into the cupboard.

She pulls down a wooden tea chest and flips it open, inspecting the different combinations of teas put together for her by her mother a while back. She finds the bag of slippery elm bark and removes it from the chest, returning it to the cupboard. She plops the tea bag into a mug and waits close by the stove for the kettle to whistle so she can stop it before it wakes the guys.

At the first sign of a high-pitched sound, Dev pulls the kettle from the heat and pours the boiling water into her mug, dousing the tea bag and releasing the sweet, soothing smell of the herbal bark. She blows over the top to release some of the heat and slowly sips the tea. The numbing effect takes place almost immediately, calming her throat. She finishes the hot cup of tea and gently sets the mug down in the sink, making her way to her bedroom to finish sleeping the night away.

THE COVEN'S SON

***

The next morning, Oak wakes up next to Alan, who is lying awake next to him on the couch. "Morning," Alan says.

Oak stands and stretches. "Morning." He stumbles to his bedroom, rubbing his eyes awake. He gathers some clothes and heads to the bathroom to shower and brush his teeth.

Alan gets up and checks on Dev. In her bedroom, Dev is sitting up in bed, her back against the headboard. Her face is pale and clammy, her hair wet from sweat. "You feeling okay?" he asks as he steps into the room.

"I've felt better," she says.

"You look it." He frowns. Her face turns sour as she points to a bucket at the bed's side. Alan hurries and hands it to her. She vomits. He pulls her hair away from the bucket and rubs her back until she is finished. "Marion should be here soon," he says, helping her set the bucket back down on the floor.

He heads back to the living room. "I hope Marion gets here soon," he says as Oak is coming out of the bathroom.

"What did you say?" he asks, towel-drying his hair.

"I said your grandmother should be here soon," Alan says, hiding Dev's condition from him so that he doesn't worry.

"Hey, do you think I could try to meet with Kyle-Ray this morning before he heads to school? I haven't seen him in a while and I want to say hi." Alan grants him permission to go and Oak puts his shoes on and heads out the door.

Alan goes into the kitchen to get Dev something to drink when there is a knock at the door. Alan opens the door, greeting Marion, who is carrying a bag full of herbs, potions, and books. "How is she?" Marion asks, stepping into the house. Alan looks down at the floor. "Oh no," she gasps.

She pushes past Alan, making her way to Dev's bedroom. "I'm here," Marion says, noticing a damp, musky heat escaping the room after the door is opened. Dev is staring blankly at the wall, white as a ghost, with deep, dark circles under her eyes. Her face is gaunt and thin. Marion takes in her daughter's condition as she enters the room, reaching inside her bag of supplies. "Dear, you look terrible. What happened?"

Dev stares blankly for a moment before answering weakly. "I don't know. I felt great for a little bit, but then I started coughing and it just got worse and worse."

Marion pulls a book from her bag and starts flipping through the pages. "I brought some things that may help." She finds the page she needs and continues to rummage through her bag until she becomes frustrated and dumps the entire contents on the bed.

Alan peeks his head into the room. "Do you need help with anything?" he offers.

"No, dear. I've got it from here. Where is Oak?"

"He went to Kyle-Ray's. Do you want me to bring him back home?"

"No, this is fine. I've got it." She fumbles with the ingredients.

"Are you sure—"

"I'm fine, Alan!"

He steps backward and out of the room, leaving her to it.

Marion feels Dev's forehead. "You're burning up." She finds a bottle containing some sort of premade solution, with a heavy film of goop settled at the bottom. She unscrews the lid and releases a pungent smell of fermented, vinegary liquid into the room. Dev nearly gags while Marion begins adding various other ingredients to the mix.

"Sorry, honey. I just can't believe the ritual is rejecting."

Marion and Dev both know that the ritual reversing Dev back to her sickly state means something more than just a common illness is at play. Marion muddles a few dried herbs into an empty cup. She pours the foul-smelling potion into the cup of newly crushed herbs and hands it to Dev. "I know it'll be hard, but you need to get this down." She picks up a fresh coconut from the pile on the bed.

"What is that for?" Dev asks, gagging slightly as she brings the tonic to her lips.

Marion tosses the coconut to the floor with a thud and waves her hand at it, causing it to roll aimlessly around the room. "I did some digging and found this tropical magic that uses a coconut to absorb negative energies from a home. The coconut will roll around the house and the water inside will pull all the bad out and keep it contained, to be discarded later."

Dev coughs, forcing more of the drink down her throat.

***

As Oak walks to Kyle-Ray's house, he thinks about everything he's been through and considers whether or not he wants to let Kyle-Ray in on the whole thing or if he wants to keep it a secret. On the way to his house, he sees a mushroom growing through the cracks in the sidewalk. He races to it and kicks it so hard it goes flying clear across the neighborhood. "I've gone from hating garlic to hating mushrooms," he says to himself, quietly laughing.

He gets to Kyle-Ray's house and hopes he hasn't left for school yet. When he gets to the front door, before he knocks, Kyle-Ray comes out. "Oh, hey!" he says, surprised to see Oak. He puts his finger up, signaling for Oak to wait a minute. He leans his head into the house and yells to his mom, "Oak is here! He's going to take me to school; you can stay home." Kyle-Ray shuts the door and turns back to Oak.

"But, I'm not—"

Kyle-Ray cuts him off. "It's fine. I was considering skipping today anyway. I didn't tell my mom about you getting in trouble, in case she didn't want me to hang out with you."

They walk to the end of the driveway and turn on to the sidewalk, heading nowhere in particular. "Where have you been? I came over and your mom's car was gone. Someone else was parked in your driveway and no one answered."

Oak looks down at his feet as they walk together. "Oh, just a short family trip. That was my grandma's car. We all rode together in Mom's."

"Oh."

Oak ponders the idea of telling him what happened but changes to a different subject instead. "Hey, is Mr. Santora okay? I heard he had an accident."

"Yeah, they told us he was okay but had a pretty crazy head injury and would be out for a couple weeks. But he is expected to make a full recovery."

They walk for a while, staying within the confines of the neighborhood.

Oak begins to fiddle with his pockets and rubs his hands together, looking noticeably uncomfortable.

"Are you okay?" Kyle-Ray asks.

"I need to tell you something." The need to tell someone about what happened wells up inside him like a balloon ready to burst. Kyle-Ray stares at him. Oak stops in the middle of the sidewalk and turns to him, grabbing his arm. "I think it's easier if I show you."

Oak grips Kyle-Ray's hand as if he is giving him a handshake. He places his other hand on top and feels the pinging of magic start to run through him. He trusts the energy and allows it to pass from himself to Kyle-Ray, showing him images and memories of the events leading up to him killing Loxias.

Kyle-Ray rips his arm away as the last vision comes to an end. He falls backward and lands in the grass next to the sidewalk. "WHAT DID YOU JUST DO?" he screams.

Oak puts his finger to his lips, asking him to be quiet. Kyle-Ray shuffles backward in the grass away from Oak, trembling. His eyes dart rapidly around, trying to comprehend all the images his mind was just bombarded with. Oak nervously reaches out to Kyle-Ray.

"NO!" He pushes himself back away from Oak, farther into the neighbor's yard.

"Kyle-Ray, please," Oak pleads, wanting him to calm down.

Kyle-Ray's mind spins from all the new memories of things he never knew existed. As Kyle-Ray crawls backward in the grass, the new information begins to organize itself within his mind. Oak watches nervously and looks around to make sure no one is around.

"The garlic," Kyle-Ray says, as one of the first memories he was shown settles into his head. He looks at Oak, eyes wide, welling with tears.

Oak starts to regret showing Kyle-Ray these memories. It looks like it is too much for him. "It's all so much," Kyle-Ray says, slowing his crawl.

Oak reaches his hand out again, offering to help Kyle-Ray stand up. Kyle-Ray takes his hand, tears in his eyes, and stands, pulling Oak into a tight, sympathetic hug. A tear falls from Oak's eye. "Is that all real? Did that all really happen?" Kyle-Ray asks, voice muffled against Oak's shoulder.

"Yes," Oak says, pulling back from the hug to look at him.

"Why didn't you tell me sooner?" Kyle-Ray asks.

"I don't know," Oak responds, looking at the ground.

"It's okay," Kyle-Ray says, putting his hand on Oak's shoulder and nudging him to continue their walk. "I don't know what to say to all this, or what to think," Kyle-Ray confesses as they reach an exit to the neighborhood.

"Do you think you would feel more comfortable if I showed you some things I can do?" Oak asks, gesturing outside of the neighborhood.

"Like, witch things?" Kyle-Ray asks.

Oak smirks. "Yes, like witch things."

Kyle-Ray nods and they walk out of the neighborhood.

They spend the afternoon together, Oak showing Kyle-Ray different tricks and explaining elements of the craft to him. Kyle-Ray slowly begins to feel more comfortable with everything and suggests they play a few pranks using witchcraft on unsuspecting people as they walk around town.

***

After a few hours, Oak walks Kyle-Ray home, relieved that he is accepting of his truth. Oak walks home, feeling amazed that he finally got everything off his chest. He opens the front door and is startled as he hears a loud bang and a coconut rolls away from him.

"Boo!" Oak jumps as Alan darts in front of him, scaring him a second time. "I have to go back to the apartment. Want to come with me and hang there for a little bit? You can set up some of your room."

"Yeah!" Oak says, turning and darting to Alan's car. They head in the direction of the new apartment. "I told him," Oak blurts

"Told who, what?" Alan questions.

"Kyle-Ray. About everything."

Alan is surprised. "How did that go?"

"He was terrified at first, but now he thinks it's awesome."

"Sounds like he's a really good friend."

Oak agrees. They drive through traffic, chatting about everything he told Kyle-Ray until they get to the gate of the apartment complex.

"Everything is inside already; you just have to move things into your room. I'm going to be doing some measuring for a few upgrades." Alan pulls into a parking space and they head to the new dwelling.

Oak immediately begins moving things into his new apothecary room. He sets up the small tables, pairing a few candles with his lamps. He piles the empty jars and bottles onto the floor to fill with herbs later. He hands his shelves to the vines he grew earlier and allows them to take hold of the shelves and hold them tightly in place. He places things here and there, moving items a few inches to the left, a few inches to the right. Then he steps back to check the symmetry of the room.

He plugs in his lamps and checks how they light the room. Then he leaves the apothecary and goes into his bedroom, watching Alan use a tape measure to figure out dimensions for curtains. His father calls for his help on a couple measurements he can't manage by himself.

THE COVEN'S SON

Oak stretches the measuring tape along different areas of the apartment while Alan holds the other end, jotting down numbers onto a notepad. Together, they decide whether the hardware in the apartment should be silver or brass. They decide on silver. Oak helps Alan count all the doorknobs, pulls, faucets, and other metallic accents they need to buy so that everything matches. They debate whether the ceiling fans and light fixtures should match everything else or not. They come to a stalemate on that one.

"We'll figure the rest out later. I'm tired. Let's go," Alan says, packing up and heading toward the door. Oak follows behind and they leave the complex and head to the home improvement store.

Oak plays around the store, collecting paint swatches from the wall of samples while Alan figures out what style and shape he needs for each upgrade.

With a cart full of items, Alan searches the aisles for Oak. Eventually, he finds him dinging a collection of trial doorbell chimes, deciding which one is his favorite. "Not buying a doorbell today. Come on, let's get you home," Alan says.

They pay and load up the car and head back to Dev's. "I'm glad we can do all this stuff together. Once your mom gets better, I'll have to get back to working like crazy again," Alan says.

"I'm glad too," Oak replies, half-heartedly, reminded that the time he has with Alan is limited. As they turn into the neighborhood, Oak asks if he can get dropped off at Kyle-Ray's house. "I want to tell him about all the cool stuff we got."

Alan agrees and drives around to Kyle-Ray's house, letting Oak out. He drives to Dev's house, parks, and heads inside.

"Alan, is that you?" Marion screams as Alan steps inside.

"Yes, just me. I dropped Oak off at Kyle-Ray's."

"Come NOW!" Marion screams, sounding frightened.

Alan rushes to Dev's bedroom. Marion is kneeling at the side of the bed. Dev's eyes are half open, staring into nothing. "Try to get her attention," Marion pleads.

Alan waves his hand at Dev's face. Nothing. He snaps his fingers. Nothing. He claps. Nothing. Her breathing is shallow and the most prominent thing you notice about her are the defined, deep blue veins showing through her translucently pale skin. Alan calls to her.

"Dev? DEV!"

***

Oak casually walks partway up the driveway where Kyle-Ray lives. He can see Kyle-Ray in the front window of his house from the yard. Oak flails his arms to get his attention. Eventually, Kyle-Ray sees Oak flailing on the sidewalk. He smiles and disappears from the window. A moment later, he emerges from the front door and greets Oak.

"Wanna go for another walk?" Oak asks.

"Sure."

They head down the sidewalk as Oak explains the new apartment and all the ideas he has for his apothecary and bedroom. He tells Kyle-Ray about how he grew vines along the walls instead of using wallpaper or paint, even though he collected some paint samples when they went to the home improvement store.

"That sounds awesome! How often will you be staying there?" Kyle-Ray asks.

"Probably only the weekends. My dad works so much during the week, he would never be home."

Kyle-Ray begins to rattle off a bunch of absurdly impossible ideas for the apothecary. Oak laughs at Kyle-Ray's overreach of how witchcraft works. He tells Kyle-Ray about the homeschooling idea to improve his abilities.

"You have to do it. You have to learn more witchcraft."

"You just want me to show you stuff."

"So?"

They turn a corner and head toward a road that loops around to the other side of the neighborhood. Oak stops as his attention is pulled to the sky. "What is it?" Kyle-Ray asks.

Oak holds his arm out. A black raven dives from the air onto his arm. "Whoa!" Kyle-Ray jumps back. "Is that the same bird from the park?"

"I think so," Oak says, studying the bird's features. The bird squawks. "DEV!"

Oak pulls his face back from the bird. "What?" he asks, shocked. As they stand on the sidewalk with the raven, a car pulls up behind them and the bird flies off Oak's arm. The car rolls down the window. It's Alan.

"Oak, your mom is unresponsive. I called an ambulance. They are taking her to the hospital."

Chapter 15

Oak's face washes over in worry and he runs to the car. Kyle-Ray follows him, but to the other side. "What are you doing?" Oak asks, getting in.

Kyle-Ray slips in the back. "I'm coming with you."

Alan drives off, not having the time to argue, and they race to the hospital. On the way, Oak stealthily changes all the traffic lights to green so that they arrive faster. Once there, they jump out of the car and race into the ER. "We're here for Dev Black," Alan tells the reception nurse.

She types away on her computer for what seems like an eternity until finally, "Ah, here she is. It looks like she is needing some tests to be run. Her airways were closing so she is being intubated right now. She's not clear for guests just yet. Have a seat in the waiting room and we will call you when she is stable."

Oak's stomach is doing flips. "She's being intubated? Like, on a breathing machine?" The nurse nods. The confirmation hits him like a ton of bricks.

Alan put his hands on Oak's shoulders and walks him to the waiting area with Kyle-Ray. "I'm going to get you boys some water."

About an hour passes before Oak sees Marion and Pepe show up in the ER, looking around. He waves and they catch his signal and come over to him. Alan stands up and shakes Pepe's hand.

Oak embraces Marion tightly, tears welling in his eyes. "Couldn't you help her?"

She wraps her arm around him and pets his head. "I tried, dear. I promise, I did everything I could." She looks up at Alan. "Any news?"

"No, nothing yet." Alan confirms. "They asked us to wait out here until they get her stable."

Marion looks worried. "Stable? You mean, she wasn't?" Alan shakes his head.

Marion lets go of Oak and reaches for a seat, trying not to pass out. They all sit in silence, listening to the kids' movie playing on the TVs around the waiting room. Another hour passes.

"Mr. Black?" a male nurse calls, holding a clipboard, standing by an electronic door that only opens with a key card. Alan and Oak both stand up and the nurse waves them over to him.

As they head to the nurse, everyone else gets up and follows, eager to hear an update. They all gather around him, waiting for him to speak. The nurse glances at everyone. "So, we got Dev stable. We don't know anything just yet, as we are still waiting on some test results. We can allow visitors, but for right now it's best if we have no more than two. I'll give you a minute to decide." He steps away, studying his clipboard.

They all study each other and Alan puts his hand on Marion's shoulder. "Go with Oak. Be with your daughter," he says, gently pushing her toward the door.

Oak looks to his family and they wave him along, to be one of the two in the room. "We're ready," Oak says, steadying his voice.

"Right this way, then," the nurse says, swiping his key card and opening the electronic door. He leads them down a plain white corridor, medical equipment scattered about. "Dev developed pharyngeal edema when she arrived, so she had to be intubated. She's also hooked up to multiple machines, so just be aware of how she may look when you go in. It can be startling."

He takes them to a curtain and draws it back, revealing Dev. She is in a traditional hospital gown, lying on a cot with wheels. A breathing tube is coming out from the side of her mouth and there is oxygen being pumped into her nose via a nasal cannula. She has an IV with multiple tubes coming from her arm and a pulse oximeter clipped to her finger. Her limbs are swollen and puffy. Her eyes are half open, but she doesn't appear to be alert or aware that she has guests.

Oak breaks down upon seeing her and immediately turns away. Marion heads past the curtain and strokes Dev's cheek. Oak walks a few steps away from the area as tears pour down his face. He begins shaking violently and cannot hold back an audible wail of sorrow as he leans his head against the wall of the hospital. His gut twists inside him and his heart feels like it's being torn away from his chest by a dull knife.

Oak realizes Dev first got sick when they were purged from the fae realm. *This is all my fault.* He hits his hand against the hospital wall. *I'm so sorry.*

A doctor heads to where Dev is lying, so Oak wipes the tears from his face and takes a deep breath. He follows behind the doctor who shakes both their hands and then explains, "So, we believe Dev is having a reaction to something she has come in contact with. We have found internal bleeding that we need to locate the source of and her airways are shut from edema. We suspect there may be an infection as well. May I ask, has Dev been out of the country recently?"

Oak and Marion look at each other, deciding on how to answer that question.

"I believe she has. Why do you ask?" Marion answers, keeping things as vague as possible.

"Well, we are still waiting for the test results, but we have a suspicion that this may be from something she ingested that is rarely found in the U.S.," the doctor states. "We will be moving her to the ICU within the hour and we should have her results by then."

Oak's face goes pale. "The ICU? It's that serious?" He knew the tubes and machines she is hooked up to looked intimidating but he didn't want to believe things were as bad as needing to be admitted to the ICU.

"I'm afraid so. I'm going to finish my rounds and I'll be back with her results as soon as they move her."

The doctor draws the curtain shut, allowing Marion and Oak to be alone with Dev.

Marion moves next to Oak and quietly speaks to him. "Help me remove her pain."

Oak sniffles a bit, unable to stop weeping for his mom. He agrees and leans over the top of the bed and puts his hands on Dev's temples. Marion begins to guide her hands just above the surface of Dev's body. She cannot absorb Dev's pain like Mallie could, but numbing her for the moment is good for now.

Oak uses his fingers to send beautiful images into Dev's mind. Walking on the beach during a warm day with a cool breeze, riding a carousel while eating fluffy pink cotton candy, lying on a hill at night gazing at twinkling stars. Her eyes fully close and when they are finished, Dev's cheeks are slightly pink.

"That is all we can do for now," Marion says, walking to Oak and setting her hand on his shoulder. He pulls her in and hugs her, sobbing. Tears begin to run down Marion's cheeks. She was holding herself together well, but the pain she is seeing in her grandson breaks her.

During their embrace the curtain quickly slides open and a nurse walks in, jotting down notes on a chart and disconnecting machines from the wall. She pulls up the guardrails on either side of Dev's bed and hooks her IV bag to a mobile stand. "Sorry to interrupt, we are ready for her in ICU. You can follow me there. She can have more visitors once we have her set up there."

She starts rolling Dev away and Marion and Oak let go of each other and follow her. Halfway there

Marion decides to go give the others an update and tell them Dev is ready for visitors. Oak stays with his mother, following the nurse.

They get to the ICU and the nurse begins setting up the area. She scribbles on a marker board and hands it to Oak, along with a marker. "Here ya go, kid. Write a few nice things about your mom so that the doctors and nurses treating her know a little about her."

Oak looks at the board. *Hi, my name is Dev and...* is written at the top. Along the bottom is an icon chart indicating different levels of pain by facial expression. *I love butterflies* is the first thing that comes to his mind. He looks at his mother as the nurse finishes setting up her equipment and covers her with a blanket to keep her warm. Dev's face looks peaceful as she dreams of the visions he placed in her mind.

The beeping and whirring of medical equipment makes his head spin. A tear drops from his face and onto the board, smudging some of the letters. He can't clear his head enough to think about anything else to say so he fills the rest of the space with a drawing of a butterfly and hangs it up where the nurse pulled it from, leaving the smudge.

Marion peeks her head in. She sees Oak sitting with Dev and waves for everyone else to enter. Pepe, Alan, and Kyle-Ray solemnly come in. They gather around and stare at Dev, hoping, wishing for a full recovery.

The doctor from before walks in, "Ah, everyone is here, good. Is there anyone else we are waiting for before I give the diagnosis?"

"No, we are all here." Alan says, eyes red.

"Right, so, I have the results of the tests. It appears here that she has tested positive for poisons from the manchineel tree. It is a deadly tree commonly found in the Central America region as well as Mexico and every part of the tree contains toxins." Everyone looks around the room, confused.

"I'm sorry, I don't think I understand," Alan says, taking charge of the conversation.

"Well, it is a bit strange, I'll be honest," the doctor replies. "We had her stomach pumped when she first arrived, because she was vomiting and we suspected it was something she ate. The tree produces a very sweet fruit and if she left the country and unknowingly ate one even though her reaction would have been more immediate, it would've made more sense. But, the results came back positive for phorbol, which is only found in the tree's sap."

Marion's face says it all and Oak's realization makes him sag so his grandmother has to hold him upright. Loxias did this. He poisoned Dev with the sap he used to seal her mouth. He knew he wouldn't win a fight with the Divine and poisoned his mother as a final attempt to seek his revenge.

Pepe, Alan, and Kyle-Ray do not understand the reaction and the doctor is just as confused. "Was there some significance to what I said?"

Marion explains that they were correct in assuming Dev had left the country but it was supposed to be a secret and she didn't understand until now, why it was relevant.

"Well, all foreign travel is important to document, regardless of the personal family consequences it holds," the doctor says firmly. "Nonetheless, I don't actually think this result would have been any different if we had known to begin with." He clips the test results behind Dev's chart and hangs it on the foot on the bed. "We will continue to monitor and treat her as best as we can. You will be contacted if anything changes."

Suddenly, Dev's heart monitor begins to beep rapidly. The doctor glances at the screen and watches it. The beeping gets faster and faster and other machines begin to sound. Soon, they are bombarded by an array of bells and chimes.

"NURSE!" the doctor screams.

Three nurses burst into the room and Alan starts shuffling the family and Kyle-Ray out of the room to give the hospital staff space to work. Marion has her hand over her mouth as Oak's face is alert with terror. Alan has to physically pull him out of the room.

Pepe comforts Marion and Kyle-Ray is respectfully quiet in the corner. Alan chews on a fingernail while Oak paces back and forth. Then, they hear it. The heart-crushing, steady alarm of a heart monitor flatlining.

The doctor steps out of the room, sweat on his forehead, and all heads turn to him. He gently shakes his head. "I'm sorry."

***

The day before the funeral, Oak packs some of his belongings into boxes. Marion is there, helping to pack up other areas of the house while Alan is at work. They've decided it's best that Oak stay with his grandma so that he can study witchcraft and not be home alone all the time. They are going to sell the house since it is too much upkeep for Alan alone. There is a knock on Oak's bedroom door.

"Dear, I am about finished for now. Are you ready to go?" Marion asks. "We can come back for more of your things later."

Oak stays quiet, grabbing as many boxes as he can carry and follows her to the car. Alan is staying in the house until it is sold, but he is not there enough during this sensitive time and Marion does not want Oak spending evenings all alone, so she had him move in early. The plan was to stay until the house sells, but Marion insisted.

They drive to Marion's house and Oak is silent the entire time. He hasn't said much since Dev's death and he hasn't slept either. He has huge dark circles under his eyes, even more so than normal. They get to Marion's house and Oak sets his things in her spare bedroom and goes into the apothecary to be alone.

Just before Marion heads to sleep she knocks on the apothecary door. There is no answer so she opens it and peeks her head inside.

Oak has made a mess of the room; it looks like a mad scientist has been hard at work. He looks up at Marion, pulling his face from a book. "Want to know why she didn't die right away?" Oak asks her, blank-faced.

"Tell me."

He flips a few pages forward. "The effects of many plants and other botanicals are highly ineffective and are drastically slowed in the realm of the fae in an attempt to hinder their magic abilities and keep them from escaping back to our world. Any effects will only be experienced gradually, but eventually are felt in full force once a witch returns to where she originally hailed." He snaps the book shut angrily and throws it across the room.

Marion doesn't know what he wants to hear, so she puts her hand on his shoulder and kisses the top of his head. "I'm going to bed. Please make sure you fix this room up when you are finished," she says, closing the door. A minute later she pokes her head back in. "Don't forget, tomorrow we are giving your mom a proper witches' funeral. Be sure to be dressed in your ceremonials."

She closes the door again and Oak swishes his hand at it, locking it. He then shuffles some of the papers around him and begins feverishly scribbling and studying late into the night.

***

The next morning, Marion opens the apothecary and sees that it is in perfect condition, even more perfect than it was before Oak spent the evening in it. She closes the door to find Oak out of the guest room and standing in front of her in his ceremonials. "Well, you're ready quite early," she says, as the funeral is only to take place under the moonlight.

"It feels right to start and end the day in this."

They waste the day lounging around and reading, sipping tea and playing cards to distract them. Oak struggles while playing Old Maid with Marion. His eyes periodically well up with tears and his hand shakes as he sets down cards. She tries to avert his thoughts with chatter about fun potions and brews she wants to try with him. When it begins to get dark, they decide to go.

"Let me grab something from my room," Oak says, excusing himself from the room. He reappears momentarily.

"Perfect. I'll grab the brooms and meet you in the car," Marion says.

Oak goes to the car to see Pepe is already inside, waiting for them. Oak gets into the back seat and Marion comes out, loads the trunk, and they head off. The funeral is being held deep in the middle of the woods of the nature trail, upon Oak's request. Mallie and Hyacinth are bringing Dev's body, having had it released to them using compulsion. She is covered by their ceremonial cloaks.

Marion, Pepe, and Oak meet Alan and Jazzy in the woods. They make small talk for a little while until they spot Mallie and Hyacinth, carrying Dev, using their brooms as a way to respectfully transport her. A traditional witches' funeral consists of the deceased being placed on top of the ground, allowing nature to reclaim the witch and recycle her magic as needed.

"Here they come, place your brooms," Marion says.

Oak, Marion, and Jazzy place their brooms onto the ground and Oak secretly places a piece of paper underneath his broom handle where Dev will lie. Mallie and Hyacinth place Dev on top of the brooms. She is laid on them, so that she does not touch the ground. Alan and Pepe watch, as they cannot participate. They pull the cloaks off Dev and put them on, adjusting her and placing her arms across her chest. Oak cannot look directly at his mom. He can't handle seeing her like this and keeps his eyes from focusing on her lying there in front of him.

"We return this witch, birther of the Divine, back to the earth from whereas we once came. Use her to feed magic and keep the occult strong. Born Dev Melt, now Dev Black, she is given to you by her coven sisters and family and by the Divine himself, head of all covens," Marion recites.

Jazzy speaks, "So mote it be."

Then, Hyacinth, "So mote it be."

Next, Mallie, "So mote it be."

Marion, "So mote it be."

Oak's lips tremble as the finality of his mom's existence is finally a reality that cannot be changed. They all wait for him. "So mote it be," he says, tears now flowing from his eyes.

Each member of the Coven bends and grips their broom handle, three on one side and two on the other. They rapidly remove their brooms out from under Dev and she hits the earth. The grass around her body turns a bright, healthy green and roots purge from the ground and wrap elegantly around her. She is pulled into the ground slowly, sinking back to the earth. Once she is fully enveloped by the ground, small flowers push from the ground. The group begins to walk away, to leave the earth to do with Dev as it pleases, but Oak holds up a hand, stopping them. He stares intently at the ground where Dev was.

There is a tiny pop under the ground, muffled from the soil. The lush green grass twitches as over a thousand monarch butterflies push through the ground and flutter into the air against the glow of the moon. They all watch as they soar and fly away, up into the sky. A single monarch lands on Oak's shoulder and then flutters away with the others. Oak wipes away a tear and smiles, sadness welling up inside of him.

"Merry part, Mom."

***

A few weeks later, the house sells.

"Moving crew is coming tomorrow. We will go shopping for your apothecary next weekend," Alan says to Oak, dropping him off at Marion's and giving him a fist bump.

Oak heads into the house. Pepe has left to another exotic country for work and Marion has gotten back to running the studio with Mallie, so the house is empty. Oak brews himself some of his grandma's blooming flower tea and takes it into his bedroom. He sips the tea and begins to read the book on alchemy that helped him to exchange Dev's body for butterflies. He hears a car pull into the driveway. It's too early for Marion to be coming home, so he goes to the door to see who it is.

He sees Kyle-Ray walking up to the front door. He's turned sixteen and for his birthday his parents gave him an old beat-up car. He opens the door to greet him.

"What kind of witchy things are you gonna show me today?" he says, holding out a box of incense. This time, it's amber and can actually be used. Oak takes it and lets him inside. Now that Oak has told Kyle-Ray he is a witch, he comes over and Oak performs the magic he has been studying for him for fun and practice.

After a fun evening in his grandmother's apothecary, Marion comes home and sends Kyle-Ray home. "Dear, you have work in the morning," she reminds him. Oak walks Kyle-Ray out and when he drives off, he gets ready for bed.

The next morning, Marion drops Oak off at Divinity before heading off to open the studio. He heads inside and puts on his apron and begins restocking the cardboard display of the book of affirmations. Behind the cash register, on the wall, there is a shelf displaying Dev's sigil-imprinted purse and her spirit camera. Below it, a plaque says "In memory of our coven sister Dev Sue Black."

Acknowledgments

I would like to recognize author Jeff Jacobson for being there to guide me in the right direction during the process of creating this book. My dad, Jeffrey, for always stepping up whenever I need him. My old lady chihuahua, for staring at me and whining during the entire creation of this book. And to the entire team at Gatekeeper Press for making this a reality.